COASTAL COUSINS

COASTAL ADVENTURE SERIES 2

DON RICH

Library of Congress PCN Data

Rich, Don

Coastal Cousins/Don Rich

A Coastal Adventure Series Novel

Florida Refugee Press LLC

Cover by: Cover2Book.com

This is a work of fiction. Names, characters, and incidents are either the product of the author's imagination or are used fictitiously. Any resemblance to actual persons, living or dead, businesses, companies, events, or locales is purely coincidental. However, the overall familiarity with boats and water found in this book comes from the author having spent years on, under, and beside them.

ESVA is a real place, with miles of unspoiled barrier island beaches that hopefully will stay that way for generations to come. Mallard Cove Marina™, Mallard Cove Restaurant™, and Mallard Cove Beach Bar™ are all figments of the author's imagination, but the names are trademarks of Florida Refugee Press, LLC.

Published by FLORIDA REFUGEE PRESS, LLC, 2019

Crozet, VA

To my son, Tyler. For years he has meant so much to his mother and me, and even more so now for his work with other people with mobility issues, especially our nation's veterans. The world would be such a better place if he had an army of clones. But he does so much by himself, having changed the lives of so many that he has met along the way.

"Rich and miserable. Now, is that an oxymoron...or, is it just the result of some dreams and aspirations that have gone completely haywire on the road to happiness?"

— FROM THE MUSIC VIDEO PROLOGUE OF KENNY CHESNEY'S "RICH AND MISERABLE" PERFORMED BY JOHN C. MCGINLEY

PREFACE

The Shore. Many places are referred to as "**The Shore**," and it can mean different things to different people. I lived in Washington, D.C. for a brief time, and when folks there referred to "**The Shore**" or the "**Eastern Shore**," they were most likely talking about the Maryland portion of the peninsula that borders the eastern side of the Chesapeake Bay. Of course, there's also the **Jersey Shore**, the **Delaware Shore**, and probably more than just a few others in the mid-Atlantic that get called by that more common and shortened name.

So, to cut down on any confusion in my books, I refer to the Virginia portion of this peninsula mostly as **ESVA** (the Eastern Shore of Virginia). This, even though I've incurred the wrath of a few locals who want it to be known only as **The Shore**. But far fewer than one percent of my readers call the Eastern Shore of Virginia home, so that's why I've taken this bit of artistic license—it's not because I don't know any better. Plus, I've seen a ton of **ESVA** stickers on cars and trucks, so it *IS* a common phrase. However, I do have more than one female character who refers to herself as a "**Shore woman.**"

But I wasn't finished there, I also ticked off a few more locals in a different location by occasionally referring to **Virginia Beach** as **VA**

Beach. Where I live in Central Virginia, it gets referred to using either spelling.

Speaking of "either spelling," you might notice that sometimes Accomack appears without the "k" at the end. That's not a typo. **Accomack** is the proper spelling of that county, and **Accomac** is the way you spell the name of the town. I have no idea why...

My location choices are important, though many are also fictional. Again, there is a good reason for this. When you stage explosions, murders, and gunfights on or about actual privately owned commercial properties (such as marinas), their owners can get so... touchy about things. And I have a strong allergy to lawyers and lawsuits.

Neither my **Bayside Resort** nor **Mallard Cove** are based on real places, though there are small sandy strips at the water's edge where each would be located. I've got a great aerial photo of **Mallard Cove**'s location on my office wall that I got from **At Altitude Gallery** in Cape Charles. They have a great website; you should check them out.

Even though I write fiction, I do my research. Because I want you to find something in each one that connects you with it and draws you into each story. These are also your stories as much as they are mine. So suspend any disbelief you might have for the next little bit, relax and enjoy this story!

PROLOGUE

T*wo weeks ago...*

The older man called his assistant into his office, motioning for her to close the door behind her.

"Is the Judge all set to be there?"

"Yes, I confirmed the appointment, and also with a private notary that will be there to witness your signature as well as the Judge's. No one from the family or the company knows anything about it, and the notary is getting a bonus in exchange for signing a non-disclosure agreement."

"Good. And Clara, I know how much Marlin means to you, but I need you to swear not to say anything about this. It has to come from me when the time is right."

"I understand."

"I know you understand, but I need you to swear that you'll never discuss any of this with him. There are... reasons I haven't told him before. Reasons only he and I can understand. At least I hope he can. I'll know soon enough."

"I swear, not a word of it will go to him from me."

"Good." The man sighed and closed his eyes as he leaned back in his desk chair. "This part is harder than dying. That's the easy part." He opened his eyes again, looking at Clara. "He'll be fine, just as he always has been. He never once came to me for anything." He looked like he wanted her to confirm she felt the same way.

She nodded, "I know. He's a scrambler and a survivor. You're right, he'll be fine. He'll take the news well."

"I hope so. That's what I'm worried about." He grunted, smiling ruefully, "In fact, that's the last thing I have left in this world that I'm worried about. How he'll react. Which choice he makes when he knows is all up to him. But I think I know what it will be. At least I hope I know..."

1

DREAMER

My name is Marlin Denton, but around the docks, they call me "Shaker." My nickname doesn't have anything to do with tremors or even something cool. I was branded with this by a friend, Captain Bill "Baloney" Cooper. I used to carry a few extra pounds until a year or so ago when I lost most of them. The nickname came at a point in time when my heaviest weight, as well as a period of extremely low tides, coincided. That day, I jumped onto Baloney's boat, the *Golden Dolphin*, landing on his teak covering board with a loud thunk before continuing down onto his deck. While the majority of my body stopped when I landed, some parts kept moving a little bit longer. Kinetic energy can be such a bitch.

Bill looked over and said, "Take it easy on the teak there, Shake-n-Bake!"

Of course, this had to happen in front of several of my other pals, Kim "Hard Rock" Collier, and Timmy "Spud" O'Shea. This also meant that my new nickname wasn't only going to stick, but would quickly get spread around the waterfront as well. I took it all in stride because I knew that objecting would only make things worse. Much worse. As in changing the new nickname to something worse. Much worse. And I could live with "Shaker," especially since my boats and I were based out of the Lynnhaven River at the time. This was across the mouth of the Chesapeake Bay. Baloney was docked at *Mallard Cove*, on the southern tip of the Eastern Shore of Virginia, also known as ESVA. I figured, "*What the heck, it's not like I see these guys every day*." Yeah, well, things change.

Along with writing articles for several national fishing magazines, I make my living guiding mostly fly fishermen. My favorite spots are in the Chesapeake Bay, inshore along the Virginia coastline, and offshore during the summer white marlin season. I have two different boats for this, which one I use depends on sea conditions and target species. My first boat is an older twenty-six-foot Gold Line center console named *Marlinspike* that's equipped with twin outboards, and a half tower. I also have a newer eighteen-foot Maverick flats boat named the *Bone Shaker*. It got named *for* me not *by* me, and you can guess by whom. Sometimes, it's better to just go with the current than try to run against it. Oh, and I have one more boat which is my floating home, a vintage restored forty-two-foot Chris Craft named *Why Knot*. Baloney didn't have a hand in naming that one, it was my father's boat and he ended up giving her to me.

As I said, I docked my "fleet" over at Lynnhaven, and life was good, up until about two months ago. Some clown named Glenn Cetta had been buying up marinas, and he finally got around to the one where I lived and worked from. When my dockage contract came up, he raised my rate by over thirty percent, and that price was only valid if I paid for an entire year upfront for all three boats. I was used to paying by the quarter year and getting an annual discount. Fortunately, Baloney had been yacking over the VHF radio about *Mallard Cove* having been bought by a couple that ran a sportfishing charter operation.

The place was a real pit, with the docks mostly falling in and only a handful of boats left over there. He said this couple wanted to rebuild the place and concentrate on attracting the biggest sportfishing fleet on ESVA, and that the dockage was still cheap. Bingo, he was speaking my language! I found out he wasn't kidding, and after meeting the new owners, Michael "Murph" Murphy and Lindsay

Davis, I signed a long-term contract. This was all about two months ago, right before all hell broke loose, but that part's another story for another day. Let's just say I found out quickly that along with some of their friends, Murph and Lindsay are great people to have your back and vice versa. They've both become great friends as well as landlords. I'm glad that Cetta was such a jerk; in the end, he did me a favor by pricing me out.

Murph and Lindsay have partnered up with some heavy hitters and are now in the process of building a big hotel and an in-and-out boat storage business onsite. They just finished rebuilding the old restaurant and bar that came with the marina, and now they are adding another. The old crumbling wood docks were quickly patched up and are now being replaced with modern floating concrete ones. I've found myself in the right place at the right time. Like my dad used to say, "*There are times when I'd rather be lucky than good.*"

"Marlin, thanks for picking me up, it's great to see you again." Dawn McAlister was a tall, beautiful thirtyish woman with long flowing red hair and a friendly personality. She smiled as she stepped from the dock onto *Marlinspike*. Dawn was one of the *Mallard Cove* partners as well as Lindsay's good friend. In a funny but complicated twist, she had also been engaged to Murph at one point. He, Lindsay, and I stopped by the upscale resort called *Chesapeake Bayside* specifically to pick up Dawn. She and her fiancée, Casey Shaw, lived there aboard *Lady Dawn*, their one hundred-ten-foot Hargrave yacht. In addition to owning part of *Mallard Cove* and several other properties down in Florida, they were the general partners in this resort and the adjoining mini estate's development. Their offices were here as well.

I smiled back and answered, "Likewise, Dawn, glad to have you aboard. Casey's not coming with us?"

She shook her head. "He had to go south on business and won't be back until tomorrow. But I didn't want to miss out on seeing what these two have found." She then hugged Lindsay and nodded to Murph. It was only over this past summer that she had begun to forgive Murph for their past issues. This was mostly because he was Casey's ex-employee, partner, and friend of over fifteen years. They had started bumping into each other again at fishing tournaments, and she realized that like it or not, Murph would always be Casey's friend. The whole issue was complex but entertaining, and best observed at a distance with some form of libation in hand.

I backed *Marlinspike* away from the floating dock, turned her, and headed out the marina's inlet. I set a course across the Chesapeake to the mouth of the Rappahannock River and the town of Deltaville. The side trip to *Bayside* had only added ten miles to our ride. Deltaville was on the opposite shore of the Chesapeake, far north of the tip of ESVA where *Mallard Cove* was located. So, the extra twenty minutes it took us out of the way to get to *Bayside* was no big deal.

As I said, Murph and Lindsay had become my good friends as well over my two months at *Mallard Cove*. At thirty-two, I was kind of midway between their ages; Lindsay at twenty-five, and Murph at thirty-five. They lived aboard their vintage forty-seven-foot Rybovich Sportfisherman, *Irish Luck*, just a few slips over from my three. They did "elite charters," meaning that their boat was maintained in top yacht condition with miles of oiled or varnished teak, and they got top dollar partially because of it. Their typical charter was at least two days long, and often would include a trip for a week or more and might include a tournament.

Unlike the other boats on "charter boat row," *Irish Luck* didn't have a sign advertising their business, and they wouldn't take just anyone who showed up at the dock. If you fished with them you had to have come with a referral from a friend. While that might sound snobbish, it was anything but. This was just a way to ensure that their charter clients were the type of people that saw their boat for the piece of floating art it was. They showed up in deck shoes, not cowboy boots. They were also appreciative of the hours of preparation and the attention to detail that was paid to ensure each trip would be comfortable and memorable. If you liked a certain beer, liquor, or food, you didn't have to tell them twice. They kept records of each client's tastes and made sure they were pampered.

Elite chartering also meant that the two of them wouldn't be stuck with any "trips from hell," forced to endure a boatload of jerks. It helped that Lindsay and Murph had won the richest tournament on the East Coast up in Delaware earlier this year, after placing second in a prestigious Virginia Beach tournament just a few weeks prior. Murph ran the boat, and Lindsay worked the fishing cockpit; together they were a formidable team. They would be headed south soon, to fish winter tournaments in the Florida Keys, Palm Beach, and Stuart before heading back to *Mallard Cove* for the spring and summer mid-Atlantic tuna and white marlin seasons. Their charter schedule had filled up fast after their wins. They had already taken a lot of time off to concentrate on the *Mallard Cove* purchase, renovation, and expansion, and were looking forward to fishing again.

But somewhere in the middle of all that the two of them had realized that year-round living aboard *Irish Luck* was likely to start taking a toll on its interior finishes, and eventually on their relationship as well. They needed a place with more room to get away from the boat, but just not too far away. They both loved the marina liveaboard lifestyle. So, Lindsay proposed a unique solution, and Murph enthusiastically agreed. They decided to buy a house barge. These are different from the traditional houseboats that usually have inboard-outboard power and are somewhat seaworthy. Barge-based houseboats are more or less like regular homes that are built on barges instead of foundations. Lacking propulsion, they usually are permanently moored because they are such a pain in the butt to move. If the hull is in good shape, a twice-yearly scrubbing by a diver is usually all the maintenance that's needed below the waterline. All the benefits of a house but without any grass to mow.

So, in addition to a couple of charters and the marina business, their last two months had also been spent looking for the perfect houseboat. The result of that search had us all taking this trip today. The thing about living around the Chesapeake is that a lot of the time it's faster to go somewhere by boat than it is by car. Today the bay had a slight northwest breeze with three-foot rollers coming out of the same direction, putting them on our starboard quarter. It should be a relatively fast, smooth, and dry trip. From *Bayside* by boat, we were looking at about a forty-five-minute crossing to Deltaville. To go there by car would easily take over three hours each way. I brought us up to a fast cruising speed after we cleared the marina's inlet. My four-stroke outboards were quiet enough so that we could hold a conversation without having to yell.

"Thanks for doing this, Marlin." Murph was sitting beside me on the padded leaning post. The women were both sitting on the console's front bench seat, talking.

I nodded. "Not a problem, Murph. You've done more than a few favors for me, so I owe you."

He looked over at me, "Have you ever been to *Deltaville East Marina* before?"

"Yeah, I have. It's like it was cut back into Stingray Point. It would make a great hurricane hole if the land around it was higher than two feet above sea level, which it isn't. Dig down a foot or two anywhere and you'll hit water. The bay will wash over it in any decent storm.

"The town is hundreds of years old and set on the end of Virginia's Middle Peninsula. It started as a boatbuilding center and waterman's town. There was plenty of tall timber for boatbuilding, and some very talented builders and designers came from there. Several generations of them in fact. Only a few of the wooden boat builders are still left there since most boats are being built out of fiberglass and epoxy now."

"Do you get a salary from the Deltaville Chamber of Commerce, Marlin?" Murph chuckled.

"I just like the place. A neat little maritime museum and a ton of marinas, but quiet as a graveyard in the winter. There's a restaurant on the main road called *Taylors*, and it's kind of the social hub in the off-season. Great seafood, cocktails, and conversation. There are just a few hundred residents living in town year-round, but the population swells to over four thousand in the summer, especially on the weekends. Seems like half of 'em are boat brokers. Lots of sailboats there, especially at *Deltaville East*. This is why I was kind of surprised to hear that this houseboat was there. Not to sound bad, but from the pictures you showed me, it doesn't fit in with their usual crowd."

Murph started grinning, and I knew him well enough to know there was a story coming. "You're right, Marlin. It doesn't fit in with all the 'blow boat' crowd, and its puke green color is just plain nasty. The story I got was that it wasn't supposed to be there for long, just for a month or so. That was over a year ago. A week after the owner moored it there, he disappeared. The marina owner couldn't find him or any of his family, so they declared it abandoned and went to court to get a clear title. Meanwhile, the marina sold, and the new owner gave the old manager orders to get it sold and the heck out of there. He has been calling him every week to see if it's gone and knows that they're going to be stuck with it through the winter if they don't move it soon. The manager is irritated, and not a fan of the new owner, so he's up for just about any offer. Now here's the part you'll really like. The new owner is our old pal, Glenn 'Birddog' Cetta."

I shook my head. "You've got to be kidding me! How is it that the guy you and I can't stand ends up owning the only houseboat that you're interested in?" Not only did I get screwed by Cetta, but he tried to bust up Murph and Lindsay's deal for *Mallard Cove*. He told the old owner a bunch of lies to get him to sell to him instead of Murph and Lindsay, but they already had a signed contract. Then he showed up uninvited on the *Irish Luck*, only to have his new Range Rover and his, uh, derriere become the target for Lindsay and a bunch of lead fishing weights after he refused to leave.

"But wait, there's more!" Murph had a sly grin. "Cetta doesn't know there's any interest in the houseboat, and I played it cool with his manager. Something I learned from Casey long ago was that when you are buying real estate, airplanes, or boats, you never 'romance' the deal. You look at it only once, then you get a contract with more 'outs' than a baseball game. You never let on how much you want something, or you're screwed before you start."

I smirked. "If you end up with this thing, just wait until Cetta hears who the buyers were. I hope you can take advantage of that scum-sucking bottom dweller!" Paybacks can be so sweet.

We cruised along in silence for a while after that, each lost in our thoughts. I was getting anxious to see this houseboat and find out if they were going to end up with a real steal.

Finally, we entered the mouth of the Rappahannock River and I made the southern turn toward the protected harbor. I pulled the throttles back as we came abeam of the point, allowing the hull to come off its plane and settle back into the water at an idle speed, reducing our wake. As we rounded the point, the channel to *Deltaville East Marina* curved off to our left, and we followed it. We took the bend to the right and spotted the marina entrance ahead. I hailed them on the VHF, and the manager directed us to the far end of the marina, all the way up next to General Puller Highway. It was in the farthest slip away from the river. If they did decide to buy this, they would have a heck of a time threading the needle to get it out of here unless there wasn't any wind. Fortunately, we were at the end of the season, and some boats had already headed south, or over to boatyards to be hauled and put 'on the hard' for the winter.

At first, no one said anything. The pictures hadn't done it justice, in a few different ways. The first was the paint color. It was far worse than it had looked in the pictures, and probably the main reason for the silence. Then, once you got past the color, it looked like it had major potential. It was huge, about seventy–four feet long by eighteen feet wide. There was a private sundeck up forward, off of what appeared to be a second-story guest room that straddled the entire width of the barge. Then at the other end on the dockside, there was a huge party sundeck with stairs that led down to a landing deck which also featured the front door. I looked at Murph and nodded slightly.

"Okay, nobody says anything positive that could be overheard. If you see something that looks like a flaw, even a minute one, make a big deal over it." Murph was on his game now.

"Got it, babe." Still, there was excitement in Lindsay's voice.

We finished tying up in an empty slip next to it just as a slightly balding older man arrived in a golf cart. "Hi, there! Denny Thompson. Welcome to *Deltaville East*. C'mon, I'll show you aboard *Key West Dreamer*."

That was when I noticed the wooden half-circle name board with a replica of the Key West Southernmost Point monument in the middle, and the boat name carved and painted along the outer edge. It was screwed to the forward exterior bulkhead. Hopefully, *Dreamer* had a fireplace where they could burn it.

Murph and Lindsay took the lead as Dawn and I followed. As hideous as the exterior was, the interior turned out to be pretty cool. The entry companionway had five steps leading down, with drawers underneath each step, and there was storage everywhere. At the base of the stairs, the main room was a nice-sized salon, perfect for entertaining. At the far right was the galley with a natural edge wood counter coated in clear polyester. Next to it was a long narrow 'head,' or bathroom. Pebble and grout flooring hid radiant heating coils, and an overhead rain shower had a retractable curtain. There was also a rectangular Japanese wood soaking tub with jets.

Back at the far end of the galley, a wall of shelves rolled aside to reveal the master stateroom which took up the entire aft end of the barge. It had a queen-sized bunk on one side, a large double-hanging locker, and a large window in the aft bulkhead. Just outside the doorway in the galley was a ladder that led up to the guest stateroom which also had an entrance from the party deck.

On the counter was a copy of a marine survey done a year and a half ago, and there were no defects noted. The surveyor said that the hull was made of fiberglass that was almost two inches thick, overkill for a flat barge that was designed to sit in a protected marina. It would probably last for several decades. Murph popped the bilge hatches and found everything dry and clean, always a good sign. All in all, the houseboat had a pretty unique and functional layout. But in reality, there were probably only two buyers for this thing anywhere near the Chesapeake, and they were standing in front of Denny. He seemed to get that part, too.

"I'm going to tell you guys the truth, my new boss has been riding my butt about getting rid of this boat. He didn't count on having to deal with it when he bought the marina, so anything he gets for it will be gravy. And personally, I don't care. Between all of us here, I'm looking at leaving after this winter. So, getting rid of this will just make my life easier between now and then."

Murph looked at Lindsay and gave her a beckoning nod. "We'll be right back." They both went out the door onto the aft deck and held a quiet conversation. Denny looked nervously at Dawn and me, and I shrugged. A couple of minutes later, Murph and Lindsay returned.

"I don't know what I hate most about this thing, the color, or the layout. We're looking at it for a fish camp that we can rent out, and I don't even know if it would be good for that. I tried my best to get Murph to see that it might work, but only at the right price." Lindsay had put on the full press.

Murph said, "I wanted to walk away from it, but she seems to think it might do. Here's the deal, Denny. Twenty grand, and not a penny more. And we'll need a month's free dockage to be able to pick our weather to get it out of here."

At first, Denny winced, since the asking price was fifty thousand. You could see him thinking and he started looking more and more like he had just been thrown a lifeline. "Let me call my boss. I'll be right back." It was his turn to go to the aft deck to hold a conversation, but this time it was on a cell phone. They could see him through the glass door at the end of the companionway, and it was easy to tell that his boss wasn't happy. He returned a couple of minutes later. "Mr. Cetta said he was insulted by your offer. He said there was no way he could let it go for less than thirty-five thousand, and you'd need to remove it within the next three days." He looked apologetic.

"Let's go, guys, this was a waste of time." Murph led everyone out to the deck and over to *Marlinspike* while Denny got back on the phone. I took my time cranking up the engines and he hung up just as I started the first one.

Denny came over to the side of the deck. "He said he'd take the twenty thousand, but only in cash, and only if you can get it out of here before he comes back up on Friday. I think he's more interested in it being gone in three days than the money."

Lindsay looked over at Denny and smiled. "Deal. We'll get it out of here the day before he shows up. We brought cash with us, too."

"Great! Let's go over to the office and we can transfer the title and draw up a bill of sale."

2

ON COASTAL TIME

Dawn and I hung back on my boat, as the three of them climbed on the golf cart and headed to the office. She looked over at the houseboat and said, "I think once you get past that awful color, it's a cute place."

I was thinking pretty much the same thing, except substitute cool for cute. "Why is it that I'm getting this vision of me holding a paintbrush?"

Dawn laughed. "Because you have turned out to be a great friend to those two in a very short period of time. And because it's probably going to happen if 'Tom Sawyer' Murphy has any say about it."

We crossed over to the houseboat and I gave it another, even closer, look. The paint appeared to be a cheap house paint, not what you'd need if it was to hold up in a saltwater environment. The color had to have been a huge part of why Cetta wanted it gone. With its proximity to both the main road and the entrance to *Deltaville East*, it made a big first impression on anyone looking for a slip. It screamed desperation — like they would do anything to fill up the marina. Since it had come in about the time that the previous owner had decided to sell, that probably was the reason. He wanted to punch up the profit numbers. But I knew that like me, Murph must have seen his share of ugly duckling boats in weird colors that became swans with a good coat of paint and some varnish. *Why Knot* had been a disaster when my father had picked her up, complete with peeling varnish and paint. The trick was getting past it and having the ability to envision what it would look like repainted. This one could be a real gem, depending on what color they picked.

Dawn was staring at the empty entrance deck, then she climbed the stairs to what I'd call the party deck. Even though I didn't know her that well, I could still see her wheels turning. Then I followed her back down to the large, open salon area, at least that is what it would be called on a regular boat. I guess in a houseboat you could call it a living room too. Again, she seemed lost in thought. She was still that way when Murph and Lindsay walked back in, and he was in a jubilant mood.

"Wait until Cetta finds out that it was Lindsay and me that bought this, he'll flip. No way he'd have let us talk him down if he'd have even sold it to us at all. Not after what happened with *Mallard Cove*, and him getting hauled in for questioning by the police over it. Just think, you couldn't build this place for fifteen times what we paid for it. I could kiss whoever painted it this color. It'll look so cool in white boat enamel with beige decks. Looks like we're going to be having a boat painting party!"

Dawn looked over at me with what was an 'I told you so' face. Then she went back to talking with Lindsay about interior colors and furnishings. Neither Lindsay nor Murph had any furniture, having only lived in furnished apartments before moving aboard the *Irish Luck*. It looked like they had the interior figured out and Murph was right, white would be a great color for the exterior.

Murph was staring at his smartphone then looked up at me. "Hey, Marlin, old buddy, old pal..." His grin looked like it came from a great white shark when it was feeding.

"Let me guess, that was your weather app."

"Yeah, and it looks like the bay should be the most calm on Friday to make our crossing."

I cringed. "Our crossing?"

"Yes. I'll pull it with *Irish Luck*, but I'll need you on the stern with *Marlinspike* to help me thread the needle out of here. That last turn up by the office is gonna be tight. You'll have to pull the stern one way while I pull the bow in the other direction. But hey, I'll bring lunch and it'll be fun!"

I knew that my charter calendar had a vacancy in four days, and they really couldn't get it out of here by themselves. "Wait, Friday is four days from now. I thought you had to have it out of here in three."

"Screw Cetta. You can't change the weather, and what's he gonna do, sue me? Denny said he would be coming up on Friday, and it's a long drive from Virginia Beach. We should be long gone by the time he gets here. It'll probably take us up to seven hours to drag this those thirty-eight miles, so we'll want to leave here early anyway. Trust me, nothing will go wrong."

I shuddered. Never say that nothing will go wrong around the water; the fates have a very warped sense of humor. And beware of anyone that says "trust me" too often. But I had a lot of free dockage coming because of a sweetheart deal that Murph and Lindsay had made me, so I couldn't say no in good conscience. I only wished that I could.

"Okay, I'll play tugboat. But it better be a good lunch."

"Trust me, it will be. Our restaurant will be ramping up for their soft opening next week, and I'll get them to make us a big takeout order. By the way, you're invited to those practice runs, as well as the grand opening. You can bring a date, too."

"Thanks." There was that "trust me" thing again. And I didn't remind Murph that I had hit somewhat of a dry spell lately. My last girlfriend and I had gone our separate ways over a year ago, long before I moved to *Mallard Cove*. I hadn't met anyone on ESVA that I wanted to ask out yet. I was figuring that might change when the restaurant opens and it hopefully becomes a draw. I'm more of an "it'll happen when it happens" kind of guy rather than the whole "desperate to find a new girl" thing. I've always found that being desperate tends to attract desperate, if you know what I mean. And life's too short to date clingy psychos unless you want your life shortened further, that is. Trust me.

They took a bunch of measurements and pictures, then we borrowed Denny's car to hit *Taylors* for lunch. The food was great, and it kept us from talking, which was a good thing. The place was full of locals, mostly watermen, especially at the bar. I overheard a few conversations and picked up a few leads on where the rockfish were hitting on this side of the bay. It wasn't really like I was eavesdropping; the volume on some of these guys had increased in relation to their beer consumption. And you can never have too many spots when you need to put your clients on fish.

After lunch, we returned Denny's car, hopped on *Marlinspike,* and idled out through the marina. Now that I had seen the size of the houseboat, I realized just how tricky getting it out of here would be. Heck, a Sportfisherman of that size with twin engines and a bow thruster would find it tough. This was going to be no cakewalk. But like I said, we're lucky that the place was now far from full, and had fewer boats sticking out of slips that we'd have to avoid.

On the trip back to *Bayside* the women again rode together up front, but now they were in full shopping trip planning mode. Since they were leaving everything on the Rybo, they had to stock both the galley and the "head," the marine term for bathroom. Plus, deck and salon furniture had to be purchased, and now they had closet space for larger wardrobes for both Lindsay and Murph. So, Murph and I just kept to ourselves, enjoying the ride mostly in silence. After we dropped Dawn at *Bayside*, Lindsay came back and stood with us for the hour-long run back to *Mallard Cove*. The two of them talked almost nonstop about their plans for the houseboat and their future. I'll admit, it was hard not to get caught up in their excitement.

An hour after we left *Bayside* we idled in through the breakwater at *Mallard Cove*. A long segment of the new floating docks was now being installed to the left of the inlet, parallel to the breakwater. This was going to be a private gated section, mostly for those of us who live aboard. This dock would only have finger piers and the boats would be backed in against it. The houseboat was going to be the first boat in the new docks, and it looked like they would just be finishing up that slip about the time that we bring it over. Murph and Lindsay had picked out a spot in the middle so they would be away from any noise from the bar, and any engine noise from boats coming and going. I was going to be a few slips down from them on the East side in the *Why Knot*. It will be nice not living right on charter boat row as it started building more traffic.

I spun *Marlinspike* around and backed her into the slip just as Bill "Baloney" Cooper returned in the *Golden Dolphin*. He was yelling orders to his mate, Bobby "B2" Smith. B2 had been with him for a few years and could do the job in his sleep, but listening to Baloney you would think it was his first day with him. That was just Baloney showing everyone that he was in charge, and B2 took it in stride.

Murph slipped the loops of our stern lines around the cleats as I shut down both engines. He turned and said, "Thanks for your help today, Marlin. I've got your next fuel ticket, as well as your beer this afternoon."

I nodded and smiled my thanks. The beer was for our regular afternoon meeting of the "Beer-Thirty-Bunch." This group was made up mostly of the captains and crews from boats in the marina. We used to meet in what had been a screened patio off the back of the restaurant. But now since the restaurant was getting back in operation, we had been evicted. Baloney had talked Murph and his partners into building us a captain's lounge next to the restaurant to take its place. It had glass windows overlooking the marina, as well as heat and air conditioning. I had no doubt that we'd all end up in the restaurant's bar on some days, but the captain's lounge would be a nice haven when the bar was too crowded.

The three of us headed over to the new lounge after stopping at *Irish Luck* to pick up a cooler, beer, and some ice. There was a refrigerator in the lounge, but only an idiot would leave their beer in it and expect it to still be there when they returned. We walked through the door marked "Slip Holders and Guests Only" and then the two of them grabbed the couch while I settled into an overstuffed armchair. We all studied the muted flat screen TV mounted on the wall we shared with the restaurant. It was set on a weather station and showed an animation of the next two days and the arrival of the first fall cool front. It was going to stall over us for twenty-four hours before moving through. Which was exactly why we were going to be late pulling the houseboat out of Deltaville.

"So, did ya buy the floatin' condo?" Baloney had walked in with his trademark cheap cigar in the corner of his mouth. As usual, it was unlit. His wife Betty had made him promise not to light up until he cleared the breakwater, making sure that the smell didn't permeate their cabin. He headed straight for Murph's beer, thankfully pocketing the cigar on the way. Baloney had left B2 in charge of washing down the boat and cleaning their charter's fish. He wasn't being lazy; this was just the normal division of labor along the docks. This was also why mates received most of the tips, typically equal to twenty percent or more of the charter fee, especially when they also cleaned the fish.

Lindsay smiled and handed him a tablet that contained all the pictures she had taken. The look on his face was priceless. In his heavy New Jersey accent he said, "Holy crap, that's one ugly color!" He thinks he lost the accent twenty years ago when he moved to Virginia, but if he did it wasn't that much of it.

He quickly flipped through the photos. "It's got potential though. So, when're we gonna go'n get it?"

Murph said, "We?"

"Well, it's gonna take two boats, so I figure ya probably already lassoed poor Shaker an' his Gold Line, an' you'll tow it with the Rybo. But you're gonna need more of a crew than just th' three of ya. Like I said, when are we gonna go over ta get it? You're already paying for my time in suds." Baloney took a long draw off his hijacked beer.

"In four days, after the front passes and the bay calms down. But I thought you had a full dance card with the *Golden Dolphin*?"

Baloney nodded. "I do, but I want B2 ta take her out some now that he's got his captain's license. With things lookin' like they'll be picking up this next season, I figure I might check out a few boats this winter. Maybe I'll get myself another one that he can run for me, and

I'll get a part-time freelance mate ta take his place on the *Dolphin* them days he gets booked."

Lindsay looked over at Murph and smiled. Expanding the small charter fleet was something that they counted on when they bought the marina. By next summer the hotel would be open, and there were other boats that were also interested in moving in. As the first dock, restaurant, and hotel you see coming off the Chesapeake Bay Bridge-Tunnel (CBBT), the draw for tourists would be there. It was just up to all of us to talk them into going fishing. And if anyone could talk, it was Baloney. He had a natural knack for his zany brand of promotion. He made sure that his yellow hulled boat's slip was in the corner, guaranteeing it was the first one you saw when driving in. And his antics got attention as well. Though he was in his early fifties, he hardly ever acted his age. He hung a black brassiere from his starboard outrigger whenever they caught a wahoo. Then every Christmas a life-sized stuffed Santa appeared on the top of his aluminum tuna tower holding a beer can in his hand. Baloney was nothing if not colorful, but he was also a very talented fisherman. The combination ensured that his charter schedule remained mostly full.

Lindsay said, "I like the way you're thinking, Bill. And thanks, we can use the help to get *On Coastal Time* back here."

That caught me off guard. "That's the new name? Pretty cool. So much better than *Key West Dreamer*. About a thousand miles north, better."

Murph said, "Lindsay thought it up. She wants to get rid of that old name board as soon as we get her tied up. Oh, hey, just the person I was going to go look for. I need the name of the sign painter that you are using here."

Murph smiled toward the door where Kari Albury was walking in. While Murph and Lindsay together were the largest partners in *Mallard Cove*, it was owned by a group, and managed by McAlister & Shaw, one of Casey and Dawn's companies. Kari had a small stake in *Mallard Cove* as well as being the project manager for McAlister & Shaw. She was a beautiful young woman, about four inches shorter than my five foot ten inches, in her early to mid-twenties with long black hair and hazel eyes. At first glance, she looked young enough to be an intern. But Casey and Dawn had recognized her abilities shortly after she came to work for them and had moved her up rapidly. *Mallard Cove* was one of a couple of projects she was now overseeing. Smart, beautiful, with a great sense of humor and personality to match. I couldn't understand why she wasn't in a relationship unless it was all the time that she spent here on her job. Lindsay had talked her into joining us in the afternoons, and I was glad that she had, I enjoyed talking with her.

"We use Accomack Sign Company. Why? What's going on?" She came over and sat in a chair across from me as Baloney handed her Lindsay's tablet. "That color is awful! But the houseboat itself looks nice. Whose is it?"

Lindsay answered, "Ours. We're bringing it over here in four days, about the time our first section of the floating dock is finished." She saw the worried look on Kari's face and chuckled. "Don't worry, I already ordered ten gallons of white marine enamel and a couple of beige deck paint. It won't look like a circus wagon for too much longer. But we need a new name board made."

Kari looked relieved. "They can do it, and they turn things around fast," Lindsay told her about the plan for fitting out the boat. Then Kari looked over at me. "Why is it that I have a feeling you have a part in this?"

"Hey, I'm just an innocent bystander and tugboat captain."

Murph added, "And an expert houseboat painter, or he will be soon, along with everybody else around here."

Kari gave me a wry smile, figuring that I was a pushover when it came to helping my friends, even new ones. I guess she had me pegged, even though I'd only met her about the same time I'd met Murph and Lindsay. The truth was, I liked her. I'd probably have asked her out except that she was way south of my thirty-two years, and like I said, pretty much consumed by her job. That, and the fact that she also lived thirty-five miles away, up near *Bayside*. Okay, that last excuse was kind of weak, seeing how it was only a forty-five-minute drive. And she *did* smile every time she saw me, but then again, I was a customer. I guess that came with the territory. Suddenly I realized that she had been saying something to me.

"Marlin?"

"Sorry, I was thinking about something. What were you saying?"

"I was asking you if you needed another crew member to help bring the houseboat over. I'm off that day, and don't have any plans."

I looked over at Murph, who looked amused and gave me an almost imperceptible nod. "Uh, sure. We can use all the help we can get. You're good around boats?"

"I'm a Shore girl. I sailed and ran powerboats long before I could even drive a car."

The look she gave me was almost challenging, and for some reason, I felt awkward. Fortunately, my phone rang at that moment, preventing me from commenting. It was Clara Edwards, my uncle's executive assistant. "I need to take this; I'll be right back." I picked up as I went out the door. "Hi, Clara, how are you?" I was expecting a brief comment or two before she handed the call off to my uncle as usual.

"I'm good, Marlin. Look, I'm calling to give you a heads up about something, and I need you to keep it between you and me." I could hear the tension in her voice.

"Of course." Clara had been with my uncle since about the time I was born, which coincided with when his company had really started expanding. She had always been a friend to me.

"Your uncle just left on a ten-day around-the-globe trip to visit the factories and offices. He'll be coming straight back to the Naples house, and you need to plan on getting down here very soon to visit him."

Sudden dread hit me like a baseball bat. "What is it? Not cancer again?" My Uncle Jack had beaten cancer back when I was a kid but had been clear ever since. The pregnant pause before Clara answered said volumes. Our family had always been very tight lipped about health issues.

"You just need to plan on getting down here soon. And we never had this conversation."

"I understand." Truth was, I didn't. "I'll call him as soon as he's back and ask if I can stop by."

"If I were you, I'd send him an email now. He has satellite Internet on the new plane, so he'll get that right away."

"Thanks, Clara."

"You know you're one of his favorite people, Marlin. This will mean a lot to him."

"To me too. I'll send that note right away."

"Good. I'll see you down here soon."

While she hadn't openly confirmed that his cancer was back, whatever it was that prompted the call wasn't good. It looked like I would be headed to Florida even before Murph and Lindsay. I started composing the email on my phone as I walked in and sat back down. I looked up after I hit send and realized that my friends were all staring at me with curious and worried looks.

"Sorry, guys, family stuff. It's all good." I could tell that Murph could see it was anything but good. I took a pull off my now lukewarm beer and settled farther back into the chair, my mind now focused on Uncle Jack.

For whatever reason, it turned out that the five of us were the only takers of the Beer-Thirty-Bunch today, less than half the usual number. I wasn't much of a conversationalist from that point on, and most of the talk was centered around the houseboat anyway. Baloney soon tired of it and left, taking along a "go beer" for his exhausting thirty-foot hike back to the *Dolphin*.

"I'd better be going too. I have an early morning back here. See you, guys, and I hope everything is all right, Marlin." Kari gave me a shoulder squeeze as she headed out, leaving just the three of us.

"I think somebody has a severe case of Marlin fever," Lindsay said.

"What are you talking about?" My mind was still on my uncle.

"Are you seriously going to tell me that you don't see it? Do you think Kari wants to help with *On Coastal Time*, or that she's looking for an excuse for some 'one-on-one time' on a boat with you?" Lindsay clearly believed the latter.

"I don't know. But going out with her wouldn't be a great idea."

Lindsay looked surprised. "Why not? She's smart, pretty, knows her way around boats, and she's attracted to you."

It hadn't been that obvious to me, though I'll admit, I had been distracted today. "Because she's managing things here. What if we didn't get along? Then I'd be in an awkward position. Besides, she's way too young for me."

"*Really*? Too young for you." Lindsay said that first word about as coolly as anything on the Arctic Circle. "You know that she's only a year younger than me, right? And you're three years younger than Murph. So, I guess the way you see things, he's way too old for me then, right?"

It was like I had woken up in the middle of a minefield. A move in any direction right now could mean things might blow up in my face. I glanced at Murph, one look at his face told me he thought this was hilarious. He wasn't going to be any help, at least not to me. "No, it's just that I've mostly dated women that were my age or a few years older than me. I don't have the best track record with younger women."

She wasn't about to budge an inch. "Yeah, well, in the couple of months since I've known you, you haven't even been to the track, much less added to any record. But I'll leave you alone about this. Obviously, I'm far too young to know enough to point out the mistakes of my senile elders." She looked at Murph. "I'll be on the boat."

3

UNCLE JACK

After Lindsay left, I looked over at Murph who had a huge grin. "Oh, you think that's funny?"

He nodded. "From where I'm sitting it is. You were so screwed, no matter what you did. She's kind of sensitive about our age difference. I think some of her friends from back in Northern Virginia originally made a big deal about it with her. Probably another reason she likes hanging with Dawn since Casey and I are both old geezers with young chicks." He chuckled.

"Then I guess this is the end of the three of us hanging out."

He shook his head. "I'll take her out for dinner, we'll have a few drinks, and most of it will be forgotten by morning. Except for the part about Kari taking a shine to you."

"I just don't see that."

"Don't feel bad, I didn't either until Lindsay pointed it out a few days ago. Unless we men are in a bar, women are so much more tuned into these things than we are."

"A few days ago, Murph? Why didn't you give me a 'heads up'? I thought this was all about today."

"Only partly about today, Shaker. But you know, I'm not much for playing matchmaker, that's not my gig. I try to stay out of all that relationship stuff. Like now. Not to switch subjects, but hey, are you okay? You seemed shaken up after that phone call."

I drew in a long breath. I don't like to share family secrets, meaning that I like keeping my family a secret. I know, that sounds strange. It's not that I'm ashamed of them, just the opposite is true. Our family history goes back a long way in Virginia, all the way to Jamestown. A Denton was even one of the English investors in the Virginia Company.

So, you might think there must be a huge family fortune, and you would be right. But it doesn't come from that far back. Over the past few centuries, several fortunes have been made and lost within my family. My great grandparents were tenant farmers. Then my grandparents started a business and did well, until the stock market crash of 1929. They went from being one of the ten wealthiest families in Richmond to being a stone's throw from being broke, literally overnight.

Then, my father's generation "redeemed the family honor," with two of the three men starting businesses that eventually became worth millions. Don't feel bad for the third one, he became worth billions. Quite a few billion, in fact.

You're probably getting visions of mansions, Ferraris, lavish yachts, and offspring doing nothing but lying around pools, soaking up rum and sun at the latest Caribbean hot spots. Don't believe everything you see on television; money doesn't just fall from the sky for a lucky few. And if you are fortunate enough to make a little money and start believing it does fall like rain, it'll dry up fast.

So, your opinion of me has probably changed now. You might even be wondering since I'm surrounded by all this wealth, why I was the slightest bit worried about how much dockage costs. The answer is because I have to; it's not my money. Remember how you "saw me" before I shared this secret with you? That's me, the real me. I work hard to make a living around the water.

So, what happened to all my parents' money? A car accident killed my mother and put my father in a long-term care facility for several years before he passed. Between that and the lawsuit from the occupants of the car that my dad had turned in front of, that pretty much drained it all. Capital gains tax took a big chunk when I was forced to sell his business for him soon after the accident. Having to accept a "fire sale" price for the business didn't help either. In fact, I was getting *Why Knot* ready to sell when Dad passed away. It would have killed me to sell her, because he and I had restored her together over a few years, and I cherish those memories. He had given her to me, and she had become my home. Those memories of the two of us surround me every day. But Dad was almost out of money, so I was prepared to do whatever I needed to in order to take care of him.

So, what about his brothers? Were they at odds? No, they weren't. My uncle Landon was gone by that time. He had developed brain cancer soon after retiring and had gone through his entire nest egg fighting to find a cure before it finally took him. Avocado pit extract injections in some Mexican clinic, something made from sheep organs in Switzerland, you name it, he tried it. The only success was on those clinics' sides, cashing his checks.

What about my dad and Uncle Jack? Well, they competed as so many brothers do. But their competition was only in business, not on the gridiron, golf course, or tennis court. It was all about who could build the bigger business, and Uncle Jack won big time. Would he have helped take care of Dad? Without a doubt, if Dad or I had asked for help. But by the point he was running out of cash, Dad wasn't aware of much of anything anymore. And it wasn't like Jack hadn't tried to help. He flew Dad to the best specialists in his plane, paying for them himself. But there wasn't anything that could be done. And Dad never wanted Jack to know that he was almost broke, so I wasn't about to betray that confidence.

In the end, Uncle Jack offered to hold Dad's memorial at his estate in Naples, Florida, overlooking the Gulf of Mexico. You're probably thinking palatial mansion again. Wrong. Highly manicured waterfront acreage with spectacular plantings and flowers, yes. But just a nice four-bedroom home that he has owned for over thirty years. Okay, it does have two detached guest apartments and a pool, but it's hardly a palace. In today's market, the value of the place is all in the acreage, and he bought that for a fraction of what it would cost to replace it today. Any buyer would demolish whatever was there anyway, even if it was only a year old. I've seen it done time after time down there. Twenty-five thousand square feet and up is the new norm. I question whether many of those owners have seen every square foot of their homes.

Anyway, we had a nice short ceremony down there, just like Dad would have wanted. I'll never forget just how lost Uncle Jack looked that day; I felt the same way. He seemed to have aged several years in that week; he really missed my dad. Still does, too.

Like I was saying about television versus reality, both my dad and my Uncle Jack lived their businesses as a lifestyle, not a job. You don't build businesses like theirs on a part-time basis, it's twenty-four/seven, full throttle. Yes, some members of Jack's side of the family do take dreamy vacations. But they work their tails off the rest of the year to afford them. Remember Clara saying that my Uncle Jack was on a trip around the world in his plane? Sounds cushy, flying off to remote locales in a private jet. Until you realize that Jack is now over eighty, and walks slowly and painfully with a cane. He takes a physician with him on long trips because of his past, and apparently now present, health issues. Walking through his factories and standing for long periods at receptions can be excruciating for him. But he sees it as totally necessary, showing that he truly cares, and his employees love him for it.

Yes, he has his own plane. His company has four in fact; all are jets. His is the largest, a brand new Gulfstream 800. Without it, there is no way he could begin to do all the traveling required to visit the offices and factories where all his ten thousand plus employees work. Yes, that number is correct. When Uncle Jack started his company, it was just him and one other guy, almost sixty years ago. He still tries to get to every office and factory at least once every other year. His son, my cousin Jack Jr., gets to each one every year. Theirs is truly a family business, and they want all their employees to know that. Kind of hard to get that point across if you've never even seen a family member. As I said, it makes a big difference to the folks that work for them.

Over a decade ago I was having a hard time finding my way, and Uncle Jack had me come and do an internship at his company in their Richmond headquarters. I learned a lot during those three months. The most important lesson I learned was that corporate life wasn't for me and that I need to follow my dream. I went to Virginia Beach, gave most of my suits to Goodwill, took out a loan to buy a used Gold Line, and never looked back. For the most part, I've been very happy ever since. Uncle Jack has been happy for me too. I think he's even been kind of proud of me. It's funny because he uses a different success gauge for my cousin Jack. It has always been about their company's earnings, not necessarily Jack's happiness. I never thought that was fair, but it was between a father and son, and not any of my business.

Anyway, I have always been close to Uncle Jack, visiting him often in Richmond. And I've flown down to Florida and back on his jets a few times when I've visited with him there in the winter. Most of the time I've driven the fifteen hours each way though. Private planes, especially jets, are promoted as luxurious and large pieces of flying jewelry on television shows. The truth is, they are just another business tool, kind of like a computer. The PC's entry into the corporate field increased the speed with which data analysis could be done, and projections could be made. The faster you get the numbers, the quicker you can make a decision. Private planes are much the same way. Instead of having to plan your day around the airline's schedule and spending six hours of that day making three connections, with your own plane you go point to point in a fraction of the time. A round trip that might take two days using the airlines now takes half a day. If your meeting runs long, your ride is still fueled and ready whenever you are. Yes, it costs a fortune to travel like this, but if you are the decision maker and you can increase your schedule by three hundred percent, it doesn't take long to pay for itself.

When Dad died, Uncle Jack sent his plane up for me. The urn with my dad's ashes and I were the only passengers. I could have bought another Gold Line for the operating cost of that one trip. But he knew the state I was in at the time and didn't want me driving that far. He surprised me by hopping aboard for the trip back. He knew that I was going to spread Dad's ashes offshore, and he didn't want me to do that alone. We left in the morning on the day after the service, just under a two-hour flight from Naples to Va Beach. If you've never flown in a private jet, you might be disappointed. There usually isn't a steward or stewardess, unless it's a full transatlantic or transpacific flight. No champagne or caviar, either. On long flights, there are usually sandwiches, packed in those clear plastic clamshell things by airport caterers. And we make our own drinks en route at the built-in bar, often before we even taxi out for takeoff. Granted, it's a *very nice* bar, but what else would you expect to find in a seventy-three-million-dollar aircraft?

After we landed, I drove us over to the boat in my old Ford Explorer Sport Trac. Two hours later we sent Dad to his final rest, in the water that the three of us had shared that one day. My first offshore trip had been here, with Uncle Jack, and it's a place that I've fished so many times since. He and I rode back to the dock in silence. After I drove him back to the foot of the stairs of the plane, Uncle Jack hugged me and loaded aboard. The nice thing about "private aviation," is that you can drive right up to the aircraft, there's no waiting, and goodbyes are private as well.

I watched as they taxied out and took off, and I transitioned from Uncle Jack's world back into my own. The one where I had to worry about charter bookings and where my next meal was coming from. Yeah, Uncle Jack was always there, and I'm sure he'd catch me if I ever stumbled, but I never wanted to ask. Ever. That would be my equivalent of total failure and humiliation.

I didn't know what to expect, I figured I'd maybe get a Christmas card from him, but I was genuinely surprised when the calls started coming. Once a week for the next six months. Checking on me. Inviting me for visits. It was humbling. He had ten thousand employees to worry about, two generations of my cousins nearby, and at least three past US Presidents on a first name basis on his phone on speed dial. But he took time out for me.

"MARLIN? Are you okay? It was like you were somewhere else."

"Just thinking back on a few things, Murph. Yeah, I'll be fine. Somebody I know is going through a tough time, that's all."

"I figured it was something like that. Hey, if I can do anything to help, just yell."

I nodded. "Thanks. You can. Go back to your boat and smooth things over for me with Lindsay. I appreciate what she's trying to do, and I didn't mean to insult her. I just know how things have turned out in the past."

Murph said, "I'll do that. I know I said I try and steer clear of other people's relationship issues, but I've spent quite a bit of time with Kari since we're now partners. If she was some airhead there's no way in hell she would be the development's project manager here. That water is deep, Marlin. I'm going to leave you with a bit of advice, then I'm bowing out. Stockbrokers have that disclaimer they love to repeat, 'Past performance is no guarantee of future results.' I think that might apply to you, too, pal. Okay, I've said my piece, and now I'm gonna go make peace. See you tomorrow."

I sat there for a while by myself and thought about what he said. But my mind kept going back to Uncle Jack. Just as I was getting up to leave I got a reply from him. He said he'd love to have me come visit for a couple of days. He'd be gone for the next ten and would be back in touch after he was stateside again. Short and to the point, like most of his emails. I know he gets a pile of them every day, so that wasn't out of the ordinary.

I headed over to look at the floating dock progress, then I looped back toward the *Why Knot* to figure out some dinner for myself. As I passed the restaurant I looked at the new deck and glass garage doors that replaced the screens on the patio and remembered Murph had mentioned that they both had been Kari's idea. Smart ideas at that. I was looking forward to the place opening. In addition to being a draw for potential charter clients, it was going to be very convenient for me on nights when I didn't want to drive or cook. Like tonight. At least I had a full day's charter tomorrow, so I'd be hitting the bunk early. Sleep would be a welcome respite from worrying about my uncle's health and having unwittingly insulted a friend. No late-night TV for me.

4

THE RALPH HOUSE

The front stalled over us two days later just as predicted, then it finally pushed offshore. My charter for that day was postponed until the next one, when we could stick close to shore, shielded against the mild west wind that had arrived after the weak front. Migrating Spanish mackerel on fly rods was a hit with the couple I fished that day. Topping them off with a nice late-season cobia by the bridge as the wind waned made for a great day.

I cleaned the fish and *Marlinspike*, fueled up, then headed over to the captain's lounge for a beer or two. Between the rain, a couple of charters, and paperwork, I hadn't been back over there since I had that run-in with Lindsay three days ago. Because I had been busy. Yes, too busy for a beer, and no, I wasn't avoiding her or Kari. Much. Okay, maybe a bit. I walked into a roomful, and Lindsay was front and center looking at me, with Kari sitting next to her on the couch.

"Hi there, stranger. I was beginning to think you had moved away to a retirement home." Lindsay had on a challenging smile.

The looks on everyone's faces but Murph's told me that I thankfully hadn't been a topic of conversation these past three days. Apparently, they were in the dark, and if I treaded water lightly here, it might stay that way. This game was mine to lose. "Nope, just doing my 'one man band' thing. Ready to make for Deltaville in the morning." Not a bad idea to remind her I was doing them a favor.

Baloney chimed in, "Looks like they got your slip ready for the *Ralph House* just in time." I had also seen the floating dock was in and secure, and that the power, water, cable, and pump-out lines should all be hooked up by tomorrow night.

Kim "Hard Rock" Collier, captain of the Kembe II, looked puzzled. "Why *Ralph House*, Baloney?"

"'Cause, it's puke green! You know, like raaaaallllpphh." He mimicked someone being seasick, hanging over the rail. If this is where the conversation was headed now, I should be safe. Maybe. If I keep my mouth shut.

Murph grinned. "It won't be for long! See those boxes over in the corner? A dozen gallons of white marine enamel, all for *On Coastal Time*, but it's gonna be used up in a New York minute." He looked over at me and winked. Murph to the rescue. "Oh, and that big box is a new stainless grill for the party deck. I figured after a good day of sanding I'd try it out on some thick ribeye steaks for anyone who helped." There were murmurs of appreciation around the room. I hoped he bought a bunch of electric sanders. Nothing motivates this crowd like red meat, alcohol, or preferably both in concert together.

The conversation stayed on the houseboat for a while before drifting over to what fish were biting and where. B2 was happy about taking another charter out tomorrow with him as the captain. I thought that maybe I might get him to run one or two for me with my extra boat. But I'd have to clear that with Baloney.

I noticed Kari looking at me a few times, and Lindsay chatting quietly with her. Honestly, I'd been thinking the whole thing over. Maybe it wouldn't be such a bad idea to spend a little more time getting to know her better. Since my conversation with Lindsay, I'd noticed that Kari was sure as hell getting a lot done around here in record time. She was direct and forceful, and the contractors all seemed to respect her. So, Lindsay was right about her being smart and pretty, but the jury was still out on the rest of it. Tomorrow might prove to be an interesting day. Then Murph's phone rang.

"Hey, Denny. Yeah, I know we were supposed to get her out of there today, but I'm no weather magician. What? No! Look, we'll be there first thing in the morning, and we'll be long gone before he even gets through all the road traffic. Yeah, count on it. Relax, we'll see you in the morning." He hung up and looked at Lindsay.

"Making friends, babe?" she asked.

"Denny. All freaked out that Birddog Cetta might get there in the morning and see the houseboat hadn't left yet. Wanted us to come over now and pull it out of there tonight."

Lindsay looked thoughtful. "You know, going over now might not be such a bad idea. Then we can get it out of there first thing. Not for Birddog's sake, but in case we run into any issues coming back, we'll have more daylight to deal with it. Between *Irish Luck* and *On Coastal Time*, we have plenty of bunks for everyone."

"I keep a change of clothes in the car, so that works for me." Kari was eager to make the trip.

"The wind has laid down quite a bit, so the bay crossing shouldn't be too bad. I've only had one beer, so that's not an issue. Bill, Marlin, what do you guys think?" After initially dismissing it, Murph now seemed more than open to the idea.

Baloney said, "Lemme go grab some clothes and talk to Betty, but I know she won't mind. Shaker, what about you?"

I wasn't about to shoot Lindsay down today. "I'm in."

THE RYBOVICH PULLED out of her slip as I was still letting my outboards warm up. Bill had jumped aboard with Murph and Lindsay, leaving Kari and me to run *Marlinspike*. If I didn't know better, I'd have figured this was Lindsay's doing. But knowing Baloney, he went with the boat that would have the smoothest ride on the hour and a half bay crossing. Since we could go twice as fast, I wasn't worried about catching up as I watched them leave before us. Kari had braided her long black hair into a ponytail to keep it from tangling and was wearing a ball cap. This clearly was not her first rodeo, just as she had said.

"Hey, Shore girl, you want to run the boat or handle the lines?" Kari didn't need to be asked twice, stepping over to take the wheel as I released the stern, bow, and finally the spring lines. She started to step aside after we were free of the slip, but I stopped her. "Get back there. This boat doesn't run itself you know." Her grin told me everything I needed to know as she then expertly took us through the breakwater and headed toward the bridge channel next to Fisherman Island. She ran fast enough to catch up with *Irish Luck* then throttled back fifty yards behind her, leaving enough room to dodge or coast if they shut down unexpectedly. She knew her stuff; I was impressed.

"You weren't kidding, you know boats."

"I wouldn't have said it if it wasn't true. I don't make a habit of letting my mouth overload my...uh...skills."

She had a big grin, watching to see how I took what she said. I matched her grin in response. We sat on the top of the lean seat with Kari reaching forward uncomfortably whenever she had to turn the wheel to make minute changes in our heading. I told her, "You can steer with a foot if you want. I usually do too. Until it gets rough."

"Didn't want you to think I was being careless with your boat or showing off." She was looking me straight in the eyes like it was a test. Or maybe just being straightforward, I couldn't read her that well yet.

"I wouldn't have suggested it if I didn't think you were a pro at this. Just wanted you to make yourself comfortable."

"I am comfortable, thanks. Great handling boat. Plenty of speed when you need it, too."

I nodded and looked ahead at the Rybo. Kari was maintaining the same separation distance. We were now passing the CBBT (Chesapeake Bay Bridge Tunnel) and starting to catch some wave action from the wide open bay. As we turned toward Stingray Point, the three-foot rollers were coming almost directly bow on. *Irish Luck* was smoothing things a bit, but we still ended up standing on the pounding deck. I set up the plotter, and it said we had just under thirty-five miles to go, which should take us almost an hour and a half at our current super slow cruise. Even in these short seas, we could go much faster, but *Irish Luck* couldn't.

I watched Kari as she scanned the gauges every few minutes, something an experienced boat operator does out of habit. Waiting until a warning horn sounds for an overheat or oil pressure failure means you are already in trouble. And half the time the darned horns don't even work. So often trouble can be avoided by seeing a subtle change in the gauge readings.

There was a real seriousness and maturity about Kari as she ran the boat, much the same as when she was directing the various parts of the *Mallard Cove* project. It was hard for me not to like and respect that about her.

We both got that one-on-one time Lindsay had talked about. We learned a lot about each other; she was born on ESVA, and I was in Richmond. She stayed within a few miles of home, while I moved just under a hundred miles away. She had an AS degree from a community college, and I dropped out after my freshman year. I didn't mention the internship at my uncle's company, nor anything about my family except that my parents were gone. She said she'd worked for four years at a CPA's office before he retired and closed his office. She got a job with Casey and Dawn soon after that and went from receptionist to sales assistant on their largest project in two weeks, and now added project manager for *Mallard Cove* to her list of accomplishments as well. It had been her design for the *Mallard Cove* property that added the second restaurant, the hotel, and the in-and-out boat storage. That part had come only three months after she started working at their management company. But Kari didn't volunteer her history with Casey and Dawn, I had to drag it out of her. She wasn't into bragging nor putting up with braggarts.

Five minutes after passing the CBBT, we arrived at Stingray Point. At least it seemed like five minutes instead of the actual hour and a half; the time just flew by, riding and talking with her. We entered the Rappahannock River and took the first inlet to the south, then a quick turn to port into a winding offshoot from the river, which soon became lined with docks and boats as we approached the marina. As we rounded the last bend and the houseboat came into view, the look on Kari's face was priceless. She started to say, "The pictures..."

"Didn't do it justice. I know." It was all I could do to keep from laughing.

"That color is so fugly..."

That caught me off guard. "What's 'fugly'?"

"F...friggin' ugly!" She was shaking her head.

"I know, right? Who would do this to that? It's nice though, once you get past the color." I believed it. Really.

"I can see it too, but damn!" She lifted her eyebrows as she shook her head. "Okay, you want me to handle the lines?"

My turn to challenge her. "Oh, sorry, I didn't realize you can't back a boat into a slip."

The look on her face read "challenge accepted." She backed *Marlinspike* in without touching a single piling. I set the lines and we walked over to the houseboat where Bill was already in full-on "Baloney mode".

"The guy who picked this color was a moron! But the boat's not that bad once you get past the color. Kinda comfortable even."

"I know, right? I can't wait to get her painted." Lindsay was at the top of her happy meter.

A few minutes later, after everyone had the grand tour, we heard someone yelling from the dock. "Hey, Captain Murphy!" After we walked out onto the landing deck we saw it was Denny. "Thanks for coming over today after all. Y'all moving her tonight?"

Murph shook his head. "First thing in the morning. Should be pretty calm by then."

"Well, I appreciate that. What are your plans for the evening?"

"I thought we'd try to get over to Taylors again. A fed crew is a happy crew, and these are all volunteers."

Denny nodded. "Good plan. If you need a way over there, look in front of the dockmaster's office, the marina pickup is there. Some of you will have to ride in the back, but hey, it beats walking. Keys are above the visor on the passenger side."

"Thanks, Denny. I guess we'll see you in the morning."

"Nothing personal, Captain, but I hope not. Mr. Cetta likes getting here early."

"Don't worry, we'll be up and moving."

After Denny left, Lindsay and Kari walked over to the dockmaster's office to retrieve the pickup. The three of us that were left set up a temporary bar in the houseboat's galley. Murph bartended, and we all raised our glasses in a toast to his new home. Then we climbed up to the party deck and perched in some of the new director's chairs that Lindsay had purchased and brought over on the Rybovich.

"That kid sure looked like she knew what she was doin' with your rig, Shaker," Bill said.

"Heck, Baloney, she runs a boat better than you!" I figured the faster we got off the subject of Kari, especially with Bill calling her a "kid," the safer tonight's conversation would be for me. Usually, he didn't like having his fishing or boating skills impugned, so this should have him changing the subject fast. I noted that Murph was looking amused. For someone who had only known me just a few months, he sure could read me. He knew exactly where I was going with this.

"That bar's not set too high, Marlin," Murph joined in, knowing that this would help derail Baloney. He had a horse in this race too. If Lindsay had heard Bill's comment, you know it wouldn't have been a good thing.

"Yeah, well, whatever. But now I see why she's doin' such a good job with the marina; she knows her way aroun' boats. Speakin' ah that, you make up a towing harness, Murph?"

"I did. We're all set for tomorrow. Even found a used bow pudding in that marine secondhand store for *Marlinspike* so they can push like a tugboat if they need to."

"What the heck's a bow puddin'?"

It was nice to see Baloney stumped on something to do with boats for once. I was able to answer this one; "You know those hemp or nylon fenders they used to use on tugboat bows? You know, before they switched over to using truck tires? Those things that look like macramé on steroids? Those are bow puddings. Getting to be a lost art, making them."

"And it's going in the beach bar as a decoration when we're through," Murph said.

A rough-looking pickup truck pulled up behind us on the dock, and it sounded even worse than it looked. Lindsay and Kari climbed out as Murph said loudly, "Bar's set up in the galley." They disappeared below, reemerging two minutes later with libations in hand, taking two of the three unoccupied director's chairs.

Murph looked at Lindsay, "I hope that thing can make it over to Taylors and back."

"Murph, it can't be four miles roundtrip."

"I know."

She chuckled. "It might not make it to ESVA, but it'll do for tonight. Whoever rides back in the bed will need a current tetanus shot though, there are some huge holes in it."

AFTER DRAINING the second round of drinks, we were off to Taylors. We grabbed the biggest table on the bar side. Bill was at his two-drink volume, talking loudly across the table.

From over at the bar a voice yelled, "Baloney!" A big bearded guy approached Bill. "You gotta be Baloney off the *Golden Dolphin*. I'd know that voice anywhere. Jimbo Morris from the *Can Do.*"

"Jimbo! Great ta put a face with ah name." Baloney went around the table, introducing all of us. "Jimbo runs ah forty-six Bertram outta Fisherman's Harbor. Pull up a chair."

"Don't mind if I do. What brings you across the bay? The food here is great, but you're a long way from home." Jimbo had an infectious smile and a way of making you feel like you'd known him forever. Bill related the story and again referred to the houseboat as the *Ralph House*. Jimbo roared. "You get that from one of the guys over here?"

Baloney shook his head as he motioned to our waitress to bring Jimbo a drink. "Nope, came up with that 'un myself, why?"

"Everybody here has been calling it that since they painted it over at Dusky's yard. The weirdest color I've ever seen on anything that floats. The guy was a little weird, too. But I guess he disappeared."

Lindsay asked, "Did you meet him?"

"No, but my brother-in-law did. He's a carpenter; the one who gutted and replaced the interior. The owner hired two guys to drag it over there with a pair of deadrises after they launched it. It was a windy day, and they had a helluva time getting it around one turn in there. The guy paid them, and that's the last anybody ever saw of him. Nobody's even stayed on the boat that I know of. Then that jerk Cetta got hold of it. He hated its nickname, the color, and everything else about it. Kept giving poor Denny hell about it not selling, as if it was all his fault."

"Sounds like him. We had our own run-in with him, a while back." Lindsay related their story, and Jimbo roared.

Jimbo proved to be good company, and he ended up having dinner with us. He was almost as full of stories as Bill, but several decibels lower. By the end of dinner, he had committed to making a trip over to *Mallard Cove* at some point next season. He, Murph, and Lindsay were also tossing around the idea of an East/West Chesapeake fishing tournament. I noticed that Kari didn't jump into that conversation. I figured I could ask her why on the ride back tomorrow.

After dinner, we all said goodbye to Jimbo and headed back to the marina. Murph, Lindsay, and Kari took the two staterooms on *Irish Luck* while Baloney took the master and I took the guest quarters on the *Ralph House*. I guess I shouldn't get into the habit of calling it that though. But *On Coastal Time* just seemed a bit long as a name. I didn't want to make waves and get on Lindsay's bad side again though.

5

CETTA

The next morning Murph cooked breakfast on the Rybovich because the only thing we had aboard the houseboat was the sub sandwiches that were going to be our lunch. Then we got about the business of prepping *Ralph House* for her tow home. Fortunately, as Murph had predicted, the wind had completely laid down overnight and we were able to "walk" the houseboat out of her slip. She had three Samson posts on both the square transom and the shovel-nosed bow. We attached the "Y"-shaped towing harness to the two outboard ones up on the bow. Back aft I snubbed up *Marlinspike*'s newly pudding–adorned bow to the center post, wrapping it and my bow cleats with heavy lines, allowing me to pivot and push the stern at steep angles. That one tight turn right in front of the dockmaster's office had me concerned. It would take a good push from Kari and me to get her cleanly around that curve.

Murph and Lindsay moved her slowly ahead, and I was able to get a bit used to how she was going to handle. Have you ever seen that ice sport called curling? The one with the huge granite rock they "toss" and the people who use special brooms in front of it to smooth the ice and try to direct it? Let's just say I now know how they feel. My two outboards have a lot of horsepower, but their small propellers are designed for speed, not for guiding a who-knows-how-many-ton houseboat. Jimbo's buddies' deadrises have much larger propellers for pushing heavy loads of fish and oysters, which would have given them a huge advantage over my Gold Line. But we were going nice and slow, and I was just nudging her one way or the other, trying to keep her in the middle. Baloney was watching from the party deck with a boat hook. He was more useful up there as another set of eyes for me, and he was giving me hand signals. If we got to the point where he needed to use that hook, we would already be screwed.

You know Newton's law of physics that says, *a body in motion tends to stay in motion unless acted upon by Marlin Denton*? That's what was scaring the heck out of me at present. This thing did not like to turn. With its high profile and flat bottom, I prayed that we could get it out of here before the breeze started picking up. We didn't need to make things any more interesting than they already were.

Murph and Lindsay had the *Ralph House*'s tow line snubbed in as close as they dared, giving them the most control possible in these tight quarters. The turn in front of the office normally had only about fifty-foot clearance across, from piling to piling. But there was a large sailboat tied up bow in which had a dinghy tied up at its stern, sticking way out of the slip and cutting that distance down to about forty feet. Remember, our tow was already eighteen feet across with a long length above the waterline. When you add in the radius of the turn, this was going to be close. Very close. And remember the guy on the other end who was doing the pulling was named Murphy. His family had their own set of laws along with Newton's. Just as he was setting up the turn, those laws came into play when a new but familiar Range Rover pulled up next to the office. A short, balding, somewhat pudgy middle-aged guy got out, took one look at the name on the Rybo, then came out on the nearest finger pier yelling obscenities at Murph and Lindsay.

"You son of a bitches! If I had known it was you that wanted that thing, I'd have never sold it to you! And I'd have never come off the damned price! You touch one damned piling with it, and I'll sue your asses!" Cetta was red in the face, and I'm sure his doctor wouldn't be happy with his blood pressure right then.

"Hey, dipshit! Instead of distracting us at the worst possible point, why don't you take your short fat ass back into your office and play with your toys or yourself, whatever you normally do! Leave us alone and let us do our job."

I'm guessing that you figured that barrage came from Murph or Baloney. You would be wrong. Instead, it had come from a very pretty brunette on my boat. One whose stock had gone up quite a few points right then. Cetta shut up for a second then yelled at her, "This isn't over!"

"Ever have your ass kicked by a woman? Oh, right, Lindsay already did. Keep yammering and it'll be my turn. Now get lost!"

I now understood how Kari had been getting warp speed and quality work out of her contractors. She spoke the same language when it was necessary. Like now.

From up on the party deck came a Jersey-accented voice. "Yeah! What she said." Classic Baloney.

Cetta turned on his heel and went toward the office. I didn't envy Denny right then. I did break my concentration long enough to glance at Kari. "Thanks. I could kiss you for that. Not the best time to be distracted."

"Isn't that what I just told him? And, who said I'd let you?" I felt a playful poke in my side. I glanced at her and got a quick rebuke. "Watch where we're going!"

She had a point, *Ralph House* had started to drift sideways toward that damned dinghy, thanks to a small puff of wind that came out of nowhere. Bill started shouting gibberish and waving his arms like a scarecrow in a hurricane. I put both engines in reverse, revved them up, and threw the helm hard over, pulling against Murph's tow line and stopping the drift about a foot away from the little dink. Out of the corner of my eye, I saw Cetta filming us with a cell phone. Fortunately, so far he was wasting his time. I did hope that he got the two-handed gesture Baloney was making for his benefit.

I backed off the throttle as we got her back in the middle. I finally started to breathe again as we hit the straight part of the channel. We still had a couple of slight bends ahead, but they were at wide spots, so the worst should be over now. Five minutes later we made our turn into the inlet that led to the Rappahannock, and five minutes after that we were headed downstream toward the Chesapeake. Lindsay had already been slowly "paying out" the tow line, preparing for our thirty-five miles across the open bay. I had both engines in forward gear at idle, not really pushing, but reducing our drag a slight bit. Hopefully, *Marlinspike* would act like a rudder set amidships, keeping the tow straight.

Baloney climbed down on my boat with a huge grin. He swatted Kari lightly on the shoulder. "I guess you an' I told Cetta off, huh?"

She smiled and said, "Yeah, Bill, we sure did." Then she looked over at me and caught the tail end of an eye roll. I got poked in the side again.

"Murph and Lindsay got about thirty yards of towline out. Little breeze straight offa th' stern, so we oughta have a smooth ride home," Baloney said. Just then the VHF crackled.

"Hey, Marlin, you read me?" It was Lindsay. Baloney beat me to the mike.

"We gotcha, Lindsay, go ahead."

"Hey, Bill, just the guy I wanted to talk to. Can you keep an eye out from the upper deck? And check the bilge every half hour. We don't want to run into any issues in the middle of the bay because we weren't paying attention."

"Roger that. I'll take care ah it."

"Thanks, Bill. We're doing about eight knots, so with luck, we should be pulling into the marina in under five hours."

"We got this! *Marlinspike*, standin' by." He replaced the microphone it its clip. "I'm gonna go give that bilge ah look. You twos yell if ya need me."

Putting Baloney on bilge watch was a classic Lindsay ploy to keep him busy. I glanced over again and saw Kari was looking at me. I said, "Last night you didn't say a word when Murph and Jimbo were discussing their tournament idea. Wouldn't you normally be involved with that?"

She nodded slightly. "The marina's management is part of my job and my responsibility. When the rebuild is finished I'll be hiring an onsite manager, but this is now a delicate balance for me. Originally, Murph and Lindsay were going to own the marina by themselves and lease out the restaurant space. Murph didn't want to give up control, but he didn't have the full vision for the property nor the capital to make the whole thing happen. Casey and Dawn talked him into letting them and the partners buy into it with Lindsay and him and then let our team run it. I guess you already know they let me have a small percentage of it."

She looked as I nodded silently. "So, with Murph and Casey being so close as friends, those negotiations were delicate, and at times, uncomfortable for me to be around, but it's all a part of doing business. In the end, we were able to come to an agreement that worked for everyone. But it wasn't as clear-cut as you might think. Casey and Dawn told me to look out for the interests of the partners, but to also be careful not to step on Murph's ego. So, it's a really sensitive position, and at times it's like walking a tightrope. If he wants to follow through with this tournament idea, which I think is a good one, I'll quietly make sure it happens and ensure that he gets all the credit.

"Lindsay was the one who gently pushed Murph into the deal. She's just interested in seeing *Mallard Cove* succeed, she could care less about any credit. But most of it belongs to her. And I'd appreciate it if none of this went beyond you."

I had learned a lot about Kari in the last sixteen hours, but the past fifteen minutes made me really appreciate her for who she was, and what she was capable of. Cetta was lucky he backed down. "Wow. Of course, it'll stay with me, and I appreciate the confidence. That's quite a lot of responsibility."

She got a sly look. "You might say it's not too bad for a youngster."

She watched for my reaction, and she got it in the form of a face as red as a boiled lobster. "Uh, I guess you and Lindsay had a conversation."

"A few of them, Marlin. Just like you two did." Her hazel eyes twinkled.

"I didn't mean anything by it. It's just that in the past—"

"In the past, you and I had never met. But hey, want to make it up to me?"

"Uh, sure? What do you have in mind?"

"How about being my date for the restaurant's grand opening next Friday?"

"Won't you be working then?"

"Technically, yes. But only by being there. The head of our restaurant management group, Carlos Ramirez, is in charge of all things food and beverage related. He and I designed the facility, and I'm overseeing the rebuild and expansion, but then he takes it from there. If I have an issue, I take it straight to him. So, I get to just sit at the partner's table, eat, and enjoy myself. I'd rather not do it alone. Are you going to make me ask twice?"

"Yes."

"What!"

"I mean 'yes, I'll go, not 'yes, ask me again.'"

"Great. Since you already live there, I'll pick you up."

I shrugged. "I can meet you at the restaurant."

"That's not how this works. I invited you out, so I get to pick you up. That's the rule."

"I was never much on rules, Kari."

"Never too late to start, not even for an old guy."

Ouch. "Remind me to have another talk with Lindsay."

She laughed, and it was a great laugh. "If you are going mention age again, I get to watch. That's a rule too."

"I think you make these rules up as you go along, like that Gibbs character on television."

"Maybe some of them."

Suddenly I had a flashback to an old relationship with a woman several years younger than me. The things I remembered about her best but tried to forget the most were the rules and games. Kari must have seen it on my face.

"Marlin, I didn't mean to make you mad."

"You didn't. You just reminded me of someone for a second."

"Someone who is part of the reason that you never asked me out?"

"Yep."

"Then I'm even more sorry than I was. I wasn't playing games with you; I was just teasing. Guess I was feeling a bit more comfortable than I should have."

"No, Kari, you shouldn't have to worry about stuff like that. It's not your fault, and I sure don't want you feeling any less comfortable with me."

"Then we're still on for dinner?"

"Of course."

She said, "I can meet you at the restaurant."

"Then I'll still be sitting on my boat, waiting for you to pick me up."

She smiled with relief after she realized that I hadn't taken anything she said the wrong way. We got back on track over the next two and a half hours by talking about our favorite boats, and I told her several funny stories about my dad and me restoring the *Why Knot*. That's when she confessed that the biggest reason she wanted to pick me up for our date was that she had an affinity for old restored boats. She had wanted a tour of mine since she had first seen it.

"Why didn't you just ask me?"

"I didn't want you thinking I wanted a different kind of tour."

I admit that took me a couple of seconds. "Oh. Ohhh. No! Don't worry, I'm not getting the wrong idea."

She laughed again. "I know that now. But without having really talked with each other, it might have been awkward. Or, felt that way."

My turn to chuckle. "Maybe so, but it doesn't now." My cell phone started ringing. I looked at the number and my heart sank when I saw who it was. My uncle's house in Florida. I answered, "Hello, Clara."

"Marlin, your uncle came back early from his trip. He needs to see you."

"I'm in the middle of the Chesapeake right now. I can start driving tonight and be there tomorrow afternoon."

"He's sending his plane for you. When can you be at the Virginia Beach airport?"

"It will be faster if we meet at the Accomack County Airport. I can be there in three hours."

"I'll see you soon then."

I hung up and realized that Kari had been right there and had heard my side of the whole conversation. She looked embarrassed.

"I'm sorry, I didn't mean to eavesdrop, Marlin. And I didn't realize that you were already seeing someone."

I was confused for a second, then I recalled what she had heard. It might have sounded like that to her. Knowing that it wasn't good news when I saw the caller ID had thrown me off.

"You didn't, and I'm not. I'd have never agreed to go out with you if I was." I sighed because I didn't want Kari or the gang to know about my family connections. As I said before, it tends to warp the way people think of me and give them the wrong expectations. But I didn't want to leave things hanging like this. I realized that I felt it mattered what Kari thought about me.

"This is going to sound so lame, but it's the truth. That was my uncle's assistant. He's ill and wants to see me. So, I have to fly down to Florida tonight. But I'm asking you to keep it under your hat, he's kind of funny about keeping any health issues private." I knew that Casey was a pilot, and hopefully by her being used to her boss flying by private plane, this wouldn't be a big deal to her. Plus, she didn't know that it wasn't a small prop plane. But in essence, by taking that plane ride I was writing a check that my ego and my bank account couldn't come close to cashing. It was part of Uncle Jack's world.

I could see her mulling over what I had said, and in the end, she decided to trust me.

"Don't worry, I've got your back. You said you had mine in the whole Murph partner thing, so I guess we're even."

I was relieved, and I guess I looked it. She put her hand on my shoulder for a few seconds to reassure me. A minute later Bill stepped aboard with three subs and sodas for all of us for lunch. I passed.

"You feelin' okay, Shaker? Never known you ta turn down lunch."

"Not hungry right now, Bill, maybe later."

By the time they both finished their lunches we were approaching the CBBT. Forty-five minutes later *On Coastal Time* was tied up in her new slip, and *Marlinspike* was back in hers. I knew that Murph and Lindsay were going to have a ton of curious friends that wanted to check out their new home, not to mention they had more gear to load aboard. I really wouldn't be missed since they'd have plenty of help. In case I was, I asked Kari to apologize and just say that I suddenly remembered I had to be somewhere. Ten minutes later I was showered, changed, had a light travel bag, and was on my way to the airport.

HALF AN HOUR later I rushed through the small waiting room at the fixed base operator's terminal and saw the copilot waiting by the security door. He nodded to someone behind the counter and the door slid open. He took my bag as we hustled toward the waiting Gulfstream. I climbed up the stairs as he stowed the bag in the baggage compartment back aft. The auxiliary power unit was running, and the captain fired up the starboard engine while the copilot closed the air-stair door and latched it. Within a minute of him sitting down both engines were running, and we were taxiing out for takeoff. I hadn't noticed the smaller Cessna jet that had pulled up in front of the terminal as I was boarding, but someone in that plane had seen me.

~

CASEY SHAW SAT in the copilot seat of his Cessna jet. The head of his aviation department, Sam Knight, was in the pilot's left seat as usual.

"Check that one out, Casey! What a beauty. That's the biggest plane I've ever seen in here. Our runway must be marginal for her; I know this tarmac sure is crowded now with just the two of us on it."

Casey watched as two figures emerged from the terminal, and headed for the airplane. He noted the tail number ending in DA and looked it up in the FAA database on his smartphone. He thought he had recognized the one man, and this pretty much confirmed he had been correct. The plane was registered to Denton Aviation in Naples, Florida. The man he had seen crossing the ramp was Marlin Denton, and he had handed off his luggage and bounded up the stairs like it wasn't the first time he'd been aboard. What was a fishing captain from ESVA doing with a Gulfstream 800 from Florida, Casey wondered. He knew Marlin from down at *Mallard Cove* and liked him, but now alarms were going off in his head. In the past, Marlin had proven that he knew how to handle weapons, and he wasn't short on guts. But he wasn't supposed to be long on cash. So many people along the waterfront had hidden wealth that came from one thing; drug smuggling. That wasn't something that Casey wanted to be connected in any way with *Mallard Cove Marina*.

6

NAPLES

The flight was smooth, and I landed in Naples just under two hours later. I thanked the crew and headed down the stairs. A large black Mercedes pulled up to the plane just as I reached the tarmac. Clara stepped out of the back door and greeted me with a hug. The hug was customary, but her meeting me at the plane was not. The co-pilot put my bag in the trunk as Clara and I both got in the back, the driver moving as soon as the second door closed.

"Sorry that I couldn't tell you more on the phone, you know how your uncle is about that."

"Yes, all too well. It's back, isn't it?"

She nodded, then teared up for a minute. "You need to be prepared when you see him. He should never have attempted this trip, but he wasn't about to give up."

"He has now?"

She nodded. "He got to London, then he collapsed. Dr. Harris made him come home. He knew the added stress of the trip..." Her voice trailed off; the implication crystal clear.

I had thought I was prepared for whatever this might be, but now with my worst fears confirmed, I knew I wasn't ready for this. I'd never be ready. Other than my dad, Uncle Jack was my closest relative. Hell, my closest friend, for that matter. We had discussed anything and everything ever since I was a little kid. He was always ready with advice when asked, but never butted in without an invitation. There was a certain comfort that I felt around him, one that I had never known anywhere else, or with anyone else.

The rest of the ten-minute trip passed in silence, then we finally pulled through the gates onto what Floridians called a Chattahoochee pebble driveway. The tires made the familiar crunching sound on the loose river rock that I recalled from back in my childhood. It was the only comfort I had felt since getting into the car. We got out at the entrance to the covered walkway. I passed both guesthouses and entered the house with Clara. We walked to the door of Uncle Jack's room, but she didn't go in with me. I walked in to find a nurse checking his pulse. He was lying in bed, and he looked like hell. The nurse said, "It would be best if you only visit for five minutes at a time."

"He just flew a thousand miles. He'll visit for as long as I want. Leave us be."

She shot Uncle Jack a withering look and left the room.

He motioned me into a chair next to his bed. "How was the flight?"

"Smooth as always, Uncle Jack. Thanks for the ride."

"Thank you for dropping everything to get here. Clara said you were out in the bay. Fishing charter?"

"Helping some friends bring home a new houseboat."

Uncle Jack nodded, not questioning, just accepting. "What did you think of the new plane?"

"A beauty. But all your planes have been beautiful."

"Ah, but this one's twenty knots faster and goes a thousand miles farther than the last one. Did you have any drinks on the way down?"

I smiled, knowing where he was headed with this. He loved his vodka. "Two. Got into your private stash."

"Private, hell! I had 'em put it out for you. Nobody touches that but you and me. Let everybody else drink the cheap stuff. I ever tell you about the time we were stuck one morning in this little airport in

Alabama that didn't have any deicing equipment? A tenth of an inch of ice on the wings when we got ready to leave that morning. No hanger there big enough to hold her, so she sat out in the freezing rain." He waited for me to answer.

He had told me, only about a dozen times. "No, Uncle. What did you do?"

"I had to be at this closing in New York, so we couldn't wait for it to get warm enough for the ice to melt. Had two cases of that other vodka. Poured it on the wings, and it ate the ice right off 'em. Lucky it didn't eat the paint, too." He smiled at the memory. "So, do I have any new grandkids in the making?"

Grandkids? Wow, this was a new one. His mind must be starting to wander a bit, confusing me with my cousin Jack. I let it pass rather than correct him. "I broke up with Tiffany last year. Haven't really dated since."

"Tiffany. Sounds like a stripper's stage name. Good thing you are rid of her. You know, you could pick up a fine woman with that Gulfstream if you play your cards right."

"I'm sure I could, Uncle. But I'm doing fine on my own. In fact, I have met a woman I'm interested in getting to know a lot better. Tough and smart; I think you'd like and approve of her."

He smiled and gave me a sly wink. "Take her for a spin in the plane when you get back. You saw it has a bed in the stateroom."

I shook my head and chuckled. "No, I'm good, but thanks anyway. You know me, if they aren't impressed with my Sport Trac truck, then I'm not impressed with them."

"Are you still driving that old heap?"

"Easy, Uncle Jack, you're talking about the truck I love."

"They haven't made those things in well over a decade. I could give you the Mercedes, I don't need it any longer."

That shook me, and I wanted to get away from any talk about him not being around. "Gee, thanks, then I could trade it in on two more Sport Tracs."

"More like a dozen of 'em." He paused and took my hand. "You're happy with your life the way it is, aren't you, Marlin?"

I nodded. "Yes. I'm doing what I love, where I love to do it."

He smiled again, but it was a sad smile. "Then keep doing it like you're doing it, and don't let anything change your life. I wish I was going to be here to see how more of it turns out." He paused, "I need to tell you something that I should have long ago." He paused again, and I now saw pain fill his eyes. Then something changed, and he started coughing. It was a deep rattling cough, and his hand tightened painfully on mine. I noticed a spot of red blood on his lip, and I panicked.

"Nurse. Nurse, help!" I stood up and leaned over him as the coughing got even worse. She came racing in and prepared a syringe of some solution. In between hacks, he managed to get out, "I'm. Sorry. Marlin. Don't. Want. To. Wreck. Things. More. Than. I. Already. Have."

The nurse gave him the shot, and within a minute the coughing eased. She looked at me and said, "You need to let him rest." Whatever she had given him must have been a sedative and painkiller. His hand went limp in mine, his deep green eyes were sunken and now glazed over. The nurse said, "He won't be able to talk again until morning. Why don't you go rest up, and then visit him again then."

I don't even remember walking out of the room, I was in such a daze. I just remember Clara leading me over to the pickled cypress-paneled Florida room. She guided me to a chair where I looked across the room and out through a huge glass window at the Gulf of Mexico and the gathering twilight. I hadn't even realized how late it was. Clara sat in a chair next to mine.

"I'm sorry, Marlin. I wish that I could have better prepared you for this."

"His mind started to wander, Clara, he seemed to be confusing me with Jack Junior. Then he said he had something to tell me that he should have long ago. He apologized to me. I have no idea why, he had nothing to apologize for."

"Hey, pal, thanks for coming." My cousin Jack Junior walked in, followed closely by his right-hand guy, Dennis Peel. "I know it's a shock. How are you coping?" I noticed that Jack's bright green eyes were fixed on mine, almost boring in like they were asking a silent question.

"I'm not ready for him to go yet, Jack. I don't think I'll ever be ready for that." I saw Jack's eyes soften a bit, and his face almost registered relief. Now I was confused again.

"I know, pal, none of us are. I checked with the nurse and saw that she had sedated him. Clara, you've been on for quite a while, why don't you go home and get some rest?"

Clara looked at me. "Are you going to be all right, Marlin?"

I nodded. "Yes. Jack's right, you've had a day of it. Go rest up and I'll see you tomorrow."

After Clara left, Dennis silently perched on a stool with his back to the bar, watching us. I never really liked him; he was a schoolmate of Jack's who eventually came to work for him. Balding and skinny with a runner's physique, he looked similar to the lawyer that got eaten in that famous dinosaur movie. Maybe even smarmier.

"The nurse said you did get a chance to talk for a while." Jack's statement almost felt like a question, expecting me to fill the void after it with an answer.

"Yes, but he seemed a bit confused. Told me the vodka deicing story again like it was the first time. Then he asked me if he had any more grandkids on the way. He had me confused with you." I could swear I saw something in Jack's eyes right then. Just for a fleeting microsecond, they seemed to register panic, then went back to their normal steeliness.

"That could be from the disease, or the meds, Marlin. He may say things that make no sense because of them."

"What are they giving him, chemo?"

Jack's eyes softened for the first time today. "The nurse is an end-of-life nurse, Marlin, specializing in keeping terminal patients comfortable in their final days. The time for chemo is over, cuz. This was Dr. Harris's recommendation. This is your last visit together, pal. He's been fading fast, but he wanted to see you one last time." Jack almost looked sorry for me, and yet Uncle Jack was *his* father. But they hadn't always had the best relationship. As I said, my uncle judged Jack by a different scale, and it hadn't always seemed fair.

I sat in the chair, stunned, as his words sunk in.

"Have you had anything to eat?"

That was when I realized I hadn't eaten since breakfast, but I wasn't hungry. I shook my head and said, "I don't want anything."

"You look like you've taken off some weight, that's good." Appearance was a very important part of both Jack's lives. When I had gained so much weight, I had endured more than a few verbal shots from both of them. Maybe it was for my own good, or maybe my weight had been an embarrassment to the family. Or both. Not that it mattered now. I didn't travel in Jack's circles. When my uncle is gone, I doubt that I'll hear from Jack. I'm sure I'll become a very distant relative, out of both sight and mind.

"I think they've got you set up in the room over the garage. You look bushed, why don't you go hit the rack and get some sleep. Maybe Dad will be recovered enough by the morning that you can have a final visit, and we'll fly you back home. Get some rest, pal."

I don't even remember getting in bed, I guess I was in a bit of shock after being told I might get one "final visit" in the morning. Jack was taking his place at the top of the family, and it was clear that mine was already at the bottom, not that I thought it would be anywhere else.

JACK WALKED over to the bar, where Dennis poured both of them vodkas on the rocks. Jack said, "He doesn't know, Dad didn't tell him. Not that it matters, he isn't specifically named in the Will no matter what. Good thing you have that friend at his lawyer's office. But if he were to find out and get a copy of it as we did, it could be a disaster."

Dennis nodded and stayed silent, listening for clues from Jack. His job was to be his "fixer," handling things at arm's length, leaving Jack with plausible deniability. So far he wasn't hearing anything needing to be acted on; everything was under control. But he was thinking about putting someone on tailing Marlin just to be certain. He knew the last thing Jack wanted was a scandal; it was bad for business. A business that he was about to inherit total control of for the first time. A business where appearances meant everything.

~

CASEY WENT from the airport over to his yacht and floating home, *Lady Dawn*. He found Dawn already on their upper deck having a glass of wine. He poured himself one and sat on a chaise next to hers.

"Lindsay and Murph have become close with that guy Marlin Denton, right?"

Dawn nodded. "The three of them have been spending a lot of time together. Why?" She had noticed Casey's concerned look.

"You know anything about him?"

Now it was Dawn's turn to be concerned. "Just what you already know. He's a fishing guide and lives at *Mallard Cove* on that beautiful old Chris Craft that you like. He isn't broke, but he's not swimming in cash. He doesn't run from danger, and he sure proved that when Lindsay got kidnapped. Seems to know how to handle a gun as well as a boat. Again, why?"

"Because I saw him getting onto a G-800 as I was coming in. It's a brand new one registered to a Denton Aviation out of Naples, Florida. I've never heard of them, but I checked, and they own four planes. A hundred million plus dollars worth of aircraft."

"And you're certain it was him?"

"Positive. Plus, in checking for pictures of those four planes on the Internet, none exist. There are pictures of almost every registered aircraft online, but not those four. They've been scrubbed off of it. That takes a *lot* of pull."

"You're thinking maybe a drug connection?" Dawn looked worried.

"Wouldn't be the first time things like that have happened. The smartest ones hide in plain sight. You know what it would cost to have a boatyard restore a wood Chris Craft up to the same level as his? You don't make that kind of money hauling tourists around in an outboard."

Dawn picked up her cell phone and hit a stored number. "Hi, Lindsay, it's Dawn."

"Hey, Dawn! We just got back with *On Coastal Time* and got her all tied up." She walked out onto the floating dock so she could hear better, away from all the well-wishers that were already on board and partying.

"Really? That's great, I can't wait to see how it comes out after you finish painting it."

"You'll have to come help." Lindsay grinned, knowing this wasn't Dawn's "thing."

"Uh, no, you don't want me to paint anything if you want more of it on the boat than on me."

"Well, come and have a wine anyway."

"We'll be there for the grand opening on Friday, and we'll stop by and have a drink beforehand."

Lindsay smiled. "Book it, Dawn-O!"

"Hey, Linds, have you seen Marlin Denton around? Casey said he thought he saw him at the airport a while ago but just missed him. He wasn't sure it was him but didn't want him to feel snubbed if it was."

"Couldn't have been him, he was our 'tugboat' and we just got here an hour and a half ago. He's around somewhere. I'm trying to help Kari and him get together, they'd make such a cute couple. She rode with him on the way over and back, and she's totally smitten. I'm working her butt off this weekend; I've got her doing bartending duty right now."

"Well, it sounds like you have your hands full so, I'll let you get back to it. Talk to you later this week."

She hung up and looked at Casey who had heard it all through her speakerphone. He was thinking.

"If they got in an hour and a half ago, he'd have had just enough time to rush up to the airport and be there when I saw him get on that plane. I'm telling you it was him. The name is too much of a coincidence. I'm going to text Kari and ask her to call when she's out of earshot."

"Be careful, Casey. If it's just something innocent, you don't want to plant seeds of doubt that might screw up their friendship. If it does, it could affect Lindsay's and mine as well." Meaning that it could also end up having a domino effect on him and Murph; he understood all of the implications.

KARI LOOKED at her phone and the cryptic message from Casey asking her to call when she was alone. She excused herself, getting Murph to take over the bar. Then she found a large stone to sit on over at the basin's breakwater, away from the party.

"Hi, Casey. Is everything okay?"

Casey had thought about different ways to handle this, but Kari was too sharp to play games with and he respected her too much. "Is Marlin Denton around?"

That threw her a bit, that he thought she might know. "Actually, no. Why?"

"When did he leave?"

"A little over an hour ago." She heard the concern in Casey's voice and decided to tell him what happened. "He told me to tell anyone who asked that he had forgotten he had somewhere to be. Again, why?"

"Do you have any idea how he is connected to Denton Aviation and a fleet of corporate jets?"

She was shocked. "I've never heard of Denton Aviation, and I'm sure he can't afford to even charter a jet. Remember, Murph gave him slip rent credits to sign up new renters, and he moved over here because he couldn't afford his old marina's rates."

"Denton Aviation owns over a hundred million dollars worth of airplanes. And I'm pretty certain I just saw him get on a new G-800 up here."

Her head was swimming now. "Okay, what he asked me to say was only partially true. On the way back over here some woman called, he said she told him his uncle was sick and he needed to come right away. I knew he was going to fly on a private plane because he told her to have it meet him at Accomack instead of Virginia Beach, and there aren't any airlines that fly out of there. He said he was going to Florida, but not to say anything." She thought a minute. "Yesterday he ran outside to take a call in private, and when he came back in he was clearly upset. He said it had to do with a family matter. Now I don't know what to think. He didn't seem like a guy who keeps secrets, but there's something off here. He can't afford his old slip's rent but flies around on private jets? I feel so stupid right now."

"Whoa, Kari, let's not jump to conclusions. There may be a logical explanation for this. And frankly, if there is we may not even be entitled to it. But it might not hurt to keep our eyes open. Could be that it is family money."

"The only family he talked about with me were his parents. After a car wreck that killed his mom, his father ended up in a care facility. Marlin said he almost had to sell his boat to keep paying for that, but then his father died. That's why this whole jet thing has to be wrong, it has to be a mistake, Casey."

"Maybe, Kari. But if he's involved in something illegal, we don't want him near *Mallard Cove*. And now he's brought in half a dozen boats of people that he knows, but we really don't. This could be another nightmare, just like that kidnapping ring that was down there. So, keep all this under your hat for now. Think about it overnight and let's talk up here at the office in the morning."

"Okay. I'll see you then." She suddenly didn't feel like rejoining the party. She went over and collected her old change of clothes from *Irish Luck* and headed home.

Back on *Lady Dawn*, Casey got hold of Sam Knight and asked him to call in a favor over at the airport. Everybody over there seemed to owe Sam favors.

7

THE NOTE

I woke up a little after 5 a.m., dressed, and headed to my uncle's room. His night nurse was sitting beside him and got up to meet me at the door. "You must be Marlin. He wants to see you. I just gave him something for the pain, so he may be a little foggy. It's good that you are here now, I don't know how much longer he'll be able to communicate. I'll be right outside if you need me." She went out of the room as I sat in the same chair as yesterday.

Uncle Jack looked even paler than he had before, and his eyes had sunk back into their sockets a bit farther. He focused on me and reached for my hand.

"Marlin. Something I need to say... should have told you... long before...now." He sucked in a deep breath.

"Just rest, Uncle Jack. I'm here. You don't need to say anything."

He shook his head. "Important. You're...my..." He started coughing again, and the nurse rushed in and gave him another shot.

"Marlin, go get some breakfast. He should sleep a few hours, then you can try talking with him again. Let him rest for now."

I went into the kitchen where Cathy the cook was pulling out bacon from the oven and had a fresh pot of coffee brewing. She had been with my uncle for years, even long before my aunt had died. I knew it was tough on her, too.

"How are you holding up, Cathy?"

"Day to day, Marlin. It helps that there are people around to cook for, keeps me busy and my mind off... things. I'm so sorry, Marlin."

I just nodded, because I was suddenly at a loss for words. Cathy made me a plate of scrambled eggs and bacon, but despite not having eaten in twenty-four hours, I was more interested in the coffee. I carried it all out to the bar and perched on the same stool that Peel had used yesterday, but my back was to the room. I was just pushing the eggs around on the plate when my cousin Jack walked in. He looked at the still full plate and the empty coffee and nodded.

"I don't feel much like eating either. Give me your cup."

I handed him my empty coffee mug and he took it to the kitchen, returning it full along with one for him as well.

"Did he say anything to you this morning? I heard you went in early."

"He tried, Jack, but he started the coughing jag again. The nurse said he will likely be out until later this morning."

Jack nodded. "Let's give it one more try together, and then you go home, Marlin. This isn't doing you any good. When was the last time you ate?"

I pointed to a small missing corner on one of the bacon strips. "Just now."

He frowned. "I thought so. Look, he knows you were here, but it's tough on him to see you go through this too. You need to let him go, Marlin. It's his time."

I covered my eyes with one hand, rubbing them so hopefully, Jack wouldn't see what was going on behind it. When I felt like I could hold it together, I said, "He's all I've got left, Jack. When he's gone, I won't have anyone. I know it's selfish of me, but I don't want to let go."

Jack put his hand on my shoulder. "You've always got me, cuz. I'm just at the other end of the phone."

For the second time today, I was at a loss for words. Jack had always been the cool older cousin when I was growing up. But his life was focused on helping Uncle Jack build the business, and mine was on school and later on the water. We were miles apart, in a lot of ways. He had a slew of kids, ex-wives, and ex-girlfriends. Some were nearly my age. Like I said, miles apart. But somehow I managed to say simply, "Thanks."

Jack walked out, and I took my plate back into the kitchen. Cathy knew better than to think the pile of food that was left was a reflection on her cooking. I left to wander around the house which was flooded with natural light from all the large windows. Most of the tables held pictures of my uncle and my late aunt with family, friends, celebrities, and even a few presidents. Several even included my ugly mug. Snapshots of an incredible life lived well for the most part.

I ended back up in the Florida room, sitting alone on the couch for a few hours. I was twiddling with my phone, trying to keep occupied. I had it set on silent/vibrate, and it kept blowing up. Murph, Lindsay, and Baloney all left voicemails or texts wondering where I was and if I was all right. There was also a text from Kari saying she would like to talk and wondering when I was coming back. I was going to have to make up a great excuse for the first three, but I didn't have a clue what I would say to Kari. I didn't want to lie to her. I hadn't, and I wasn't planning to start. I was so preoccupied that I hadn't noticed Clara come in and sit down in the chair next to my couch.

"I hear you're heading home."

She startled me. "You've heard that too, eh? I'm going to see him one more time and then I'm supposed to leave. I guess it's best for him. Apparently, I'm stressing him out a bit by being here."

She shook her head. "He has been fighting to be awake and aware while you're here. The coughing is bad." She leaned forward, indicating I was to do the same. In a low voice, she continued, "But they've been keeping him doped up, and I swear it's on purpose. That damned Dennis Peel has been in charge of the nurses; he was even the one that brought them in. Why Jack allowed that I don't know." She leaned back as I sat there in shock. It was the first time in my life that I had ever heard Clara curse. She had to be really upset for that to happen. As I was pondering what she had said, Cousin Jack appeared in the doorway.

"Marlin, it's time."

I swear he almost glared at Clara, and that was another first for me. I got up and followed him into Uncle Jack's room. The nurse wasn't in sight, which I thought was odd, since he was there all alone. Uncle Jack was awake but seemingly unable to talk. I held his hand, but it was still. He didn't grip mine as he had before. I could see his eyes follow mine, but the light within them was dimmer than it had been.

I sat with Jack standing behind me. I leaned forward and told my uncle that I loved him, and I thanked him for everything he had done for me throughout my life and that I'd miss him, but we'd see each other again in the blink of an eye. I stood up and saw that his eyes had welled up like mine. He had heard me.

After they were alone again, Jack Denton Junior looked at his father, "So, you weren't able to tell Marlin your big secret. Too bad, because I'm not going to tell him either. You'll just have to tell him yourself if he ends up in the same place as you. And I'm not so sure he will. Maybe he'll forgive you, but I won't."

With that, Jack Denton Sr. closed his eyes, not wanting to look at his namesake ever again.

I honestly don't remember the car ride to the airport. I do know that I was alone. I never saw Clara again before I left. Jack had someone pack for me. He put that reassuring hand on my shoulder at the end of the walkway before I climbed into the car. My bag was waiting in the backseat next to me. The noise of the Chattahoochee river rock under the tires that had sounded so familiar and comforting on the way in sounded almost alien when I left.

When I got to my seat on the plane, there was a cardboard case strapped in on the one across from me where my uncle normally sat. On top of it was an envelope with my name written in his handwriting. One of his personal notecards with the initials JD on the front cover was inside.

Dear Marlin,

I'm writing this on my way back from London. By now we've had our talk, and I hope that things went well. Please find it in your heart to forgive me.

I've instructed the crew to give you my last case of that vodka we always shared together, and there's a fresh bottle in the bar for your trip back. I only wish that I was there to share it with you. Know that you are very much admired, and if I have any regrets it's that we didn't fish together more often. I'd have loved to give you another greasy, fried pork sandwich.

JD

Forgive him? For what? I was more grateful to him than anyone else on the planet. I didn't understand what he meant by that, and now I never would. But when I got to the bit about the pork sandwich, that did it. I lost it. Uncle Jack had taken me white marlin fishing off Virginia Beach when I was eleven or so. I'd never been offshore before and started to get a little queasy in the cockpit with all the diesel fumes wafting around while we trolled. I retreated into the cabin where he was reading sales reports.

He was always working, even when he was out having fun. My favorite picture of him was taken about the same year. He was waist deep in the Gulf in front of the Naples house, a cigar in his mouth and one of those old green and white computer printout sheets in his hands. That's how you build a multi-billion dollar business, not just by just hoping, dreaming, or thinking about it.

Anyway, on that first fishing trip, I lay down on the couch in the salon. Uncle Jack saw that I was kind of green and asked me if I wanted one of the "greasy, fried pork sandwiches" that he'd brought along. That was it, I was up and out, back in the cockpit leaning over the side, throwing up my toenails. As luck would have it, that was when my very first white marlin chose to strike. Those sandwiches always went with us from that day on.

On the flight home, I did my best to put a huge dent in that bottle Uncle Jack had left me in the bar. I didn't really think about the thirty-mile drive I had ahead of me once we landed. Hell, I couldn't have driven thirty yards. As it was, I didn't have to. Waiting for me at the bottom of the plane's stairs were Kari, her boss Casey Shaw, and some other guy who looked like that narrator from the Big Lebowski movie. Oh, crap. So much for keeping a low profile.

It must have been an impressive sight, my pulling up in a big Gulfstream, and then almost falling down the stairs with that open bottle in my arms. To top it all off, I puked on Casey's shoes. Then everything went black.

"I JUST HAD a text from the airport, that Gulfstream is due back in about an hour. One passenger aboard."

"Thanks, Sam. Do you mind meeting us there? Maybe you can get some info out of the crew." Casey knew that crews are usually laxer about talking with other pilots, and everyone loved talking to Sam Knight, who looked a lot like that actor, Sam Elliott. Then he and Kari would see what they could get out of Marlin.

The three of them were waiting when the Gulfstream pulled up, but they weren't expecting what came next. One very inebriated Marlin Denton almost plunging headfirst down the stairs only to be caught under his arms by both Casey and Kari.

"Hi, everybo...every...ralllph. Oh, crap. Cleanup on aisle one."

Casey was shaking vomit off one shoe while he and Kari gently lowered a now passed-out Marlin to the ramp. One of the crew came down the stairs with a cardboard case while the other went to fetch Marlin's bag.

The captain asked, "Are you friends of Marlin's? I can't leave him here like this alone without any help."

Kari replied, "We are, but we're just a little confused. I've never seen him like this."

"Neither have I miss, and I've been flying for his uncle for years. I've had Marlin aboard dozens of times, and usually, he's only good for a drink or two on long flights. But please don't judge him too harshly, since he's having to deal with his uncle's condition. Marlin's a good man. I'm going to miss him."

She nodded like she knew what that was all about and was relieved to see Sam and the copilot coming their way with Marlin's bag. She carefully removed the bottle from his arms and found an engraving in the glass on the back. *"Distilled especially for Jack and Marlin Denton."* She recognized both names, but the first one raised more questions than it answered. They loaded the case, Marlin's bag, and an unconscious Marlin onto a baggage cart and rolled him to Casey's Jeep.

I WOKE up in a chaise lounge on the upper deck of Casey Shaw's yacht. It was a chilly morning and despite the blanket that someone had thrown over me, I was still cold. There was a plastic bucket next to me, fortunately empty, and no signs of any off-target accidents on the deck, nor on me either. After what happened yesterday, I was wishing I was dead. I kind of felt halfway there, too. So much for ever seeing Kari again, and now I was going to have to move the boats.

"Good morning, Marlin." It was Casey, carrying a plate of pastries and a tall glass of orange juice that he set on a low table next to me. "You might try sipping the orange juice and slowly nibbling on some of the pastries. Right now, carbohydrates are your friends."

"My only friends, Casey. First, let me start by saying that I'm so sorry, and I'm getting out of here right away. Or whenever I find my truck. Please tell me I didn't drive here. And speaking of here, I'm assuming this is *Bayside*, right?"

"Marlin, just stop and relax. You have more friends than you realize. We talked to the plane's crew, and we know what you are going through. Just forget about it, nobody is judging you. Yes, we're at *Bayside*, and no, you didn't drive here. Your truck is still at the airport, right where you left it. There was no way we were letting you drive anywhere in that condition." He pulled my keys out of his pocket and handed them to me.

Still, I was mortified. You don't forget things like what happened on the tarmac. "I owe you a new pair of shoes."

"Nope, wash and wear deck shoes. They've already been through the washer, and they're fine."

"I'm so embarrassed. I can't apologize enough to you and Kari."

"It's us that owe you an apology." It was Kari, she had walked up behind me.

"Oh, hi." I was hoping to have been able to sneak away without having to face her. Cowardly, I know. But the last thing that I felt this morning was brave. "How do you figure *you* owe *me* an apology? I don't remember you puking on me."

"We thought you might be involved in something illegal, and that's why you were hiding the planes. It's why we were at the airport when you came in."

"I wasn't hiding the planes, they're not mine to hide. I was just trying to avoid anyone finding out about my uncle."

She nodded. "We know that now. I'm sorry for suspecting something so bad about you. But you have to admit, most people don't hide their wealthy family connections."

"I'm not most people, Kari. I'm not wealthy and don't want to pretend to be something I'm not. Most people, if they knew I was related to Uncle Jack, would figure that I'm rich too, or that I might become that way when he dies. But our family isn't like that. For generations, the Dentons have passed inheritances straight down to our kids and grandkids, and not to brothers, sisters, nieces, nephews, or cousins. It's our way.

"This is partly why I didn't make my family relationship public. People expect things from you that you can't do, and they think you have things that you don't. Things that you can't afford, and don't even want. Or, they want to use me to get introduced to my uncle. It's why I just keep to myself and the gang at the marina, though now I guess I'll find another place to tie up."

Kari looked surprised. "Why would you leave? We haven't told anyone, and we're not going to. You can trust Sam, Dawn, Casey, and me. I mean, if you still want to."

"My head hurts, and right now I can't even trust this pastry to stay down. But I do appreciate y'all keeping this in confidence. I've got a lot to sort out over the next little bit."

Casey said, "Please accept our apologies, Marlin, and I hope you'll stay at *Mallard Cove*. I know you've been a big promoter and believer in what we're doing there, and though it might not feel like it this morning, we really appreciate that. Stay up here as long as you want, and Kari will follow you back to the marina whenever you want to go. I hope I'll see you there on Friday night."

After Casey left, Kari asked me, "Are we still on for Friday night?"

"Sure, if you want, and if you have a pair of barf-proof shoes."

I took her grin as a good sign.

"So, you'll stay at *Mallard Cove*?" She looked truly concerned, another good sign that we were still friends, reinforced by a look of relief when I nodded.

A few minutes later we headed over to the airport where I quickly got into my truck. I was hoping to avoid being identified by the ramp guys as the knucklehead that made the mess they had to clean up out on the tarmac.

Kari followed close behind me in her car, since I was still a bit shaky from the alcohol poisoning. I had adapted a version of my story for the gang in case I was asked about my absence. It lacked the names of my relatives, and any mention of a jet or being in Florida. I would lead them to believe I had been in Richmond without actually outright lying about it. After all, my uncle did live there part of the year.

When we pulled in I saw that fortunately, Baloney and Hard Rock both had charters, so their slips were empty. *Irish Luck* was deserted, so Lindsay and Murph must be over working in the *Ralph House.* I suddenly thought better about it, deciding that wasn't a good idea for me to call it that after all.

"Do you feel up to moving *Why Knot* over to the other side? I'll be glad to help, then you can start enjoying more privacy. At least your aft deck will be facing the breakwater and away from all the hotel construction noise. We're going to be ripping out this part of the old dock tomorrow or the next day anyway." Kari's suggestion was a good idea. Better to get the move done since they had already broken ground on the hotel, and there was a lot of hammering and heavy equipment noise happening. I wasn't a big fan of noise today.

Before Kari gave me a lift to the airport this morning, she must have enjoyed her car ride to work. As soon as she turned the ignition key a country song came out of the speakers at an ear-shattering, brain-damaging decibel level. She grimaced and mouthed "sorry" as she quickly turned it down. After I switched over to my truck, I had driven back to *Mallard Cove* with my radio off. It was amazing how loud my street tires were.

"I think that would be a great idea, I'll take you up on your offer of help, thanks." We climbed aboard and I opened the engine room hatch down in the salon, sticking my head down below deck level. She knew what I was doing; trying to detect any gasoline fumes. I know that a lot of people have electronic gas fume detectors, or they run their engine room exhaust fans that are supposed to be sealed and explosion-proof. I'd watched two boats blow up because of those darned fans. But I don't know of anybody who has ever blown up a boat by sniffing a bilge.

I started both engines and then closed the hatch. Kari and I put *Why Knot's* dock box aboard, then we took her across the basin and backed her into her new slip, or rather, my new address. Right before I killed the engines, the port one sputtered a bit, which I had anticipated. I was trying to run the old gas out of the auxiliary tanks because it had been in them since early summer. So, the starboard tank shouldn't be too far behind the now empty port one.

"Thanks for the help, Kari. And thanks for keeping everything else under your hat."

She put her hand on my shoulder again. "I'm just sorry that Casey and I jumped to stupid conclusions, Marlin. If you need somebody to talk to, just call me. My phone is never turned off."

I nodded, then watched as she turned and climbed down onto the new concrete floating dock, heading for the restaurant. She glanced back at me and that's when it hit me, I probably should have offered her that boat tour for her help. Being perceptive and thoughtful are not my strong suits.

"Marlin, where were you? At least you got back just in time," Lindsay yelled across the two empty slips that separated us. "Come on over, there's painting to be done!"

I guess painting would be kind of therapeutic, and I had run out on them abruptly, so helping them out today would be a good thing. I changed into some painting clothes that already had their share of enamel and varnish and headed over.

"Where have you been? You missed the 'sanding party' yesterday. She's all prepped and ready to paint."

Fortunately, Lindsay was more focused on their progress than my lack of attendance and mumbled response. Boy, was I ever thankful that the "sanding party" had been held yesterday instead of today. I could just imagine a half-dozen electric jitterbug sanders all going at once, sounding like an amplified beehive. My head couldn't have survived it. Of course, right then the big diesel pile driver on the barge crane started up. It was driving the first of the huge galvanized pipes into the bottom over on the new charter boat row's floating dock. Each strike of that hammer sent out shockwaves of noise that beat right into the core of my brain. Fortunately, I had brought over a set of radio headphones that were well insulated from outside noise.

I got to work while listening to a smooth jazz station with the volume on low. I was rolling white epoxy primer, which covered the green pretty well. The irony of helping erase "puke green" wasn't lost on me. I started from the little private sundeck in the bow, reaching what I could with the roller attached to a pole. Murph and Lindsay worked from below on a small maintenance raft, painting the sides down to the two-foot section of gray barge hull that was exposed, and which would be left in that color.

I saw that the nameplate was already gone. During a lull in the pile driving, I asked, "No more dreaming of Key West?"

Murph replied from the raft, "That ended up behind the beach bar. It was too cool a sign just to throw away. That's where the pudding ended up, too. A little more nautical décor out there."

Ordinarily, I'd be excited about the idea of an outdoor beach bar opening up. Maybe later, I thought, as that damned pile driver started back up.

WE FINISHED with all the primer just as Kari showed up with paper sacks filled with bacon cheeseburgers and french fries. She winked at me, knowing that this high carb, high fat lunch was just what the doctor ordered for my fuzzy head.

"First food out of the kitchen. Let me know what you think so I can pass it along to Carlos and the crew."

We all agreed; the burgers were some of the best we'd had. Between the food and sweating out a lot of yesterday's overindulgence on this cool almost fall feeling day, I was beginning to feel halfway human again.

I hadn't heard from Clara, Jack Jr., or anyone else down in Naples, so I assumed that Uncle Jack was still with us and fighting. My heart sank every time my phone rang, but there was no way I was going to call down there for an update. I still wasn't ready to lose him, even though I knew I'd never see him again on this planet.

Murph thankfully interrupted my thoughts. "Ready to get back at it? Time for some high gloss polyurethane yacht paint for this pretty but stationary vessel. Let's roll on some liquid beauty!"

We all stood, and Kari headed back over to relay our comments to

Carlos. This time she didn't just glance back, but turned and smiled, confident that I would be watching her. She was correct.

"Quit staring at her butt and get back to work." Lindsay had snuck up to ambush me, and it worked. She laughed as I jumped and blushed simultaneously, and then gave me a sisterly shove. Two things kept me from denying what she had said. The first was that it would only encourage her teasing, and the second was that it was true. I hurried to escape back to my solitary starting point on the sundeck.

8

WEB STREAKER

We had just finished painting when Baloney and Hard Rock returned from their charters. We got a long-distance, long-winded, verbal critique across the basin from Baloney, starting from the time he cleared the breakwater until when he backed into his slip. Then we got two visual "thumbs up" from Hard Rock and his mate, the Mad Gaffer. We ignored Baloney but appreciated the other honest appraisals. The transformation was unbelievable, morphing from the *Ralph House* into a floating swan. We still had the beige nonskid left to go on the decks, but that wouldn't take long on another day. For a big ungainly floating box, she was starting to even look slightly nautical.

"I'm so glad you painted this thing! I had to keep closing my eyes when I walked by to keep from ruining my color vision for the rest of the day. And she didn't come out half bad." Jack "The Ripper" Grayson was a nationally renowned maritime artist and member of the Beer-Thirty-Bunch. He was on his way from his boat over to the captain's lounge for the afternoon conclave.

I liked Jack a lot. He and Baloney were old friends, and they usually picked on each other, nonstop. His art studio was a corner of the salon in "Reba" the sixty-foot sport fisherman where he lived aboard with his wife Carol. They would be around for a while longer before throwing off the dock lines and heading south for the winter, then they'd be back again in the spring.

"Why is it that the one person in this whole place who has the most experience with paint didn't volunteer to help?" Murph poked him.

"My brushes are too small. And then Baloney would want me to paint the *Dolphin* and sign it so that he could sell it!" For years Bill had been after Jack to give him a painting. Every year for Christmas Jack gave him an unsigned sketch. It drove Bill crazy because with them being unsigned, he couldn't sell them. Signed, each one would be worth about what he grosses in a solid month of charters.

"You guys coming over?" Jack had a six-pack of Heineken in one hand, his favorite beer.

"Got a couple of things left to do first, then maybe we'll be over," Murph answered as Jack kept walking.

"What's left to do? We're almost through cleaning up." I was ready to be done for the day.

Lindsay said, "Kari's coming over after work to set up our Internet access and install some security cameras onboard. But you can go on over with the beer crowd if you want."

Without missing a beat I said, "No, I think I'll stick around and see if she needs a hand."

"It's okay, Marlin, we can help her." Lindsay had the needle going again, with a sly smile to match.

Since I was facing Lindsay, I didn't know that Kari was walking up on the dock. "No, Linds, you know us old guys don't know much about these new electronic thingamabobs. I think I'll hang around and see if I can pick up a few pointers."

"Oh, like that pointer you got when you were watching her butt this morning?"

"I did not. As I keep saying, I'm not a teenager like you!"

"And I can't believe that you went back to that whole age thing again." Lindsay scowled.

A shrill whistle sounded from the dock where Kari was standing with a pile of boxes on a cart. "Am I going to have to separate you two? Marlin, how about giving me a hand with these boxes? You can look at my butt later." She had an amused look on her face.

I glared at Lindsay who now looked smug, happy that she had successfully trapped me. Murph was over by the guest quarters door, staying out of the fray but enjoying the floorshow. I went down the stairs to the entrance deck and started grabbing the boxes that Kari passed over to me. "I didn't know that you were into all this electronic stuff."

"I'm not 'into' it, but I know how to make it work. I set up the network at our office at *Bayside*, and the one here at the marina and restaurant. I also designed the layout for the camera security system around the docks, but I'm having a company install them." She pointed to several poles that I had seen being put in place today. "You know us kids and our electronics." Lindsay wasn't the only one who knew how to throw a verbal jab.

I wasn't now falling into her trap too, so I ignored it. "If there are already going to be cameras on the docks, why add these?"

"More coverage. The ones on the poles only catch the docks and long shots of the boats. We'll record those feeds in the office and slip renters will be able to access it all live from wherever they are using their PCs, tablets, and phones. It's a nice perk for them to be able to remotely check on their boats any time of the day or night. But the system I'm installing here is going to be on a virtual private network for Lindsay and Murph. It'll cover both the party deck, the entrance deck, and the middle of the basin from their bow up to the breakwater inlet, all in high resolution, live over their network, and stored on a hard drive onboard. Again, nice reassurance for them when they are down in Florida this winter. I'm also setting up a high water alarm in the bilge that will send an alert to their phones if there is a problem. You should think about one for *Why Knot*."

If I wasn't impressed enough with Kari's abilities before, I certainly was now. "I guess that probably would be a good thing. I'm not really 'electronics literate.' And I just learned to tap into the marina's Wi-Fi, now that we have one."

"How have you been saving your articles and stories to the cloud?"

"I'm not. I don't know how to do that."

"Then I guess you'll be buying the pizza tonight while I set it up and show you how."

I was still not one hundred percent recovered from yesterday, and I had a charter in the morning, but a quiet evening in having pizza with Kari was definitely appealing. And I guess I needed the cloud thing. Whatever that was.

"I don't do anchovies."

She smiled. "Good, because neither do I. Now let's take those boxes down below."

AN HOUR and a half later she was finished, and I had learned more than I thought I'd ever know about security camera systems. Then we rode together in my truck to pick up a pizza to bring back from a place just up the road. I grabbed a couple of beers and we sat on my back deck to eat. The beer helped with the leftover fuzziness from yesterday.

"How did you know about my articles and stories?"

She smiled. "Because I've been reading them for years. Told you I'm a Shore girl. I've been fishing since I was three or four, and I've been reading about fishing since middle school. And before you say it, that was longer than a year or two ago."

"Ouch. When are you two going to let go of that?"

"When it's not fun anymore, or when it stops bugging you, whichever happens first." Her grin told me she didn't expect that to happen anytime soon. "It was your stories that first attracted me to you. They were honest and showed a love for the water that seemed to match my own. Then when I met you, I saw that you didn't have the swagger that so many of the more successful charter crews get. You've built a following without getting a big head about it, and that's kind of rare around the docks, as you know."

I thought about making a self-deprecating remark right then but decided to just drop it before I said something dumb. Then as we were finishing our last slices my phone rang, startling me. I checked the caller ID and was relieved to see that it was my next day's charter customer. He only wanted to double-check our meeting time. After I hung up Kari looked over at me.

"I meant what I said earlier, Marlin. Call me anytime you need or want to talk. I can see that this waiting is wearing on you."

"I will, thanks. It's tough to accept that even though he's still breathing, he's really already gone. It's like losing my dad all over again. But you don't need to hear all this negative stuff."

"That's what friends do. They are there for their friends when they are needed. I hope I'm both for you."

Kari suddenly got a very insecure look, like she was thinking she had stepped over a line or said too much. My turn to reassure her, so I put a hand on her arm, squeezed, and nodded. She was a friend, and I did need her around. She looked relieved.

I was looking forward to Friday night and an "official date." Though hanging out with just the two of us was proving to be easy and relaxed. I didn't feel like I had to be on my best behavior; I could just be me. Maybe it was because she was the one who had been attracted to me first, that took so much pressure off. I didn't know where this was headed, and right now I didn't care. It was going to be whatever it would be. But it was nice to have somebody to hang with where I didn't feel I have to continually make conversation. That was the first for me in recent memory, and I liked it.

We headed down the companionway stairs into the salon. I gave Kari the nickel tour of *Why Knot*, starting with my stateroom aft, the guest stateroom in the bow, and the galley in the forward third of the salon. She loved the attention to detail that my dad and I had put into her restoration, right down to having the Chris Craft letters on the wood header over the galley re-chromed. Finally, we ended up at my built-in desk and laptop. She got the chair since she would be doing all the work.

"Okay, what's your password, Marlin?"

"To what?"

"Uh, your laptop?"

I could hear the implied "duh." This wasn't going to go over well. "Um, I don't have one. Just open it up, it'll come on."

Kari looked at me like I was from another planet. I told you this wasn't going to go over well.

"You really should have one. How about anti-virus? Please tell me you at least have that installed."

"That I do. Came with it. I always practice safe web." I thought I was being funny. She didn't. It turned out that what I thought was protecting me wasn't actually doing much, and I was the equivalent of an Internet streaker. I had been going pretty much bare butt in front of the entire web surfing world. I had never paid much attention to the cookie issue either. By the time she fixed all that I had omitted or ignored, she had honed that "you must be from another planet" look to a fine edge. Hey, I may not know all this Internet stuff, but at least I know boats, fishing, and navigation.

An hour and a half later my computer was running faster, and safer, and the important stuff was backed up on "the cloud" somewhere in Idaho or "I don't know" where. When she asked me if I had ever backed anything up, I pulled out a thumb drive from my desk drawer. It had most of my pictures and stuff. I was proud of myself for being so proactive. I got "the look" again.

"You do realize that all your data was suspended over a potential saltwater grave by a hull made of sixty-year-old wood, right? And that thumb drives and saltwater don't mix?"

I gave her my own look which silently said, "I'm not saying anything more, because it would only make me look dumber than I feel right now."

"You can relax; I've got you covered by the cloud. But you really might want to spring for one of those high water alarms."

"Kari? Paaaal..."

She smiled, figuring out what was coming. "Hey, Marlin, would you like me to pick one up and install it for you as I did for Murph and Lindsay?"

"Would you mind? I'll pay you back and throw in a day of fishing for all that you've done." Not that I couldn't install it myself; after all, it comes with directions. Not that I usually read those things. But Kari seemed to like working with this wireless stuff, and who was I to deny her more fun?

"I'll take you up on that whenever we both have a day off. I'd love to fish with you. I've always said that it's less about the catching than it is about the company and the conversation."

I nodded because I love putting my clients on fish, but more importantly I like showing them a good time on the water. Sometimes that means filling fish-less voids with conversation. Whether you're a mate on a sixty-foot sportfish or the sole crew member on a flats boat, connecting with your angler is important. But Kari and I had already discovered that silence could also be part of our conversation, so this was a fishing trip that I'd be looking forward to.

"You want another beer?" I asked.

"What I want is to hang out with you a while longer, but what I had better do is head home. I have a ton of details to finish up tomorrow before the restaurant's soft opening on Wednesday, and you have a full-day charter to get ready for." She was the one who had filled in my schedule on that cloud thing too.

Kari was serious about her business responsibilities and understood the demands of mine. But I was looking forward to Friday night, and hopefully a lot more days and nights after that if things went well. As I walked her out to the aft deck, we discovered that the daylight was almost gone. The integrated LED lights on the new power pedestals had already kicked on up and down the dock and lit up a little bit of the water around each one. I watched as she left, and no, I wasn't just watching her butt. She gave a quick backward glance, smiled, and kept walking.

As Kari disappeared, I looked at my phone for any messages from Naples and was relieved to find there were none. I guess I kept hoping for a miracle, that somehow I'd wake up tomorrow and get an email from my uncle saying the doctors had made a mistake. I didn't want to be alone. I knew that my cousin said that he'd be there for me, but it wasn't the same. I wasn't ready for this.

~

ONBOARD A CHESAPEAKE DEADRISE boat that was anchored out beyond the breakwater a cell phone rang.

"Situation report." The gruff-sounding voice on the other end of the call was all business.

The boat's sole occupant replied, "Lights on the Chris just went out, so he's settled in for the night, alone. The girl left half an hour ago, the tracker on her car shows she's headed north. He's pretty predictable so far."

"Good. Let's hope it stays that way. Keep on him."

"Will do."

9

THE GRAND INQUISITOR

The next morning Kari and Carlos had finished going over some last-minute restaurant details and she was headed over to the portable construction trailer that served as the project office. Lindsay intercepted her halfway across the marina parking lot.

"So, did you make any headway yesterday?"

"That was a nightmare! He had no backup nor much in the way of anti-virus protection." Kari looked serious.

"You know that wasn't what I was talking about," Lindsay said in a conspiratorial tone.

"I'm not trying to 'make headway.' We're friends, and that's good."

"Oh, friends. That's nice. Hey since you're just friends, Baloney said that his mate Bobby and his girlfriend were bringing her cute, single brother with them to the soft opening at the restaurant tomorrow night. I'll get them to introduce you two."

"Linds, I'm good. I don't have time to date anyone right now anyway."

"Good, huh? And I thought you had a 'date' with Marlin for the grand opening on Friday. But if you don't have time, I know someone else I could get to go with him."

"Okay, look, I don't want to play the field and go through that drama again. I do like Marlin, yes he's my date for Friday, and hopefully there will be more dates beyond that with him. If not, I'll worry about that when the time comes. Or not. But yes, we're friends."

Lindsay had her smug face on. "I get it. You're friends. With benefits. Just make sure he doesn't forget his other anti-virus protection."

"No! Not with benefits. Look, I like where things seem to be headed, and thanks for helping me. But I need to wait and see where this goes, if it even goes anywhere, okay?"

Lindsay laughed. "If you two could only see yourselves from outside looking in like the rest of us. By the way, he's coming with us to dinner tomorrow, friend."

"I like my view just fine, thank you. And I'm glad he'll be there, even if it isn't an official date. I like hanging out with him as well as you and Murph. That's the best part about this, whatever this is. It's comfortable."

MY CHARTER TODAY was with a long-time client, Paul Levine. He used to have a big Rybovich "back in the day." He used to have a lot of things back in the day until his wife got a better divorce lawyer than he did. I liked fishing with Paul; he was one of those easy-going clients who were just happy to be out on the water. It made the day go fast for both of us, and it helped that I was able to put him on a mixed bag of big bull-sized black drums, mid-sized redfish, bluefish, and mackerel. The big stripers haven't started to move in yet, but he and I are both looking forward to when they do.

As we pulled back into the marina I saw that the contractors had finished installing the new floating dock which ran parallel to the restaurant at the west end of the basin. Finger piers sticking out from it created the individual slips. Their installation had been the largest source of my audio nightmare yesterday. This morning I had taken *Marlinspike* out from her old slip on the wooden dock over on the north side. But now I was bringing her back to her new slip at the concrete floating dock to the west. Eventually, as this dock fills up, the diners at the restaurant will be looking out into the cockpits of almost two dozen charter boats, including my two.

As usual, Kari had worked her magic, having new signs made for all the charter boats and getting them all installed at the dock today. They were uniform in size, shape, and color, with our boat names, and phone numbers, and had the *Mallard Cove* logo at the bottom. All except for Baloney, that is. It was in his dockage agreement that he could keep his old, much larger sign that featured a full-sized, stuffed bull Mahi, better known as a bull dolphin. He had repainted it every year himself, using a can of silver spray paint. The color made it look more like an oversized mullet than a Mahi. In return for keeping his old sign which Kari then had professionally re-lettered, he also agreed to let her send the Mahi to a taxidermist to have it repainted in its normal colors. Along with his premier corner slip, this sign now screamed that he was "special," and that he was the top dog on the docks. I didn't begrudge it to him, at least not much. He had been instrumental in bringing more new boats into *Mallard Cove* than anyone else. Except for me, of course. Then again, he had signed me up, too. Adding my three boats tipped the scale in his favor.

As the first boat back in, this meant I was also the first one to use the new fish cleaning table. It had been installed today alongside Baloney's slip. I was washing the table down after Paul left with his fillets. Baloney arrived and backed the *Dolphin* into her new slip. Some straggler laughing gulls that hadn't yet left on their southern migration had been competing with school-sized rockfish for the carcasses and scraps that I had thrown back into the water. The birds screamed at the boat that now blocked them from their free dinner. Baloney looked down from his flybridge.

"Big night tomorrow, Shaker. Can't wait ta see what they've done wit' the place. I know the food'll be good, judgin' by that barbecue two months ago."

None of us had been allowed inside after the renovations had begun, and paper still covered the windows. They were building suspense for the opening night.

Carlos had catered a promotional party a couple of months ago as part of Lindsay and Murph's push to get the word out about the ongoing renovations. That food had left Baloney talking about it for weeks afterward. He had been salivating ever since he heard about the soft opening practice runs. Baloney added, "Carlos food an' two free drinks each! Can't beat that."

"Nope, I'm looking forward to it. Hey, speaking of free, you want to give me a hand for a minute? I've got to go move *Bone Shaker*, my dock box, and rod vault over from the old dock."

"That'll take more'n just a minute, Shaker. You'll owe me, even more'n ya do already."

"How do you figure I owe you?"

"'Cause I talked ya inta comin' here. Your life's changed for th' better since ya got here."

I didn't want to argue, because he was right about some parts of my life being better. Of course, he didn't know about the bad part, and I wanted to keep it that way.

We ended up making two runs over to the new slip, one for each of the fiberglass boxes because there was only a limited amount of space on the bow to carry them. The smaller box had all my boat maintenance stuff, the other longer one had all my tackle and rods. I needed Bill's help because there was no way I could handle them all by myself.

"We scored with Murph, Lindsay, an' company, Shaker. Did ya see my sign? It's never looked that good. Now we got a great place ta eat and drink, an' new docks and I hear the hotel's construction is ahead ah schedule. We won't have any open slots next year unless we block 'em out ourselves."

I wished that I was in a better mood to celebrate with him. But after Paul left, my mind drifted back to my uncle. And I hadn't seen Kari, who was obviously busy. I doubted I'd see or hear from her until tomorrow night.

"Earth to Shake-n-Bake! You hearing me?"

"Sorry, Bill, I was thinking about something."

"Yeah, an' I was sayin' that I'm gonna add another boat next year for B2 ta run. We're on th' ground floor ah somethin' here, Shaker, I can feel it."

I knew he was right, but I couldn't think about all that now. So, I just nodded and smiled, and didn't bring up the idea of B2 running my idle boat. I wanted to be as excited as Bill was, but that would have to wait. I hung out on the dock a little while longer listening to him ramble on until he finally headed for the Beer-Thirty-Bunch. Then I went home to *Why Knot*. I plopped down on the built-in couch in the salon and decided to call Clara for an update. I was stunned to hear a recording announcing that her company cell phone had been disconnected. This had been her number for almost two decades. I knew that she should be in Florida near my uncle, but I decided to call her direct line at Denton Industries in Richmond.

"Anna Jackson."

"Uh, hi. I was trying to reach Clara Edwards."

"I'm sorry, Ms. Edwards is no longer with the company."

I felt like I had just gone down the rabbit hole. "This is Marlin Denton. Do you have a new number where I can reach her?"

"Oh hello, Mr. Denton. No, I'm sorry. She retired yesterday, and we don't have her new contact information."

"I see." I really didn't. "What department are you with?"

"I'm one of your cousin's assistant executive assistants."

"Can you tell me how my uncle is doing?"

"I'm sorry, Mr. Denton, you'll have to ask your cousin about anything related to your uncle. I'm not allowed to comment on that. Would you like me to transfer your call to his cell phone, or would you like to leave a message with me?"

"Um, if you could transfer me, that would be great."

There was a pause then, "You have reached 804-555-3025. Please leave a message at the beep."

"Hey, Jack, it's Marlin. Sorry to bother you right now, but I was just trying to check on Uncle Jack. I tried calling Clara, but they said she left the company. Please give me a call when you have a second. Thanks."

I thought back to the look Jack had given Clara the last time I'd seen her, how he'd glared at her. Then her cursing about Dennis Peel, saying that he had been put in charge of the nurses. I'd have bet everything I had that she didn't voluntarily retire. It was inevitable that things would change after my uncle was gone, but as far as I knew, he was still with us. This didn't feel weird, it felt almost...sinister. I know that sounds overly dramatic and even paranoid, but I don't know how else to describe it.

I almost jumped out of my skin when my phone rang a minute later. I thought it might be Jack Jr., but it was Kari.

"Hey, I stopped by the group, but Baloney said he saw you headed down the dock. Everything okay?"

"Yeah. I just didn't feel like going there today."

"You feel like some company?"

"I thought you would still be on the go tonight."

"No, Carlos has the restaurant ready. I'm back to focusing on the other construction projects now. But I was thinking about you." I could feel she regretted that last sentence as soon as she said it.

"Well, fair warning that I'm probably not the best company right now, but I do have a cold beer in the fridge."

"I'll be right over." She sounded relieved as she hung up.

It was true that I had a lot on my mind. But it was also true that Kari already knew about my uncle. Maybe if I unloaded it on her, she might help me make some sense out of this, and bring in a new perspective. Kind of like Lindsay claimed to have about Kari and me. She showed up two minutes later.

"Hey. I hope I didn't push myself on you." She looked worried.

"No, I was glad that you called, it was good timing. Grab us a couple of beers and let me tell you what's going on, and get your take on things." I wanted her to feel welcome as a friend, not a guest. Otherwise, I'd have gotten the beer myself.

She brought over two bottles and then sat beside me on the couch, turning a bit so that our knees touched. I know that we are new friends, but I felt I could trust her, and she is super smart. So, I value her opinion. Besides, she already knew most of what I'd been trying to keep secret, so why not the rest? She kept saying, seemingly hoping, that I could call her at any time to talk. To be honest, right now I was feeling the most alone at any point in my adult life. I guess I needed to be able to trust someone, and I hoped I wasn't making a mistake by telling her. My gut was saying that I wasn't.

She sat in rapt attention as I related all that happened in Florida, including my conversation with my uncle and how he confused me with Jack, and my interaction with my cousin. Then when I got to my calls this afternoon, I could see her tense a bit. So, it wasn't just me, unless I was telling it in an unintentionally prejudicial way. When I finished, she sat quietly for a minute, taking a sip of beer before speaking.

"I thought I fully understood why you got plastered the other afternoon, but now I really get it. I'm sorry about all you're going through, Marlin. I think you have some very legitimate concerns, but also some of these things might turn out to be quite innocent.

"As harsh as this sounds, your uncle is not going back to his office. The sooner changes get made within the company to reflect that fact, the quicker things will get to their 'new normal' over there. They are too large a company to come to a standstill even over his loss." She paused a bit and took another sip.

"I think what bothers me most is the note that your uncle left you on the plane. Why would he want you to forgive him? He obviously intended to have a serious talk with you about whatever it was, and it sounds like that might be at least partly why he sent for you. It sure sounds like you were given 'the bum's rush' after you got to his house, though not by him. Was it to keep you from having that conversation because your cousin didn't want it to happen? That's a real possibility if it was something he wanted to be left alone. But if this Peel guy is that much of an influence on your cousin, enough to be the one directing the nurses, he might have had a hand in running you off. Maybe it was just him behind all this, and not your cousin. If your uncle's assistant was so trusted by him for so long, and she didn't trust Peel, then you probably shouldn't either. You think he might have known what your uncle planned to say, and was trying to keep that from happening?"

"I don't know, but it does feel kind of like that."

"What about the crew of the plane? Would they have left that note and case of vodka onboard for you if your cousin had told them not to?"

"I doubt it. But Jack may not have been aware of it. Apparently, my uncle gave them direct instructions on the way back from London. Jack has another plane with his own crew, and he wasn't with my uncle on the trip. If I had to guess, I'd wager that Jack didn't know about it and might not even now.

"Uncle Jack obviously had something he wanted to say, but every time he tried, that cough came on and then they sedated him. I guess I'll never know what it was."

"I'm sorry, Marlin. Both about your uncle and my not being much help right now. I think the best advice I can give you is to just trust your gut."

"You're wrong about not being of help. This is very important to me; that you are willing to help me sort this out. Even though we haven't been friends that long, I don't have anyone else that I feel comfortable enough to share this with. I trust your opinion and appreciate your advice." So, now she didn't hold the only patent on instant regret about having said something. The last thing I wanted to do was scare her off and lose my only confidant. I was surprised when she reached over and silently took my hand. I think it surprised her, too. That it had been a natural reaction. I squeezed it slightly. "Hey, the least I can do after dumping all this on you is make dinner. I mean, if you don't already have plans."

She squeezed my hand back and said, "No plans, but I'll only stay if I can help."

I grinned, "You mean more than you already have? It's a small galley, and two would be tight. Just kick back, and I'll prep something we can do on the grill. Crab stuffed flounder and asparagus sound okay?"

"Better than okay, more like delicious."

"Well, don't expect Carlos-level cuisine, but I think my version is pretty good." I liked cooking on the small stainless gas grill attached to the aft deck railing. There's something about grilling that is so relaxing, and after having dumped all my crap on her, I needed to do something to lighten things up. It turned out that it was just what the doctor ordered, as she took over the grilling part. She reminded me that "growing up as a Shore woman," she had grilled more than her share of fish. Ordinarily, I wouldn't have surrendered control of my grill, but I trusted her advice, so I decided to trust her with this, too. It turned out to be a great call. "Kari, your timing was perfect. This is the best flounder I've ever had. Cooked perfectly."

Her smile was as wide as the fish was good. "Then it's the best *we've* ever had."

After dinner we sat out on the aft deck for about an hour, talking about fishing. If it was as I suspected, a ploy by her to get my mind off things, it worked well. When we stood up after she said that she needed to head home, it seemed only natural when we hugged. Whatever perfume she was wearing fitted her perfectly, with subtle notes of jasmine. I breathed in her fragrance and didn't want to let her go, but after a minute I did. That minute was the best I'd felt since I'd gotten on the plane to go to Florida. This time when I watched her walk down the dock, it was with the hope that she would be coming back soon.

After she was out of sight, I did a scan of the docks and the water beyond the breakwater. Off in the distance, I saw a single white anchor light and recalled that it was the same spot where I had seen a deadrise anchored both today and yesterday. I made a mental note to check the spot after it moved. I didn't know what they might be fishing for right there, but they must be having some luck. Paul had rebooked me for a half day tomorrow starting at nine a.m., and hopefully, that boat will be gone by the time we go out.

The next morning I was up early and checked my phone for missed calls or voicemails from my cousin, but there was nothing. I walked out onto my aft deck and saw that the deadrise was still anchored in that same spot. I am sooo going to check it later; that has to be a red hot spot.

"Hey, Marlin! We're headed over for breakfast at the restaurant, want to join us?" It was Murph, over on the entrance deck of *On Coastal Time* with Lindsay. They must have finished up the interior painting and spent the night onboard.

"Yeah, that would be great, thanks."

I met them on the dock, and we walked up together, then sat out on the deck. It was a little chilly, but the sun was out, the sky was clear, and we were all in long sleeves.

The paper was still on the restaurant windows, and I wasn't allowed to peek inside yet. The "great reveal" would be right before dinner this evening. Murph went inside for a minute, then returned with a waitress, menus, and Carlos, who joined us for coffee.

According to Murph, Carlos was part culinary genus, part circus ringmaster; everything that was needed to run and build a burgeoning restaurant group. And, as I discovered over our piping hot coffee, a hell of a nice guy. It was obvious that he and Murph were long-time pals. Both of them had come up from Florida with Casey Shaw, so they had a unique and yet similar history. Carlos hung out with us until our orders arrived, then he visually checked each one, watching how the waitress handled us. Then he said goodbye and headed back inside.

"Nice guy."

Murph nodded. "Great guy. He was wasting his talent as a fry cook at this little marina restaurant down in Florida, kind of a tiki hut. He dropped everything to come with Casey and me, to run the restaurant at *Bayside*, which didn't even exist at that point. One heck of a leap of faith. But that's Carlos. If he believes in you, he gives a hundred and ten percent effort."

Kind of reminded me of Kari. Shaw sure had some talented and dedicated people around him.

"I saw that Kari left your place a bit late last night." Lindsay smiled and cocked one eyebrow.

"Impromptu hanging out. The timing just kind of came together."

"Did you now? Eek!" Lindsay hadn't seen Kari walking up behind her, and about jumped out of her skin when she felt both of Kari's hands on her shoulders.

"Hi, Linds. Or, should we call you the 'Grand Inquisitor?' So, was there a question in there that you want to ask me instead of Marlin? I'll be happy to tell you something, or to do something."

I could see that Kari wasn't happy that I was starting to get grilled by our mutual friend. I could also see that once again, Murph was going to stay as far out of this as he could. Smart man. I intended on following his lead. Like that would be possible.

"I was just commenting that I saw you pass by on the dock late last night. Marlin said it was a case of your timing coming together. That's all. A purely innocent conversation, nothing to get upset about. Unless you're touchy about things. Like timing." Lindsay was grinning widely at being able to turn the tables on Kari. She didn't realize that she had met her match.

Kari walked over next to my chair and faced Lindsay. "I'm not touchy at all about our timing." She looked down at me, smiling as she reached for my hand. "Correct me if I'm wrong, dear, but did you or did you not say that our timing was perfect last night, and we both said that it was the best that we've ever had?"

Oh, this was fun. "I can honestly swear that I did say both things. And I wasn't lying either; it was indeed the best that I've ever had. But that's usually not something that a gentleman says to anyone who wasn't there at the time."

Kari leaned over and kissed me then said, "I can't wait to see you again tonight." She winked so only I could see it, then smiled at a drop-jawed Lindsay. "See you later, Linds. And don't bother asking for more details, because a lady never talks, either."

She headed inside the restaurant. Kari was indeed smart, and someone very special. It was all I could do to smother a laugh and a grin. Murph looked amused, and Lindsay looked like she was still trying to process what had just happened. Truth is, so was I, at least a little bit.

I thanked Lindsay and Murph for a very enjoyable breakfast and walked over to the dock to prep *Marlinspike* for Paul's arrival. A few minutes later I got a text from Kari, "That was so much fun!"

"I enjoyed it."

"Are you talking about pranking Linds, or the kiss, Marlin?"

"Both."

"Me, too. See you tonight."

This was now going to be a very long half-day charter.

10

THE BRUSH OFF

When Paul and I cleared the breakwater, I saw the deadrise was still where it had been the past two days. I cruised over by it and saw a man on the back deck but he went below as I got closer. I didn't want to get too close, but I wanted to get a view from my side scan sonar and fish finder. It couldn't reach exactly under the deadrise, but what I saw puzzled me. Or rather, what I didn't see. There didn't seem to be any structure to attract fish; in fact, no fish were showing at all. Yet the guy had two rods sitting in holders on the covering boards. Not very many rods for a boat of its size, even with only one angler aboard. Curious.

We headed over to the first manmade island at the CBBT, where the tunnel end meets the bridge. There I did see some fish on the screen. We dropped some pearl and white jigs and ended up with our first "slob" rockfish of the season. I texted Baloney and Hard Rock, telling them to get over here. It wouldn't be long before word got out that the fish were in, and I wanted the first pictures on social media to be from the *Mallard Cove* charter fleet. Half an hour later they had put their anglers on some nice school-sized rocks and a couple of "slobs." I got some phone videos of both of them in action before Paul and I headed back in. I stayed out a little longer than scheduled because we really got into the fish, and Paul was having a ball releasing them. He knew I stretched the time, and his tip reflected it. But these were the trips that were the highlight of the season, for both of us.

There was no sign of the deadrise as we rounded Fisherman Island. I dragged through where he had been, and again, the sonar found nothing. That's not to say that there couldn't have been an occasional shark or school of fish that might pass by, but it certainly wasn't a hot spot, not enough to warrant camping out for two days. I wondered if it might be one of Glenn Cetta's people, spying on the marina. But why?

"He made me. Came cruising by real slow, looking the boat over."

The voice on the phone said, "You'll have to switch over to watching from the woods until the bar opens, then you can camp out in his backyard without him knowing it. The trackers are still running on his truck and the girl's car, right?"

"Yep. Still good."

"All right, get outta there. We know what his routine is, and he's not that tough to watch."

Yeah, not that tough for you, boss, the boatman thought. *You're back on land while I've been cooped up on my boat off the point for days.* He hung up and started his engine then cranked up his hookless fishing lines. It was time to go sit in the woods.

I went over to *OCT* a little before six p.m. While I wasn't Baloney, he wasn't the only one who could come up with nicknames, and *On Coastal Time* was too darned long to keep saying. Murph and Lindsay were up on their party deck, and I climbed the stairs to join them. Murph made me a vodka on the rocks with what my uncle would call that "other vodka." The thought of it made me smile.

"You sure are smiling a lot today." Lindsay was still trying to figure out exactly what was going on with Kari and me.

"What's not to smile about?" I smiled wider.

"Hi, guys!" Kari came up the stairs wearing a light blue oxford, black jeans, and boat shoes. And wearing it all well. Very well. Her mid-back length raven hair had an almost dark blue sheen against the pale blue cloth. I think I must have looked about as slack-jawed right then as Lindsay had been at breakfast. Kari smiled, then sidled up and kissed me while taking my hand. Whether it was for Lindsay's benefit or not, at that point, I didn't know, and frankly, I didn't care. I looked at her and got a smile with no wink. I'll admit I was a little confused, but still happy. I realized I hoped this wasn't just a show for Lindsay.

"You two aren't going to do that all through dinner, are you? The whole 'public display of affection' thing and the 'goo-goo eyes?'" Since Lindsay was unsure whether this was a put on, she jabbed and probed, watching for us to flinch.

Instead, Kari ignored Lindsay, took my drink, and tasted it. "Nice!"

"Another vodka, coming right up." Murph poured another and handed it to Kari, then she and I sat on the cushioned wicker couch, part of a set that Lindsay and Dawn had picked out for this deck. Kari slid in close to me as I draped an arm over her shoulders. Lindsay scowled.

"You two can cut the act. If you think I'm buying this as being real, happening this fast, I've got a CBBT bridge section to sell you."

Kari looked at me. "Marlin, do you want to cut the act?"

I shook my head. "Not me. How about you?"

"Who's acting?"

"Well, okay then." This time I kissed her. I heard gagging sounds coming from Lindsay's direction, but we were too busy to look. Coming up for air, Kari sighed and leaned her head on my shoulder. I make it a point never to sigh. Then I sighed.

. . .

I WAS THE GUINEA PIG. Out of the four of us, I was the only one who hadn't seen the interior of the newly renovated and expanded *Mallard Cove Restaurant & Beach Bar.* Which meant we had to go in through the front door, rather than from the dockside. It also meant that all three of them would be staring at me, trying to judge my reaction to the place. News flash, I was stunned. The new exterior siding was faux wood made from concrete, painted to look like weathered wood. Inside, the front room had been turned into a bar area with tables, but the wall that had been between the old patio and the restaurant was gone, and in its place was what looked like an ultra-wide Sportfish's transom and cockpit, complete with exhaust pipes, a waterline, and faux bottom paint. In gold leaf with a green outline were the words "*Irish Luck*" and the hailing port underneath reading "*Mallard Cove, VA.*" Extra deep teak covering boards with polyester resin on top served as the bar surface, with seats on the parking lot side, so they all faced across the bar and toward the water. The other side had an open service area with a low knee wall, providing a view of charter boat row. The now enlarged patio area was the main dining room, with several garage-style doors on tracks, featuring huge double-paned glass sections that overlooked the new deck. The doors were closed tonight because of a nip in the air. There was a private dining area through a doorway over to the right. It was behind the most stunning feature yet, which was a huge built-in saltwater reef tank that separated the two rooms. Special lights simulated sunlight during the day, and moonlight late at night. The colors of the live corals were indescribable, almost neon.

"I'm totally blown away. The view, the aquarium, even if the food was mediocre this place would be a destination. But having tasted some already, you guys are going to be printing money in the basement with this place. Wow."

All three looked relieved, and Kari squeezed my hand. Lindsay couldn't have seen that.

We were seated over by one of the garage doors, looking out over charter boat row. Our drink order came, but we weren't offered menus. Murph explained, "Carlos always tried out new dishes on

Casey and me. So, we'll probably get four different items that we're supposed to share between us. I hope you guys don't mind, it's kind of his thing." None of us did.

Before our food arrived, Murph and Lindsay got up to go circulate among the tables, saying hello to friends, boat owners, and friends of friends who turned out for the first soft opening. Baloney was holding court at a table in the corner, and I knew they would be tied up there for a few minutes. When we were alone Kari looked over at me and said, "Please tell me if you were acting tonight."

I didn't know if she was backtracking now or what. I shook my head. "I'm not much of an actor. Is that all it was for you, just an act to mess with Lindsay?"

She looked straight into my eyes. "This morning a little of it was. But I like you, and like being around you. I've been thinking about you all day and looking forward to this dinner. So, no, Marlin, it wasn't an act. Isn't an act."

I hadn't realized that I was holding my breath until I exhaled. She saw this and smiled.

DINNER WAS EVEN ABOVE EXPECTATIONS, both the food as well as the company. Carlos had outdone himself with these dishes, pairing Chesapeake seafood with Caribbean sauces, adding twists to meat dishes, and making sliders out of his special Chesapeake Sea Cakes. Then the four of us shared two slices of house-made orange mango cheesecake and key lime cheesecake. Yes cheesecakes, not pies. All of it was unbelievable. Murph and Lindsay were beaming as they got up and said goodnight to us, then went around the room again, doing host/owner duty.

Kari and I went out the door leading to the deck, looking at the charter fleet, now lit by floodlights on the new dock. My two boats had never looked so good at night. That's when my phone went off. The caller ID said it was Uncle Jack. I picked up.

"Uncle Jack?"

"No, Marlin, Dennis Peel. Your cousin wanted me to let you know your uncle died today around noon. There will be a memorial service in Naples on Monday at eleven a.m., but if you want to attend, you'll have to find your own way to get here. The planes are already full of family friends and other relatives. Good night, Marlin."

I was in total shock. I mean, I knew this was coming, but I still wasn't prepared for it. The tears started running down my cheeks, and I don't even remember walking back to the boat. I do know that Kari walked silently with me, sensing what had happened. I pulled out that bottle of vodka I had opened on the plane and poured us each a glass. We sat on the salon sofa, and I related the conversation.

"I don't understand. I mean, I wasn't really expecting a plane ride down there, but he died at noon, and Peel said that the planes were already full of family and friends. Meaning four planeloads of people were told before I was. And my cousin didn't have the decency to call me himself, he had his flunky do it? What the hell did I ever do to him to deserve such a slap in the face like that? My uncle is gone, and it feels like a knife in my heart; like I lost my last parent. It sounds like my cousin doesn't even want me at the service. Well, I'm gonna be there, Jackie boy! He was my uncle, my blood, and I loved him like a father. You may never want to see me again, Jackie, but you're gonna see me on Monday."

I realized that I was ranting, and Kari was still right there, holding my hand. I looked at her and said, "You've seen me at my worst. Falling down drunk for the first time like that in years, and now tonight a raving friggin' lunatic that's mad at the world and who has a screwed-up distant family. Why are you still here? You should be hauling ass right now from this mess."

She looked at me for a long time before she answered. "Because, Marlin. Because this is as bad as it gets, according to you. So, now I've seen you at your worst. Big deal. Wait until you see me with a bad case of PMS, friend." She gave me a wry smile, and I couldn't help but smile back a little.

She continued, "And I'm here because right now you need a friend, and it sounds like I fit that description better than just about anyone else in your life. True friends don't run off when their friends are hurting like you are right now. And because I already told you today, I like you, and I don't want you to ever doubt that. So, why don't you refill our glasses, come back to the couch and rant and rave or tell me anything you want, say anything you need to get off your chest. Then tell me stories about the good times with your uncle. I'm right here, Marlin, and I'm not going anywhere."

THERE WAS a little light peeking through the porthole in my stateroom. I was hungover but not as bad as I had been on Monday. Of course, I hadn't had nearly as much to drink last night, either. Then I realized there was an arm tucked across my chest, and it wasn't mine. It all started coming back to me as I realized I was still fully clothed. I looked to my right and saw Kari looking back at me, still in her clothes as well.

"Hi there."

I felt as awkward as I had ever been while still wearing clothes. "Hi."

"Any regrets?"

Okay, it just got more awkward. "Did we do anything that either of us needs to regret right now?"

"I didn't. We just talked. Or rather, you talked, I mostly listened."

"Oh. Sorry about that."

"Don't be. I encouraged you to."

I couldn't recall what I talked about. "I'll be honest here, Kari. I don't remember much about last night. Did I say anything 'morning cringe-worthy?'"

"The only thing I can think of is that you like me, and want to see more of me."

"So, I didn't say anything I regret then."

She smiled. "Good, because I told you the same thing, and now I don't have to cringe either." She tucked in closer to my side and tightened her arm across my chest. "I'll tell Casey that I'll be out next Monday and Tuesday."

"Why?"

"I'm assuming that we'll be driving down to Naples on Sunday, and won't head back until sometime Monday afternoon."

"Wait, we?"

"You don't think I'm going to abandon you to go into that viper pit all alone, do you? Marlin, I told you last night, I'm your friend. I'm not running out on you at one of the toughest times of your life."

"Can I ask you something?"

"Told you last night that you could say or ask anything."

"Are you always this assertive with people you like?"

"Why, you think it's a bad thing?"

"Just please tell me, Kari."

She hesitated, "No, I'm not."

"Then why me, and why now?"

"Because I want to help you. Maybe more than I've wanted to help anyone before. Because you touched something in me last night. I saw you stripped of all your defenses, in such intense pain, yet you were still concerned about me, telling me I ought to run rather than stay. And at that moment I saw someone I realized was worth sticking around for. So, here I am."

"Kari?"

"Yes, Marlin?"

"Thanks."

11

CHANGES

Jack Denton Jr. opened the envelope addressed to him in his father's handwriting. In it he found a new Will and Testament, directing that twenty-five percent of his shares in the family trust be divided between his grandchildren, and the remaining seventy-five percent be divided equally between his children. His children, not his child! Jack Jr. was his only publicly acknowledged heir. If this got out, it could ruin everything.

Jack could have his lawyers argue that the old man was senile except for the fact that there was also a video included in which his father repeated the terms. He was flanked by a highly respected Henrico County judge, a friend who attested as to his father's sound mind. With seventy-five percent of the family trust which owns the business, Jack Jr. was assured of control. But if Marlin inherited half of those shares, it would take only four of his seven kids teaming up with Marlin to boot him out of the company altogether. And four of them were minors, with three of his ex-wives as their mothers. Women who despised Jack, and would now vote those shares for their minor children over the next several years until they came of age. He needed a plan, and he needed it fast.

~

Of course, when we headed up to the *Cove* for breakfast, Murph and Lindsay were just emerging from *OCT.* There's that timing bit again. This time though, Lindsay looked at us curiously rather than suspiciously. Then again, we weren't hand-in-hand, either. She peeled Kari away from me, and I paused to let the two of them walk on ahead and have the private "girl's talk" that I had already anticipated would come at some point. Murph walked up beside me and cocked his head a bit.

"You don't look like you are in a mood to celebrate, after walking down the dock early in the morning with a girl who's a knockout. Trouble already in paradise, buddy?"

I didn't want to have to explain about my uncle. "Hungover."

He nodded sympathetically. "Lindsay's still trying to figure you guys out."

"That makes three of us." We followed the women at a distance. One of the things I like about Murph is that he doesn't jabber on just to hear himself. He's a good friend, and I felt a little guilty about not telling him the whole story. With my uncle gone, it put me at a much farther distance from his side of the family, not that there's anyone left alive on my side. It's one thing to have a billionaire uncle and an entirely different thing to have a herd of rich cousins. Distance makes the difference. So, maybe in time, I'll feel comfortable about telling him the story, just not today.

The four of us had a nice quiet breakfast out on the *Cove*'s deck, and afterward, I walked Kari to her car. She had an office day scheduled up at *Bayside*.

"Would I be pushing it if I asked if you were busy later?"

I shook my head. "Not at all. Nothing planned today nor this weekend, other than fishing tackle and boat maintenance."

"Mind if I come by after work?"

"I was hoping you would. I feel bad about how last night ended."

She gave me a sly look, "I hope you aren't talking about the part where you woke up next to me."

I chuckled. "That was the good part. You know what I mean. And there's no way I could repay you for putting up with that, having to deal with me and my family drama. But I could start by making us dinner again tonight."

"You don't owe me anything, but I'd love to have dinner again with you."

"Done."

She kissed me, got in her car, and drove off. I watched her car turn and head north, then I went back to the docks. Lindsay was up on the restaurant deck and waved me over. Murph was nowhere in sight. I knew what was coming.

I sat opposite Lindsay who had ordered coffees for both of us. After the waitress was out of earshot she said, "What's really going on with you two?"

I could dance around the question, or get angry and accuse her of meddling, but I knew this was about friendship, not gossip.

"Honestly, we're trying to figure that out ourselves. So, I can't answer that question. I'm not trying to avoid it; I just don't have the answer."

"You know she's my friend, Marlin, and I just don't want to see her get hurt."

"Neither do I, Linds, she's my friend too. And I'd like to think that you and I are still friends and that you wouldn't want to see me get hurt either."

She paused. "We are, and I don't."

"You know I was hesitant about this. I didn't know if we had enough in common. And don't get all pissed off again, but yes, the chronological age thing. But I learned quickly with her that there is age, and then there's *age*. Some people act theirs and other people don't. Some people can be more mature and stable. Like Kari. And it turns out that we have more than a little bit in common."

She didn't look convinced. "And you learned all this about her in a week."

"Most of it, yes. And she's learned more about me in two days than you have in the same two months that you and I have known each other. Yet you feel that you know me enough to have this conversation."

"Yeah, I know. You worked fast with her." She wasn't happy.

"Can I ask you something?"

"I guess."

"Something personal."

"You can ask, but I don't know if you'll get an answer."

"Did you and Murph first sleep together soon after you met?"

"What happened between Murph and me was completely different."

"I'll take that as a yes. And how about his reputation as a player back in Florida, did you know about that?"

"I figured that he might have had a past."

"And you didn't know that he was engaged to Dawn at the time."

"What the hell does this have to do with you and Kari?"

"Well, you two are good together, despite everything."

"Murph ripped my heart out before we finally ended up together. I don't want her to go through what I did. Now she's jumped into bed with you right off the bat, and you guys don't even know each other."

"So, you are comparing me to Murph."

"You already have!"

"Lindsay, I probably should get up right now and walk away, but you are my friend, and I'd like to keep it that way. So, I'm going to tell you a few things. First, don't worry about Kari, she's not a kid; she knows what she's doing. Second, I'm not, nor have I ever been a 'player.' It's not in my makeup. Third, I'm not interested in seeing anyone else other than Kari. By the way, you've jumped to the wrong conclusions partly because we led you there on purpose, to get you to back off a bit. The timing and 'best we've ever had' comments were all about grilling out."

"Grilling out. I suppose you had a 'grilling marathon' and that's why she stayed over last night."

"No. I lost someone last night who was very close to me; a mentor. I was and am still pretty broken up about it, and she didn't want me to be alone. She stayed as a friend, not a lover. At a time when I was at my lowest. That tells me all I need to know about her. She's an incredible woman, a very strong woman, and now a great friend. And yes, I learned that in this very short amount of time, and I'm grateful for all of it."

"So, you two haven't..."

"Remember what I said about being a gentleman? I meant it. And, Linds, if you remember when you were kidnapped, I was one of the ones who got shot at while coming to rescue you."

"You were after the guy; you didn't even know I was there."

"But I knew it was *about* you. We all wanted revenge because of what we thought happened to you. And yet now you are more worried about me hurting Kari than her hurting me. Kind of a double standard, don't you think? Because I've never done anything that should make you believe I'm capable of doing that. Thanks for the coffee." I got up and left her to think about what I'd said.

"We need to take things a step further. An accident, and it has to happen this weekend, no later than Saturday night."

"You know this goes way beyond the surveillance rate. I have to put a specialist on it."

"Of course."

"He's been seeing that woman. This might make things more difficult."

"Or, it might help sell the idea of a tragic accident if both are involved. I'm not concerned about any collateral damage."

"I'll take care of it."

"Have a good day?" Kari was climbing aboard the aft deck. She had on jeans again, but this time she wore a big long-sleeved sweatshirt. I was glad she dressed for comfort, instead of to impress. We passed that point last night. This was "hanging out at home" time.

"Hey. Got a lot done on the boats, had the oil changed in the truck for the trip, oh, and got ambushed by Lindsay right after you left."

"Um, yeah, I heard about that. She called me when I was on the way down. Sounds like you made some good points, and I think she'll back off now. You really wouldn't tell her if we slept together?"

"That bothers you?"

"To be honest, for a split second I thought it might have been because we hadn't. Male ego and all that. But only for a split second. I could have avoided telling you this, but I wanted, no, I needed to be upfront with you about it. I know you didn't tell her because you wouldn't, even if we had."

I smiled in answer to that.

"About the trip, I hope you don't mind, but I needed to tell Casey why I was taking two days off."

"I figured you would. It doesn't matter, because Casey already knew about my uncle after I poured myself off the plane last weekend."

"He still feels bad about that."

"He couldn't feel worse than I still do; at least he didn't vomit on me."

"It turns out that he has to go down to his office in North Palm Beach for the day on Monday in the Citation. He's offered to drop us in Naples, and pick us up on the way back. He thought it might help make up for us jumping to conclusions so quickly as we did."

"That would be great. Tell him thanks, we'll take him up on it. Or, did you already?"

"Would you be mad if I did?"

"Let's just say I'd be surprised if you didn't."

"Then you won't be surprised." She came over and hugged me. "Sorry about Lindsay."

"Don't apologize for Lindsay, she's my friend too."

"I'm glad you still feel that way." Lindsay was climbing the steps on the finger pier which led up to my deck level. She had a bottle of white wine in hand. "Truce?" She handed the chilled bottle to me;

Roseland, from King Family Vineyards in Crozet. "It's Kari's favorite. I figured you might not know that yet."

I went over to the Yeti cooler by the rail and pulled out a matching bottle. "I might surprise you. Though I've found that I have a hard time surprising Kari."

"You just might yet. Well, I wanted to pop over and say I'm sorry. I thought about what you said, and I guess I have been using a bit of a double standard with you."

"Never be sorry for looking out for a friend. But never forget that you and I are friends, too. Hang on, I'll open this and we can all have a glass."

"Thanks, but I'll have to take a rain check. Murph and I have to entertain more guests at the *Cove*. Last of the soft openings tonight you know. But we'll see you two over there tomorrow night for the grand opening, right?"

"Count on it." Kari had wrapped her arm around mine. I guess it was a solidarity thing. I liked it.

WHILE WE SIPPED OUR WINE, I brought out some smoked fish dip and crackers, along with two beautiful ribeyes. I had bought the steaks today and pre-seasoned them, letting the spices work their way into the meat. Now I wanted them to warm up before they went on the grill along with two baked potatoes.

"Great fish dip."

"I got the recipe from Murph. I think he stole it from Casey. Made it with some of the mackerel and bluefish I caught last week. Always better when the flavors mingle for a few days."

"About the best I've ever had."

"Yeah, well, don't say that around Lindsay, or I'll be explaining all over again."

She laughed. "I guess we did look guilty, doing the walk of shame this morning."

"I wasn't. Ashamed, that is. I don't care what other people think. Except you."

"You know what I mean, Marlin."

"Yep. You were ashamed to be seen with me. I get it."

"You know I wasn't!"

"You react so well to teasing."

She wanted off this subject. "If I eat that much dinner, I'll be out like a light."

"If only you had brought your clothes for work tomorrow and the grand opening, you could've stayed here tonight and not had to drive home. And that's not a pass, it's just trying to save you a seventy-mile round trip, half of it late at night."

"You sure that's not a pass?"

"I'm not into making short-term arrangements."

She smiled. "Want to help me get my clothes out of the car? Don't look so shocked, you thought of it too. As you pointed out, I'm working here tomorrow anyway, and this saves me an hour and a half on the road. Plus, I'll be safer this way."

"Yeah, but now I'm wondering if I will."

She slugged me in the arm. "If you don't want me to stay, just say so, and I won't."

I wrapped my arms around her. "I know that you stayed last night because I was kind of lost, and thanks for that. It was nice waking up next to you. It's been quite a while since I've woken up next to anyone, because like I said, I'm not a short-term kind of guy. I know that must sound like a line but it's true, I'm not into one-nighters. I don't need that kind of insecurity in my life. I'm not the chest-thumping, bedpost notching type."

"Good, because I'm not a short-term gal, either. I haven't had time for a relationship for quite a while. Hadn't met anyone that I wanted to make time for. I'm focused when I'm at work, it's so important to me. Casey and Dawn took a big chance when they hired me; I had never done project management or sales before. I'm learning as I go, with their help. But, Marlin, after we started spending time together I realized that when I wasn't at work, I felt alone for the first time in a long time. That went away when I was with you. I want to spend as much time as I can with you, as much time as you are willing to make for me. Am I scaring you yet?"

"No. Because I feel the same way. I told Lindsay today I don't know anyone else I'd rather see, and that's the truth."

"Good, because I feel so much at ease with you. I mean look, I showed up for dinner tonight in a sweatshirt, and we haven't even been out on an official date yet."

"And you look great in it. But I'm not into 'official anything.' Call it whatever you want, but I'm not into numbering dates or deciding what's official or not. As far as I'm concerned, we've already been on a few dates. And you are the only date I've ever let run *Marlinspike*. If you're really at ease around me, then you should wear whatever you want to, and are comfortable in. And I'll do the same. Deal?"

Kari had a wide smile. "Deal. I knew I liked you for a reason." She looked at me questioningly, "What is it?"

"I just remembered something I told Uncle Jack that I forgot to tell you."

"What?"

"I told him that I had met someone who I wanted to get to know better. He knew about you."

Her face softened as she realized how important this was to me. "I'm really glad, Marlin. I wish I had met him."

"I wish you had too, Kari. He'd have liked you, and I think you'd have liked him."

I LIFTED my head to see over her to the digital clock on the built-in nightstand. It read five-fifteen a.m. I lay my head back on the pillow as she said softly, "Hey."

"Hey. Sorry, I didn't mean to wake you."

"You didn't. I've been awake for a few minutes."

"Buyer's remorse wake you up?" I was worried until I heard her chuckle.

"Nope, not at all. I just usually wake up early."

I said, "So do I, especially when I have to go fishing."

"What do you do when you wake up and don't have to go out?"

"Most of the time I lie here. Sometimes I can get back to sleep."

"You're not fishing today, right?"

"Nope."

"Good. You're not going back to sleep, either."

I WAS MAKING breakfast when she came up from the stateroom. I poured her a cup of coffee, but before I could turn around and hand it to her she hugged me from behind.

"I didn't realize that you were so domestic."

"It has kept me from starving to death. We didn't use to have a restaurant here, remember?"

"So, I've heard."

I turned and faced her, looking her up and down. Tan slacks and a long sleeve blouse with a windbreaker. "Wow. You look great."

"Just work duds."

"Work duds that you rock."

She took the coffee mug. "Coffee, breakfast, and compliments. A gal could get used to this."

"I hope so."

"Marlin, has anyone ever told you that they feel like they've known you years longer than they have?"

"Not lately, if ever, Kari." I grinned. "But it sounds nice."

"It is."

12

NO MORE BUG PROBLEM

Kari came out of the "head" in a stunning teal dress, looking like a Hollywood star. I was bowled over.

"Do I look okay?"

"No. We'll just have to stay here. There will be other guys there, and they don't need to see you like that."

She wrapped her arm around my neck and kissed me. "And only one that I care about looking good for."

"Is he bigger than me?" I got slugged on the shoulder for that one.

Dinner was a blast. We sat with Casey, Dawn, Murph, Lindsay, Cindy Crenshaw, a partner in *Mallard Cove* and head of McAlister and Shaw's hotel and hospitality group, and Rikki Jenkins, the chief partner in ESVA Security. They provide security for *Bayside*, many private corporations, as well as several high-profile individuals and events. They share the office building with Casey and Dawn's company at *Bayside*. It was an eclectic and very interesting group.

The night turned out to be a fantastic success, with the waiting list for a table at one point stretching up to an hour, making it standing room only in the bar. Carlos was there, overseeing the kitchen, and watching the condition of the plates as the busboys brought them back in. Almost all were empty, the sign of a successful restaurant. The signs were pointing to the *Cove* being a hit.

Casey, Dawn, Cindy, and Rikki had ridden down together but had arrived too late to check out *On Coastal Time* before dinner. We all headed back to the houseboat where Lindsay started pouring wine, so we could toast their new home. Unfortunately, she ran out before filling the last glass, but then I remembered that bottle she left on *Why Knot*, and I volunteered to go retrieve it. I went aboard and started opening the salon door. I never knew what hit me.

THE EXPLOSION TOOK out all the glass in the salon, ruptured the overhead salon roof, and blew Marlin off the aft deck and into the empty slip next door.

After seeing the explosion from *OCT*, Kari ran full speed down the dock, screaming Marlin's name. Upon reaching the Chris Craft and leaping up onto the aft deck, she saw it was vacant. She looked through the open companionway where the door had been blown off. The automatic halon fire suppression system in the engine room was still operable; a blanket of flame extinguishing gas was rising and snuffing out the fire that had spread from the engine room into the salon. Turning back around she spotted one of Marlin's shoes lying on the deck, halfway to the railing. She looked over the side and thought she saw something disappearing down deep in the water, at the edge of the circle of light coming from the dock's power pedestal. As the others were racing up the dock, she dove over the side in the direction of whatever it was. The water was black and cold, but she searched frantically until her lungs screamed for oxygen. She surfaced, getting a lungful of fresh air, and dove back down immediately as Murph jumped in next to her. She was almost out of air again when her hand touched what felt like fabric in the inky blackness near the bottom. She grasped the material and tugged a large form upward. When she reached the surface, she realized that she had hold of Marlin's sleeve. She found his head and pulled his face above the surface. He wasn't breathing. Murph surfaced next to her and helped pull Marlin to the dock where the others hoisted him out and started CPR. He started breathing on his own soon after that but was still unconscious. After what seemed like an eternity, an EMS team showed up and transferred him onto a gurney. They raced him down the dock and loaded him into an ambulance, then headed across the CBBT to the hospital with Murph, Lindsay, and Kari following right on their bumper.

An hour later, Casey, Dawn, Cindy, and Rikki arrived. Dawn embraced Kari, and asked, "Have you heard anything?"

"No. They said the doctor would be out when there was news. I guess that with him taking so long, that's a good thing. That he's not..." She leaned on Dawn, not wanting to finish her sentence as Lindsay hugged the two of them.

The doctor came in and asked which one of them was Kari. She grabbed both Dawn and Lindsay, bracing for the worst.

"Marlin is asking for you."

"He's alive?" Kari was suddenly hopeful.

"He is, and you can see him after we complete the CAT scan. He has a concussion and a dislocated shoulder. We're going to keep him here for a couple of days for observation. The paramedics said he was pulled out of the water after a boat explosion. How long was he underwater?"

Murph answered, "Maybe two minutes."

The doctor shook his head. "That's amazing. His lungs don't show any signs of water, so the explosion must have stopped his breathing before he went in. Whoever pulled him out and got him breathing again saved his life. Oh, and he's a little singed from the explosion, missing one eyebrow and some hair, but that will all grow back soon enough. Kari, I'll have someone take you to him in a few minutes."

Everyone was extremely relieved and in awe of Kari's heroics that had saved Marlin. But Rikki had some news, and she also needed some answers.

"Kari, Casey filled me in on Jack's family connections and said there was some kind of a recent disconnect. Can you tell me the details?"

"Rikki, why do you want to know about all that?"

"Because this was no accident. We'll know more after the fire marshal and the State Police complete an investigation, but the boat was rigged to explode. Fortunately, the fire wasn't that severe; it didn't fully destroy the trigger mechanism that was attached to the doorway, so they have some evidence to work with. As soon as I spotted it, I secured the scene for them, and got everyone off the boat and away from it after we put out the rest of the fire. Someone tried to kill one or both of you. Do you have any idea who it may have been?"

"No! There were some rough family edges with his uncle dying, but no threats or anything along those lines. And the only people who knew I was staying with him are right here, so it can't have been me they were after. But I can't imagine why anyone would want to hurt Marlin, he's the sweetest guy in the world."

A nurse came in asking for Kari, then led her off to see Marlin.

Murph addressed Casey. "What 'family connections' are you guys talking about, Case?" Lindsay looked confused as well.

"He wanted this kept quiet, but he's Jack Denton's nephew."

"Jack Denton? As in the multi-billionaire from Richmond that just died? That Jack Denton?" Lindsay was incredulous.

"The same." Casey nodded.

"To think that I gave Marlin discounted slip rent because I thought he was just scraping by. Boy, he suckered me. I thought he was a friend." Murph felt deceived.

Casey said, "He is just scraping by, Murph. He just happened to have a wealthy uncle. That has nothing to do with his situation. I made the mistake of jumping to conclusions, too, and Rikki did some checking for me. He didn't deceive us; he is exactly who he looks like he is. This is why he never told anyone. And now he's lost his home and almost his life."

"And when whoever did this finds out that they failed, they might come back to finish the job," Rikki said.

Casey said, "Set up protection for both Marlin and Kari, Rikki. I'll take care of the bill. And see if your crew can help the cops find whoever did this. We need to find out why. Maybe it was a case of mistaken identity. Or something else. But we need to know whatever it was or is."

"Got it, Casey. I'll have someone with both of them twenty-four hours a day until we catch them." Rikki went out into the hall to make some calls.

"I TOOK care of that problem. Saw the flash and heard it from offshore."

"You sure?"

"Trust me. No more bug problem."

"I'll let my customer know."

KARI CAME into the room where I had been brought after the CAT scan. From the looks of her hair and what had been that beautiful dress, I gathered she must have been the one who jumped in and saved me.

"Nice night for a swim, wasn't it?"

She grabbed my hand. "I've never been so scared in my life. When I saw *Why Knot* explode, I ran over just as fast as I could. I saw you weren't onboard and got a glimpse of something sinking. I wasn't even certain it was you."

"But you dove in anyway?"

She nodded.

"I owe you my life, Kari."

She gave me a wry smile. "It's a little too soon to see if I want to collect on that debt, don't you think?" She winked.

I squeezed her hand and smiled back at her. "How bad is my boat?"

"Honestly, I only got a brief look at it when I was searching for you. But we won't be sleeping there anytime soon."

"Fixable?"

She knew how much that boat meant to me, having restored it with my dad. It was all the memories that were tied to it that couldn't be replaced.

"Marlin, let's worry about the boat later. We need to get you well, and out of here first."

"Yeah, but where do I go from here?"

"We've got a houseboat with an empty guest room you two can use as long as you want." Lindsay walked in with Murph, Dawn, and Casey.

"Starting in a couple of weeks we'll need a boat sitter for the winter anyway, and then y'all can have the run of the whole place," Murph said.

It's so great to have friends. Especially ones as good as the folks who were standing in my room right now. I wanted to say something, but I didn't trust my voice at that point. I nodded instead. Rikki Jenkins came in and walked over to my bed, giving me a chance to compose myself.

"Hey, Marlin, how are you feeling?"

"Like my boat blew up under me, Rikki. I've always been so careful around gas engines, but now this happens." I saw her give the others a questioning look.

"Um, about that, this wasn't your fault. Someone deliberately sabotaged you. It appears the salon door was rigged. Can you think of anyone who might want to hurt you?"

"What? No! Nobody." My head was spinning, and I couldn't tell if it was from the concussion or finding out someone just tried to kill me, and almost succeeded.

"Well, until this gets sorted out, someone from my team will be with you and Kari at all times."

"Thanks, Rikki, but I can't afford that. As you already know, I own a pistol and I can take care of myself and the two of us." I had been with her when she took down Lindsay's kidnapper.

"Casey is taking care of the tab, and I'm only billing him at cost so don't worry, he's getting the family discount. You can relax now; we've all got your back."

The doctor came in then, telling everyone that they needed to leave and let me rest.

They all started to file out after telling me they'd see me in the morning. All except Kari. "I'm not going anywhere. I'll sleep in that chair." There was a recliner in the corner of the room, and I knew better than to argue with her. Besides, I wanted her here with me. Maybe needed is a better word than wanted. Seeing her was reassuring in a lot of ways.

"MARLIN? Sorry to wake you, but I need you to look at a picture. Do you recognize this man?" I opened my eyes and saw Rikki, holding up what was an infrared picture of a man in a kayak by the bow of my boat.

"No, I don't. Is he the one who tried to kill me?"

"We think so. The marina's cameras aren't linked up yet, but we lifted this one off the houseboat's recorder. The guy disabled your bilge pumps and then cut the supply lines leading from your tank selector manifold to your engines, letting gas fill the sumps underneath each one. He must have wanted them to overflow, and let the gas run into the entire bilge where it would have gone all through the boat. Had that happened, we probably wouldn't be having this conversation right now, the vapor would have been all through the boat instead of just the engine room. But there wasn't enough gas in the tanks to even fill the engine sumps."

"Yeah, I always run the saddle tanks dry right before winter to get rid of any old gas. Then I refill them so that they don't get any condensation building up in the cold weather. One engine started sputtering after we docked the other day, so the second tank couldn't have been too far behind before it ran out."

She nodded. "That makes sense; there was only enough gas vapor to blow the windows and door out of the hatchway. It kept the fire damage to a minimum. Your halon system put most of it out, we got the rest with a hand extinguisher. Most of the damage happened from the explosion when the vapor lit off. But usually, it's the fire that follows it that destroys boats."

Kari had gotten up and was now standing next to me on the opposite side of the bed, looking concerned. I looked back at Rikki; she knows boats.

"Think it can be repaired?"

She looked a little worried. "As I said, the main damage was amidships. Both staterooms had smoke damage, but again, fortunately, no fire. Hull seems to be sound; she's not taking on any water. But you are going to need to rebuild the salon, galley, and the ruptured salon roof. Insurance will probably total it. You had insurance, right?"

I nodded. Most marinas require liability insurance, but fortunately, I had damage insurance too. Hopefully, I have enough. If they total it, I'll buy it back. I intend on fixing it myself anyway, it'll be cheaper that way. And I don't fish that much in the winter, so I'll have time.

"What time is it?"

"A little after 5 a.m. Again, I'm sorry to wake you, but on the chance that you knew the guy, we needed to find out who he was as soon as possible."

That made sense. I asked her, "Have you been to sleep at all?"

"Not yet, I'll grab some shuteye later. Oh, and you remember Tony and Dave who kept an eye on Murph and Dawn a couple of months ago? Tony's out in the hall. Dave will swap out with him later this morning."

"Rikki, I can't thank you enough."

"Thank me by getting well and getting back to the marina, I hate hospitals. Besides, you had my back two months ago; I can't thank *you* enough."

I had boarded a boat after Rikki; it belonged to a psychopath who had shot at us. I was just backing her up as she removed him from the tax rolls, permanently. To say we have a mutual admiration between us would be putting it mildly.

After Rikki left, Kari climbed back into the chair and went to sleep. I wanted to, but my mind wouldn't shut off. Before I saw that picture, none of the whole "somebody is out to get me" thing felt real. Now I knew it was, and what the guy looked like. I also knew he was a stranger. I kept wracking my brain, trying to think of any reason anyone would want me dead. I drew a blank. I had an old girlfriend way back in my past who I parted ways with on less than ideal terms, but she wasn't a psycho, nor capable of harming anyone.

I kept thinking about my call with Dennis Peel. It was strange, but not threatening. More like a door slam than a threat. Still, it bothered me.

13

BREAKING OUT

I looked over at the chair and was startled to see Dave looking back at me.

"Hi, Marlin. Sorry if I gave you a start. Lindsay showed up an hour ago, but you were asleep. She picked up Kari and took her back so that she could get her car and some fresh clothes. Said they would be back in a few hours."

"Dave, I want to be out of here in a few hours. What time is it?"

"A little after ten a.m. Don't count on them letting you out of here today, that was a bad concussion. Had one like it once. Took a few days until everything was right again."

I knew Dave was former military. I didn't ask, but I was willing to bet that his concussion didn't happen on this side of the world. And I didn't have a few days, I was going to be at my uncle's funeral if I had to go there still wearing a hospital gown.

The doctor came in a few minutes later and repeated pretty much verbatim what Dave had said, minus the part about having had a concussion himself. I told him that I might stay one more night, but I'd be gone by breakfast in the morning. He gave me a "we'll see" look, and I gave him my best "don't screw with me" look. I really don't have a good one of those, so it was mediocre at best. But one way or another, I was leaving tomorrow at the latest. Dave gave me an amused look after the doctor left.

"This isn't funny, Dave."

"You being hurt isn't funny, Marlin. You're telling the doctor what to do, now that's funny."

"I'm serious. I have a funeral to go to on Monday."

"I know you do, Rikki already told me to make sure I had a black suit ready because I'm going with you. But in the meantime, please do what they say and rest. I'm here to protect you, and that includes protecting you from yourself if I have to."

A FEW HOURS LATER, a lieutenant from the State Police came by. He interviewed me about the explosion, wanting a list of my charter clients, anyone that I had any disagreements with, and asking if I had seen anyone or anything strange around. That's when I remembered the deadrise that had been anchored out, fishing in a bad spot. He took down a description of the boat, but it looked like any one of the hundreds of deadrises running around the bay. After he left, I decided to rest my eyes for a minute. I woke back up to the sound of hushed voices, now coming from Tony and Kari.

"What time is it?"

"Sorry, we woke you, Marlin." Kari looked chagrinned. "It's a little after eight."

"At night?" Had I really slept most of the day?

"Yes. I had them leave your dinner tray. You need to eat something if you want to get out of here in the morning."

"I don't 'want' to get out of here, I'm 'going' to get out of here. I hate hospitals. I'm not sick, and I want out of here before I catch the plague or one of those skin-eating diseases that live in hospitals. This room is probably crawling with germs."

Tony started silently and quickly for the door, no doubt to sit out in the hallway where it was safer, where sick people didn't linger, so there might be fewer germs. I wanted to go with him, that way I'd be that much closer to the car.

"I learned something about you I didn't know; you're a lousy patient," Kari scolded.

"You're not the first person who has told me that today."

"I bet. How do you feel?"

I answered, "I feel like getting out of here."

She rolled the tray table over and started spoon-feeding me. I wanted to argue, but my dominant right hand was attached to the arm that now resided in a sling for the time being. Using my left hand to try to feed myself would probably end up as a laundry disaster. Plus, she looked like she was enjoying it.

In between bites, I asked, "Did you bring me back any clothes?"

"I did. But you don't get them until tomorrow at the earliest."

I said, "I'm out of here in the morning if I have to go bare-assed. I'll buy you breakfast out somewhere."

"News flash, friend, whenever we leave, I'm driving us back to the marina and you are going straight to bed until we leave on Monday. I was able to get your clothes off the boat, and I had your black suit dry-cleaned at the one-hour cleaner place, so it's ready for Monday. I also had the rest of your clothes cleaned and washed to get rid of the smoke smell."

"Is the boat that bad?"

"It's not great, but we can fix it. I accessed your contacts in the cloud and sent your insurance guy an email to start the claim process. And my cousin Carlton has a boatyard a few miles from *Mallard Cove*, we can have her hauled and put in a heated shed there so we can work on her in the winter."

"We?"

She looked at me funny. "What part of 'I'm a Shore woman' didn't I make clear? Yes, we. I'm going to help when I can make time. And I probably lay varnish down better than you, anyway."

"If that's a challenge, then it's accepted." Kari just kept getting better and better. "Did you happen to check out the bunk on *OCT*?"

"For?"

"Size."

She gave me that sly smile again. "I did, in fact. Plenty of room for two."

"I like waking up and seeing you in the morning. Seeing Dave in your spot in the chair this morning was traumatic."

She laughed. "I had to go get things organized if we were going to get you out of here tomorrow."

"Aha! You admit you have signed on with the morning breakout plan."

"I didn't say morning." She paused and grinned. "The doctor did. If, and only if you eat a good dinner and have a good night."

"Are you staying?"

"Yes."

"Then I'll have a good night. Now let's kill that applesauce."

AFTER GETTING RELEASED the next morning I didn't go straight to bed. Over Kari's objections, I went to check out *Why Knot*. I just needed two minutes to determine that we could indeed fix her. I hoped that Kari was as good with repairing vintage boats as she was with managing real estate. It was going to take both of us working as a team if we were going to get her put back together by the time Lindsay and Murph got back in the spring. I didn't want to impose on them by staying on the houseboat any longer than necessary.

Back at the houseboat, I argued that a chaise lounge out on the party deck was just about the same as reclining in bed. Besides, there was plenty of fresh air, and flights of returning waterfowl to watch for. Kari agreed, with the stipulation that I go inside when the temperature dropped. Dave took a seat in a chair by the stairs where he could see anyone approaching. Kari settled on the padded wicker sofa that was next to me, using the wicker coffee table as a makeshift desk. I saw she had brought along a canvas bag filled with papers from work. She noticed me looking.

"I want to make up the time I'm losing at work tomorrow. It's the least I can do since Casey's flying us down and back."

I nodded kind of absentmindedly. She put her papers down and looked at me questioningly. "What?"

I paused a minute, about to enter water I wasn't familiar with, hoping I didn't look foolish while doing it.

"Marlin, what is it?"

"You know I'm not really up on all this computer stuff."

"Trust me, I do. Aren't you glad we backed up your computer and phone to the cloud since both were destroyed by the blast and when you went into the water?"

"Well, that's what I was just thinking about. I'm phoneless until after we get back tomorrow and I have time to go buy a new one. So, I could be losing business by not being able to answer it, since I do mostly everything by phone."

She saw where I was headed. "You want a website and online signup for your charters. Great idea."

"That's not all. The whole charter fleet is trying to promote *Mallard Cove* and the restaurant because it's good for our business, and vice versa."

Kari was starting to see where I was headed with this. "Since your calendar is in the cloud, it can be accessed by a central system, like the marina office."

"Right. And if all of us put our calendars in the cloud thingy, then the office could take phone reservations for us, in return for a small flat fee. And we can also have our own online signups when people prepay through our websites. It could show them what dates are already booked. I don't know how many calls I get from anglers wanting dates that are already gone. It wastes a lot of my time."

I could see Kari light up over the idea. "On the marina's website it could show the available boats by date and then you click on the boat name to be taken to their reservation page. You know, Marlin, half the battle of making a great web-based system is knowing what to include in it. This is great."

"It's also another tool to lure additional charter boats here." I felt like an Internet genius.

"What's this new tool?" Murph asked.

He and Lindsay were climbing the stairs with takeout from the *Cove* for the five of us for lunch. Kari explained our idea, then Murph and Lindsay added to it, suggesting a password-protected section for higher-end charters like theirs that aren't open to the general public but only to their established private client base.

After lunch, I felt the best I had since the explosion, even though there was someone still running loose who wanted to kill me. But Dave had our backs and had just gone to check the dock after Murph and Lindsay went over to work on *Irish Luck.*

I smiled because I had impressed the heck out of my girlfriend with a good business idea. My girlfriend. This was the first time I had thought of her using that phrase.

"Hey, Kari, can I ask you something?"

She looked up. "Sure."

"How do I introduce you tomorrow?"

She smiled. "You can start by saying 'This is Kari.'"

"My *friend* Kari?"

"If you say, 'My friend with benefits Kari' you'll need a sling for your other arm."

"Okay, how would you introduce me to your family?" Did I just say something about getting introduced to her family, like not at a funeral? Oh, crap.

She put her papers down and crossed her arms, grinning. "Oh, I get it. Mister 'I don't number dates' who isn't into 'official' dates now wants a title. How about 'My favorite floater?' Though, you suck at floating since you sank."

She looked amused now. I was sorry I brought it up and felt heat rising in my face. I leaned back and started scanning the skies for waterfowl. I had to say something to change the subject.

"I haven't heard a laughing gull in days nor seen a pelican now for a week. The Canada geese will be here soon. Time for the fall shift change."

She picked up a group of papers and went back to reading. "I know. My boyfriend keeps tabs on all things waterfowl related and keeps me officially updated."

Okay, so I'm about as smooth as eighty grit sandpaper, but I got my answer. And she enjoyed teasing me. Win/win.

14

LAWYERING UP

I hate my 'funeral suit' because that's pretty much all I use it for. Basic black, hotter than hell in the summer in Virginia, or in the humid early fall on the west coast of Florida. Kari's black mid-calf dress looked somewhat cooler and yet somberly stunning. At least, I think that's a thing, "somberly stunning." Then again, she would look good wrapped in burlap.

As we walked across the ramp toward Casey's plane, Dave handed me his phone. Rikki wanted to give me an update. "We've got a name to go with that guy in the picture. Gary Shifflett. Ever heard of him? The state police lifted a set of his prints off two GPS trackers we found hidden on both your and Kari's cars. His mugshot matched up with the person in the kayak photo."

"No, I haven't. So, he has a record? For what?"

"Being a leg breaker over in Virginia Beach. He's mostly worked freelance for loan sharks and bookies. Looks like he's branching out into bombings and murder for hire now. And unless one of you two has a gambling problem or loan shark debt that I don't know about, someone else has hired him. State police have issued a warrant for his arrest. It's only a matter of time before he gets picked up, and then we'll find out who's really behind this."

"So, he was keeping tabs on both of us, not just me?"

"Looks that way. We just need to figure out why."

I handed the phone back to Dave. We all climbed into the Cessna CJ-3, Dave in the back row, Kari and I in the middle, facing forward, Dawn in front of her, facing aft, and Casey took the aft-facing seat in front of me. Dawn decided to go with Casey at the last minute, another flexibility plus of having your own private aircraft; the passenger list can change easily and instantaneously.

It wasn't the first time I'd been in a Cessna jet; Uncle Jack's first plane was an earlier Cessna model. This CJ-3 was a real performer for the money, cruising at over four hundred sixty miles per hour at forty-five thousand feet. We would use less fuel on this entire trip than Uncle Jack's G-800 would use just getting to its cruising altitude. Our flight time to Naples would be around two hours, only slightly longer than my last flight in the big Gulfstream.

On the way down, Kari told Casey and Dawn about the new website reservation idea, and they were enthusiastic about it. They were interested in adding more marinas to their property portfolio; tools and details like this would give them that much more of an edge over the competition. They liked having Kari on their team, and it was clear she had a real future with them. I doubt I'd have been on their plane if she didn't.

We landed in Naples just ahead of a Gulfstream G-150, a mid-sized jet that was similar to the CJ-3. I stepped out into air that was so humid you needed a machete to cut your way through it. As I did, the Gulfstream pulled up next to us on the ramp. But I didn't pay any attention to it and the fact that its tail number ended in DA. I was too busy thanking Casey and Dawn, who were about to re-board and head over to Palm Beach. Two people disembarked from the 150 as Kari, Dave, and I started walking around the nose of the Cessna, toward the private terminal.

"Cousin Marlin!"

I looked over and saw my cousin Carter Denton, Jack Jr.'s oldest son. He was tall and handsome and had recently joined Denton Industries. Now twenty-five years old, the papers were already calling him one of Richmond's most eligible bachelors. I walked over to him with Kari and Dave following.

"Hi, cuz. You're looking good." I saw that Virginia Supreme Court Justice and family friend, Mark Powell, was standing next to him. "Hi, Mark. How's the hunting?" Mark was an accomplished big game hunter, having scored trophies from around the world with a bow, shotgun, rifle, pistol, and even a few using marriage licenses.

"Probably not as good as your fishing. Good to see you again, just sorry about the circumstances."

I introduced Kari and Dave just as Sam Knight started to taxi out in the Cessna, hitting us lightly with the thrust from its engines. Carter looked questioningly at it, then over at me.

"Whose plane?"

"Friend of mine who's also Kari's boss. Beat's driving down."

"I was hoping you might ride with us, and we'd get a chance to talk since Mark and I were the only ones aboard this flight. But Dennis said that you weren't coming."

Dennis believed I wasn't coming? I thought he expected that I'd make my own way here. I wondered if Jack was behind it all and if Dennis was just doing as he had been told. Suddenly the thought popped into my mind that maybe Dennis thought I'd be dead, and that's why he said I wouldn't be coming. A quick glance at Kari confirmed that she shared the same thought.

"He must have gotten me confused with someone else. It's a rough and mixed-up time for everyone right now."

Mark asked, "Speaking of a rough time, what's with your arm?"

"Boating accident. Nothing as spectacular as falling out of a tree stand though. All healed up from that?" Two deer seasons ago Mark had fallen almost fifty feet when a climbing peg next to his tree stand had given way. Despite breaking numerous bones including his pelvis, he managed to crawl back to his ATV and somehow drive it slowly back to a farmhouse. Mark is one tough guy.

"I can now very accurately give you two days' advance notice of any incoming weather systems." He grinned.

I like Mark, he has one of the most brilliant legal minds and is fun to drink and talk with. He's one of my cousin Jack's most trusted friends, and before his being picked for the State Supreme Court, he had been Denton Industries' outside counsel.

"You have a car?" Carter asked.

"We're going to call a taxi."

"We've got plenty of room, there's only the two of us." A black Mercedes Sprinter van with dark tinted windows idled next to the Gulfstream.

I accepted for the three of us, Kari and I climbing in the front bench seat with Carter, while Dave and Mark took the next row back. Carter and I shared numerous stories about Uncle Jack on the fifteen-minute drive over to the house. As the van pulled up to the gates, we were waved in by two security guys with earpieces and bulges under their coats.

"Carter, what's with all the security?" I asked.

"Someone at the office accidentally let the time and place of the service slip to a reporter, and it got picked up on the newswires. Dad freaked out because the little ones are here, and are easy targets for kidnappers. If you aren't in this van, or aren't on the guest list and have a photo ID at the gate, you aren't getting in."

I looked over at Kari, who nodded. *This* was another reason why I never told anyone about being Uncle Jack's nephew. In my case, I doubted that any kidnappers would take my IOU.

Once again, the sound of the loose driveway pebbles under the tires instantly brought back memories, the last one painful. We pulled up to the entrance of the breezeway, and I saw Jack waiting, probably expecting only Carter and Mark. He smiled at me as I opened the door.

"Marlin, I'm glad that you made it after all! I was upset when Dennis said you weren't coming." He hugged me, being careful of my arm and asking about it. I gave him the pat "boating accident" response. I introduced Kari, who he looked over like a lion looking at a gazelle, and then Dave, who I said was a friend. I got a very curious look back. He sent Carter and Mark inside, saying that he needed to talk with me. Kari had taken my good arm, and it was obvious that she had no intention of leaving my side. Dave had taken a position at the top of the steps, where he had a clear unobstructed view of anyone coming near us.

"What the hell is going on, Marlin? First, you aren't even going to show up, and 'friend,' my ass. Your pal Dave was part of the security detail at an event I attended in Richmond two weeks ago. It's obvious he's protecting you, and you thought this was necessary here at my dad's house? Does this have something to do with your arm?"

It was either the best acting job I'd ever seen in person, or he really didn't know.

"You also thought security was needed, that there might be a threat here since you have a perimeter set up. Any reason for that, Jack?" I countered, almost bitterly.

"A security leak at the office. But you still haven't answered my question."

"Somebody tried to kill me and possibly Kari as well by blowing up my boat. If it hadn't been for her jumping in the water to save me, I'd have died. The police have identified a suspect, but he's still at large. Until he's caught, some friends have decided to provide security for Kari and me."

"My god! I'm glad you're okay. I was worried that something was wrong when Dennis told me that you said you didn't need a seat on the plane because you weren't coming."

I raised my voice. "I didn't tell him I wasn't coming, he called to tell me that if I was going to show up, I'd need to get down here on my own. I thought you had told him to keep me away!"

Jack glanced around and waved my voice down. "I'd never do that. You and Dad were so close. Why didn't you call me directly?"

"I left a message on your damn cell phone!" I was really hot now.

"My new number? The Florida one?"

"No. It was an 804 area code, the one in Richmond. Someone in your office transferred me to it."

Jack shook his head. "I had to switch phones because whoever leaked it about the place and time of the service also apparently leaked my phone number too. I never got your message, only a voice mailbox full of reporter's interview requests. We have several new people in the office, and things have been a bit confused. I'll give you my new number before you leave."

There were an awful lot of coincidences happening around Jack and me. Things weren't adding up. But I knew one thing for certain; Dennis Peel had lied to me, and apparently to my cousin as well.

"Dennis lied to me and you, Jack. I'm going to get to the bottom of this and find out why."

"Not here, and not right now. This isn't the time or place, today is about my dad. Trust me, I'll get to the bottom of it with Dennis after this, and you're going to leave that to me. How did you get down here? You must have been at the airport since you rode in with Carter and Mark."

Kari spoke up. "My boss, a friend of Marlin's, dropped us off on his way to Palm Beach. He's going to pick us up on the way back."

"Why don't you three ride back with Carter and Mark, and not have to put your friend out? That way you can stay as long as you need here, and I know that Carter would like to spend more time with you, Marlin, and do some catching up. Let me do that for you all since things got so turned around on this end." Jack gave us a confident look.

I glanced at Kari, who nodded. Then I told Jack, "Thanks. I appreciate it."

"Good, let's go over to the lanai, that's where the service is going to be held. Dad loved the view of the water from there so much."

We walked up the breezeway and through the front door. We could see through the glass doors on the other side of the dining room that several dozen chairs had been set up on the lanai and the brick patio beyond. As we walked into the crowded living room, Kari took my hand. Just then, Dennis Peel came in from the Florida room, stopping in mid-stride when he saw me, the color draining from his face. It was like he had just seen a ghost, or someone that he expected would already be a ghost by now.

I started toward him, but Jack put a hand on my shoulder. The wrong shoulder. I don't know if he did that intentionally, but it hurt like hell. As Dennis spun on his heel and retreated into the other room, Jack said quietly, "Not now, cuz. Remember, you're going to leave that to me, and trust me on this one."

I looked at Jack, who was watching my eyes, searching for both agreement and the trust he asked for. I guess he finally found them when I nodded and looked away. My only choices were to let Jack handle it or go tear into Dennis myself immediately. Doing it myself meant destroying the serenity of my uncle's memorial service for everyone gathered here. I wasn't about to do that. Suddenly, Kari was squeezing my hand, hard. That's when I realized that I had unconsciously tightened my grip on hers when I saw Dennis, and it was hurting her. I mouthed, "Sorry." I turned back to Jack, but he had already started making his way around talking to everyone, "working" the room. He was so good at this, but it was something that I detested.

My mind kept going back to Dennis, who had now vanished. At the very least, he was guilty of trying to keep me away from here. I wanted to know why. Was it a coincidence that Jack's number and the service information had been leaked, and that my call had been directed to the one number that was now being ignored? My head was spinning, and I couldn't think straight. Things were still a little fuzzy from the concussion, and this wasn't helping.

Kari read my face and said, "Do you need to sit down?"

"Yeah, I do." We walked out through the sliding glass doors over to the second row and took the two seats next to the aisle. Dave moved over by the lanai side wall, where he had the best vantage point over us.

A couple of Jack's youngest kids came over and hugged me, girls both about seven years old. They were with their nannies, as neither of their mothers was invited nor allowed to attend the service. Once you're out of the family, there's no coming back. Oh, and I'm assuming you've done the math on the similar age of the girls and the number of mothers. Let's just say Jack's a charmer and leave it at that.

Two of my other cousins were a boy and girl in their early teens, so it was a shock when they came over and chatted me up. I guess that for some reason I was their "cool" cousin, much the way that Jack had been mine. The age difference between me and them was similar to that of me and him. They told me to "friend" them on social media, which scared the hell out of me, worrying about their security. Hopefully, Jack or their mother (they had the same mother) was keeping an eye on that. Jack's other two kids were in college (another mother, also Carter's) and each gave me a quick and polite hello as they passed by before moving to their seats. Carter came over and insisted that we come sit with him in the front row. Carter has always been my favorite ever since he was a kid, and now you can see why. It suddenly hit me that Kari and he were close to the same age. Kari gave me a strange look.

"What are you thinking about, Marlin?"

"Huh? Oh, nothing. Not a thing. Why?"

"You had a very funny look on your face."

"Not me! Nope. My mind was just drifting. Post-concussion and all."

She gave me a sideways look and dropped it.

I wanted to change the subject, and fast. "Hey, you want to text Casey and tell him we don't need a ride?" She looked at me like I was a simpleton. "Oh, right. You'll probably have already done that, huh."

"Yeah, huh."

Carter was amused. "You two are really good together. You must have been seeing each other for quite a while."

Kari smiled. "There have been days when it seems like an eternity." She squeezed my hand again, winking at me.

"I'm glad we're all riding back together. We never get to see each other, Marlin, and I miss spending time with you. We should fish together soon. Maybe I'll come over in December when the big rockfish are running."

"Let's plan to. Call me with a date so I can block it out on my calendar."

"I will as soon as I'm back at the office."

The minister took his place in front, with his back to the Gulf. He did a nice, short service, then invited Jack up to say a few words about his father. After Jack was through with a couple of humorous anecdotes, he called me up there. I went reluctantly because it really isn't my thing. But somewhere between my chair and the front, it suddenly came to me. I told the story about the greasy fried pork sandwiches and my first white marlin. There were chuckles throughout the crowd; it was so representative of Uncle Jack. Family, work, and what the family calls "Denton humor."

When I finished, a shadow suddenly crossed over the patio. Everyone looked up, and I followed their gaze. A flight of seven pelicans in a "V" formation was flying by when one peeled off from the middle of the right side. That lone pelican circled us twice directly overhead, then flew straight out into the Gulf, finally disappearing from sight. You could have heard a pin drop. Jack came over and embraced me with a tear in one eye, whispering one word in my ear, "Dad." I only nodded because it didn't seem right to say anything beyond that.

I returned to my seat and Kari whispered, "I've never seen a pelican do anything like that. They always stick together, parallel to beaches."

Again, I could only nod. I was choked up because I knew Jack was right. Uncle Jack had let us know he was okay, and that he had moved on. Think what you will, but I'll believe it as long as I live.

After a buffet luncheon where the pelican's behavior was a prominent topic, we were all ready to leave. Kari and I went to look for Jack to say goodbye and found him talking with Steve Cashman, our insurance agent. Cashman and Jack had been on the tennis team together in college, and Uncle Jack and Cashman's father had been life-long friends. Both Jacks had their insurance with him, which is why I did as well; it wasn't because of Steve's "charming" personality. He was what I'd call a "professional mooch" with an exceedingly high opinion of himself. That skinny snake must have snuck in right before the service; I hadn't seen him before now. But after seeing the way he looked at me, I realized that he had been there all along, but must have been avoiding me. I suddenly had a very bad feeling.

"Hello, Steve. I'm surprised I didn't see you before this. Did you get the e-mail about my boat claim?"

"This isn't the place to talk about that, Marlin. I'll call you tomorrow."

Jack picked up on Steve's vibe, sensing a dodge. "Don't stop on my account. It's good that you are both here, you can deal with this face to face."

It felt like Jack was announcing two fighters in a boxing match. I was ready to be the first one out of their corner. "I agree, Jack. What's to talk about, Steve? I just need an adjuster to look it over, so I can get a check and start on the repairs."

"Um, well, about that. I checked with the police, and since they can't rule out terrorism, you might not be covered. There's a terrorism exclusion in your policy."

Carter and Mark had walked up behind Steve. Mark's eyebrows went up at the mention of terrorism. The two of them had prior history, and it wasn't pretty.

"What exactly happened to your boat, Marlin?" Mark looked concerned.

"I didn't want to say anything, but it exploded, Mark."

"That's how you got hurt?"

I nodded. "Apparently someone has it in for me and tried to kill me."

Now Mark looked concerned. He turned to Steve and in a mocking voice he said, "So, you think it's Al Quida that's out to get Marlin?"

"At this point, the police haven't ruled anything out, so my carrier isn't inclined to pay."

Mark looked back at me. "Do they have any suspects?"

"Some guy named Shifflett. I've never heard of him nor seen him before."

Mark turned back to Steve, "Well, there's a terrorist's name if I've ever heard it. I guess that this is their new master plan, killing off all the Virginia fishing guides?" He was disgusted. "Marlin, we'll call my old law partner on the way back to Virginia. I'm sure he'll represent you for a percentage of the punitive award you are going to get from Steve here and his carrier. Then again if they're smart, they'll settle, and fast."

The look on Steve's face was a mixture of fear and loathing. He said, "I'll try talking to them again. Maybe there's some wiggle room."

"Wiggle fast. You've got until we land to get an appraiser lined up. If not, let your office know they're going to be served with papers."

Steve turned on his heel and walked away. Jack smiled as he said to Mark, "While I'm glad you're happy as a judge, I sure miss having you as my attorney." He looked like he had just seen a prize fight. He loves winning and winners.

"That's because you and I always won together, Jack." He had a huge smile, and I wasn't sure if it was from the memories of working with Jack or having verbally beaten Steve over the head.

As Jack walked us out to the end of the breezeway, it hit me that this was the last time I'd ever be here. Jack already had a place in Jensen Beach, over on the East coast of Florida. No doubt he would sell this house, and whoever bought it would tear it down and build one of those new "McMansions." The finality of it made me sad, but I wanted a picture of Jack, Carter, Kari and me together at the breezeway. Mark took it on Kari's camera, and I put on a fake smile that lied about how I felt right then.

I WAS glad that Kari got to talk with and know Carter and Mark on the flight back. She already knew the rest of my favorite people, and now she added the last two. I didn't add much to the conversation; I wasn't in the mood to chat. I missed Uncle Jack, and that hit me again hard after we took off from Naples. Despite the flight back home in the G-150 and having been at Uncle Jack's house, I realized that I had never felt like I was in his world this trip. Because it didn't exist anymore. It had always been like a protective bubble around me when I was with him, making me feel that anything was possible. Now, that was gone. I could have dumped everything on him about Dennis Peel. He would have instantly known what to say and do, giving me sage advice. Now I had to trust that my cousin would get to the bottom of things as he had promised. But something was nagging at me like I had missed something. Something important. It felt like whatever it was lay just out of reach. I hoped I would figure it out before it hit me over the head as Mark had with Steve.

15

THE BLAME GAME

Instead of stopping at the marina, Kari headed over the CBBT, with Dave following right behind in an SUV.

"Where are you going?" I asked.

With a grin, she answered, "To get you out of that funk you've been in since we left Naples, and back to being upbeat. We're going to the electronics big box store in Virginia Beach to get you a new laptop and phone. Then we'll pick up some Chinese food, take it back to the houseboat, eat, then get you reconnected with the world."

"You're still staying with me, right?"

"I wasn't planning on going anywhere unless you're kicking me out." Kari glanced at me as if she was half expecting a response to that.

"I figured since you've seen my crazy family, it might send you fleeing to the hills in sheer terror, or back to your place."

"We don't have any hills nearby. And lately, my place has been with you, and I figured it still is. Don't mind me if I pat myself on the back, but I'd like to think that I've been a tad helpful, and I'm not just talking about pulling you out of the drink. But if I'm overstaying my welcome..."

"No! You're not. I'm just...I don't know...it's been a hell of a week. I appreciate you being there with me. I couldn't have gotten through it all nearly as well without you, and I'm not just talking about the 'saving my life' part, either. I'm glad that our friendship has evolved into more than just that. I really don't want you to go anywhere."

"I never figured you for the mushy type," she teased.

"I'm not. I guess I'm trying to say thank you. For a lot of things, but most of all for being here, and sticking with me."

She gave me a very serious-looking glance. "I can't think of any place I'd rather be. I chased you, remember?"

"Yeah, before finding out exactly what you were getting into. Especially the family part."

"Today wasn't bad, Marlin, and your family isn't bad. A little unusual maybe, with a whole zip code worth of waterfront and their private air force, but not bad. I like Carter, and the rest of Jack's kids are nice as well. Some seemed a bit reserved, but they just lost their grandfather, so it's not a fair time to judge them."

I shook my head. "That was about normal. What about Jack?"

"The jury is still out on a few things with him. One thing is certain though, he has a certain charm about him when he wants to show it. When he does, I can see why he has so many kids and all those exes. I'd hate to see his monthly child support and alimony bills." She glanced my way again. "What? Don't get nervous, but he looked at me like I was raw meat."

I snorted. "That's Jack. I know not to trust him around you."

"I hope you know that you can trust *me* around *him*."

"I do. But do I trust him about Dennis Peel?"

"That's part of why the jury is still out. I only got a glimpse of Dennis, but he was certainly surprised, no, make that *shocked* to see you."

"Because he thought I was dead?"

"I thought that at first. But now I can't be sure. Remember Carter saying that if you weren't on the van from the airport, you had to have a photo ID and be on the guest list? What do you wanna bet Dennis put that list together, and that you weren't on it? So, if we had shown up in a car, we probably couldn't have gotten in anyway. Dave and I certainly wouldn't have been on that list. And you don't have Jack's current phone number to call for help in getting us cleared."

"Didn't. But I do now, he gave it to me on the way out."

Kari said, "But that's a possibility as to why Peel looked shocked. By the way, you never said hi to Clara while we were there."

That's when it hit me. "Something had been bugging me, but I couldn't put my finger on it. That must be it; Clara wasn't there. Damn, I feel so guilty for not realizing that."

"You shouldn't feel so bad; like you just said, you've had a hell of a week. It's amazing that you can remember anything at all after getting your brain scrambled. Most people would still be home in bed."

I shook my head. "I bet that was Dennis Peel's doing, too, her not being there."

"It sure seems like he could be behind a lot of things," Kari said.

"That, or he's carrying out those things for Jack. I just wish I knew why if he is. I wish Jack had let me go after him myself, right then. But he was right, today was all about Uncle Jack."

JACK HIT a number on his speed dial. "What the hell were you thinking?"

The voice on the other end was slightly indignant. "I was thinking that I was protecting you!"

"Don't hand me that crap, you thought you were protecting yourself and your position! We don't do *that*; we don't hurt people. Especially not Marlin. It's one thing to keep him at arm's length, at least until things are settled, but he's not to get in any way physically hurt, are we clear on that?" Jack was trying to control his anger.

"Yes."

"Call off your dogs, and I mean right now. With the police closing in, that could easily lead back to you, and then it's a short jump over you to me. Whoever you used needs to take a trip out of the country. Clean this mess up, and I mean like *yesterday*." Jack hit the "End" button.

I LOVED WATCHING Kari work with electronics. After we had gotten back to the houseboat she had first plugged my new phone and laptop into their chargers. We ate our Chinese takeout while the batteries got topped off. Then we sat on the bed together while she started loading both devices with the data she had so fortunately saved to the cloud. She handed over my new smartphone, and I started going through a few voicemails. The last one was from a terse-sounding Steve Cashman, letting me know that an appraiser would be out in the morning and that I could expect an expedited check in a few days. I replayed the voicemail on speaker so that Kari could hear it. She got a huge grin.

"I'm glad we're going to be able to fix her. I know she holds a lot of memories for you, Marlin, and now she does for me too. One bad one, but a few good ones, and one very good one."

"Only one?" I needled her.

"Yep. The other times I was just faking it." She burst out laughing at my indignant look. She was better at teasing than me.

"Speaking of fakes, I'm going to be looking for a new insurance company tomorrow. I know Cashman will be sure to stiff me on renewal rates, now that I've made a claim. Insurance is such a racket, like legalized extortion." I was still fuming over him trying to weasel out of paying me.

"We have a great agency that we deal with for the resort and the marinas. They handle the boats and autos, too. I'll get our agent to call you, you'll like her."

"I'll like her if she's cheaper than Cashman."

Kari chuckled. "I get the feeling everyone is cheaper than Cashman, except when it comes to paying out claims."

My phone rang, and it was Rikki, so I put her on speaker. "We don't have to worry about Shifflett anymore. The sheriff just found him in the parking lot at the end of Poquoson Avenue at Messick Point over by Newport News. He was shot in the back of the head at close range, and his body was dumped there."

I guess I shouldn't have been shocked, but I had been expecting him to get caught or maybe shot by the police. Instead, someone had beaten them to it. "You think he picked the wrong legs to try to break?"

"I think that blowing up your boat may have been his first and last murder for hire job. I bet that whoever was really behind it saw him as cheap and expendable. That's probably why he was picked for it in the first place. I'm thinking that whoever hired him is now cleaning house and tying up loose ends. That's why they were able to get so close behind him to take that shot; he knew and trusted them. They've got to know that your guard is up now and that we're watching over you. Fortunately, it was a total amateur hour. If whoever hired him had used a pro, you'd be dead now. They were out of their comfort zone, whoever it was." Rikki sounded calm.

I had caught something. "You said 'was' Rikki. Like past tense, as in not around anymore."

"I think that's right. You have to ask yourself why his body was dumped where it was found. It's remote, and not a popular spot this time of year, but I guarantee not a day goes by that someone doesn't go down there. So, why not dump him in the swamp, or out in the Chesapeake?"

I knew where she was headed with this. "They wanted him found."

"Exactly, Marlin. They were sending us a message that they took care of things and have called off the hit. If they were still coming after you, then why go out of their way and risk getting caught in a public place dumping a body? Why let us know they wouldn't be using Shifflett again so we might start watching for someone else? They would stay quiet until they struck again. Whoever it was is done, and I highly doubt they'll be back. We'll keep the guys with you two for a few more days, but I think you are in the clear. Carry your pistol from now on though, just in case."

I closed my eyes and tilted my head back, breathing deep. It felt so good hearing this from Rikki, I trust her judgment, she's a pro. I'm willing to bet my life on her being right. Which is exactly what I'd be doing. "Thanks for everything, Rikki."

"Hey, don't make it sound like I'll never see you two again. We need to get together soon. Up until the point when you went for a swim, that was a fun night."

Kari said, "It was, and we never did get to make that toast. We all need to get together before Lindsay and Murph head south. I'll set something up and be in touch. And thanks, Rikki."

"That sounds great. I'll call Casey and Dawn and bring them up to speed. Meanwhile, you two can relax a bit."

After I hung up, Kari went back to loading the laptop as I silently removed my arm sling. I hugged her from behind as she made an almost purring sound. Then she stiffened.

"Hey! You aren't supposed to take that sling off for another few days."

I nibbled an earlobe. "It's not a real hug if I don't use both arms."

She turned around halfway, putting her arms around me. "I said it before and I'll say it again, you are a rotten patient."

I smiled. "Yes, but I make up for it in other ways." I kissed her as she closed the laptop with one hand. I didn't need to email anyone tonight anyway.

THE NEXT MORNING, we were both awake in the pre-dawn as usual, but not in that much of a hurry for breakfast. We ended up over at the *Cove* a little after seven, eating inside where it was warm. There hadn't been a frost yet, but I was willing to bet we'd see one before Lindsay and Murph leave in a little less than two weeks.

For me, fall is the most exciting season in the Chesapeake. The brilliant foliage as a backdrop against the water isn't something that is quickly forgotten. And the huge flights of arriving ducks and Canada geese are simply breathtaking. Don't get me wrong, I love it when the pelicans and the laughing gulls return in the spring. But they kind of trickle in quietly, and if you aren't watching for them you might suddenly realize one day that "Oh, they're back." That never happens with the geese. The volume of sound of hundreds if not thousands of them squawking in huge geometric formations overhead is incredible. And the flights of the arriving tundra swans and their haunting warbling calls, though fewer in number within their formations are equally as stunning.

It turned out that Kari loved the "seasonal shift change" as much as I do. That didn't come as a surprise. This morning over breakfast we made a pact to get out on the water as much as possible after work, to take in as much of this spectacle as we could. But today she planned to call her cousin, and after work, we would tow *Why Knot* over to his boatyard. I had back-to-back charters starting tomorrow, and then an open weekend when we could start on her in earnest. So today I'd start packing up all of my salvageable personal items, meet with the appraiser, and get the old girl ready to tow.

The appraiser showed up a little before ten, and as much as Steve was a jerk, this guy was just the opposite. He was also an old wood boat aficionado. Five minutes into his inspection he deemed her to be "totaled." Meaning that I'd be getting a check for the full agreed-upon replacement value. I asked him what the salvage value was, which he had estimated to be barely above zero. There isn't a big market for exploded, slightly burned old wooden Chris Crafts. I made a deal to buy it back for the salvage value minus the estimated cost of towing to the breaker's yard in Portsmouth. Then he gave me a signed copy of the agreement, and left a happy man, having saved his company the hassle of having to tow it out of here.

I looked at the bottom line, eyed the damage again, and figured I could make the repairs for less than half of that. I'd tuck the rest away because I'd had an idea percolating in the back of my head ever since Baloney had B2 running a few charters for him. I'd run it by Kari, Murph, and Lindsay, to see what they thought.

I was walking over to the *Cove* for lunch when my phone rang. It was Jack.

"Hey, cuz, I hear that you all had a great time chatting on the plane. And the guys were impressed with Kari. Carter said he thinks she's the one you should hang onto."

"Don't jinx me, Jack. Did you catch up with Peel?"

"That's part of why I'm calling. Telling you the planes were full was all his dumb idea of how to protect me." Jack had his smooth, soothing voice on, the one he usually reserved for hot-looking women.

"Protect you? From what, from me? By blowing up my boat?"

"Absolutely not, he swears that he had nothing to do with that. Frankly, I believe him; violence is not really in his makeup. And you weren't the only one that he was excluding. Somehow he thought that it might be more painful for me if any family other than my kids were there. I think he thought it would be easier for you, too, if you weren't around for the service."

"For me. Easier. Who the hell is he to decide any of that? You tell that son of a bitch that the next time I see him, I'm gonna break his face! Violence isn't normally in my makeup either, but I'm more than willing to make an exception in his case."

"Marlin, I'm ultimately to blame for all this. I let him handle too many things when I was concentrating on taking care of my dad, and it kind of went to his head. You know how some people get a little power and they take off with it. So, it was my fault for letting it get to that point. I'm sorry about that, Marlin, but he's not whoever was after you. Let's put Dennis in the past. I'll make certain that he never comes near you again."

I was still really pissed, and not quite ready to believe this story. Some parts of it just didn't match up. But Jack was now charging forward.

"Marlin, Dad left me a note saying that he wanted his ashes spread in the same place that you two took your father, and he wanted you and me to do it. Can I hire you to do that this weekend?"

"No, Jack, you can't hire me. But you can ride along with me."

"At least let me pay for the fuel."

"No, this is totally on me. He never really let me do anything for him in life, it was always him doing things for me. Now it's my turn." I was getting choked up again. That's the funny thing about grief, it hits you when you least expect it, or just when you think that you have it all under control.

"Okay then, pal. Saturday work?"

"Yeah, the weather is supposed to be good, and we have a front coming through Sunday afternoon, so the winds will be picking up all day. Saturday's our shot."

"Text me the address, and I'll see you around what, nine a.m.?"

"I'll see you at nine, Jack. Thanks for the call."

JACK TURNED to the person next to him. "I didn't want to do this. I don't like who he is, and how this threatens both of us, but this is something I've never been a part of before. We needed to find another way before you moved ahead without telling me anything, damn it!"

"Play the blame game all you want, but now this has to be finished, there's no other way. With this now going to hit the paper, we can't take the chance. I'll take care of it, and I'll find out who leaked it, too."

16

THE COMMODORE

Tuesday is supposed to be a slow restaurant day. Apparently no one in lower ESVA got the memo. Kari and I had to sit at a high top in the bar, as the dining room of the *Cove* was completely packed. I told her about the appraiser, and she was ecstatic. Then I told her about Jack's call, and what he said about Peel.

She asked, "Do you believe him?"

"Honestly, I don't know what to believe. Is it possible that this is true? Yes. Plausible though, is a whole 'nother subject."

"Well, at least he's keeping in touch. You didn't expect that." She looked hopeful.

"Maybe only because it was at my uncle's direction. Remember, he did leave me a note. Could be that he left one for Jack, too. I just don't know, but at this point, I don't care. I finally get to do something for Uncle Jack, and he won't even know it."

"I wouldn't say that. Keep your eyes peeled for pelicans."

At first, I thought she was teasing me again, but her eyes said something else. I hoped, no, I *believed* that she was serious. And right.

Lindsay and Murph walked in, and we pulled another high top up against ours. I told them about the insurance settlement, and they were happy for me.

Lindsay asked, "You two need help getting her over there? Murph and I are available."

I was pleased, "Absolutely. She should tow easily behind *Marlinspike* but getting her all tied up once we get there might prove to be a handful for just Kari and me."

Murph said, "You're on the hook for the beer."

"You've been hanging around Baloney too much," I replied, with a grin.

AFTER LUNCH I went back to boxing up my stuff from *Why Knot*, getting her ready to move. I rented a small storage unit at a place just up the main road.

The thing about doing such menial tasks like boxing stuff is that it gives you lots of time to think if you're so inclined. Me, I'm *over* inclined. I tend to overanalyze things when I'm alone. I was running and re-running Jack's conversation in my head. Something was wrong, but it seemed to be just beyond my grasp. I did glean one thing from it right off the bat, he said that I wasn't the only one Dennis had excluded. Probably meaning that Clara was another. Though I couldn't help but remember the scowl that Jack had shown the last time I'd seen her.

Kari had just climbed aboard when suddenly I knew what kept bothering me. Jack had said about Dennis, "...he's not whoever was after you." *Was* after me. Past tense, as in no longer a threat. How could he have known that? I hadn't told him about Shifflett being murdered, so as far as he should have known he was still after me. Present tense.

"An 'Ah ha!' moment, Marlin?" Kari had just arrived, and she was getting good at reading me. She looked amused until I told her about what I remembered about my conversation with Jack. Amusement then switched to concern as she became pensive.

"You know, that might not mean what you think it does. It could be that he meant past tense because the bombing was in the past."

"Maybe, but it just doesn't feel right." I wasn't a hundred percent convinced in either direction.

She had her serious face on. "I know one thing; I'm not letting you go out fifty miles offshore alone with him."

"Not *letting* me go? Like I need your permission?" I started to get my back up.

"Marlin, I'm just doing for you what I hope that you would do for me if our roles were reversed. Ever since Rikki told you to carry a gun, I've been carrying mine too. It's as much for your security as for my own. In this whole thing, I'm the one on the outside looking in, giving me a perspective that you don't have. Which might just save your life."

She started to reach out and take my hand, then thought better of it after seeing the still angry look on my face and dropped hers instead. She looked straight into my eyes. "The other morning, I said that in you I found someone worth sticking around for. That meant fighting side by side, and even being assertive when I see something that could be dangerous that you can't see. It's a side of me that's never shown itself before because I've never been involved with someone that I felt was, for lack of a better word, *worthy* of it.

"I'm sorry if you're reading this the wrong way. I'm not normally a controlling person, Marlin, except at work, where it's part of my job. I just don't want anything more to happen to you. I'm scared, for you and us, and the idea of you going offshore alone with him just feels wrong."

I didn't know what to say or do right then, I just stood there, not moving. I guess she was expecting me to say something, but I wasn't sure of what it might be. The last thing I wanted to do was stick my foot in my mouth, so I didn't say anything. After a long, pregnant pause, Kari looked both sad and disappointed, having read me wrong. She turned and started to make her way back to the dock.

"Please don't go, Kari." I had just learned a hard lesson. Forget about putting a foot in your mouth; sometimes you can shove your whole leg down your throat by not saying anything. When she turned back around, I saw the tear running down her cheek. My heart broke. I went over and hugged her. "The other night you said that I could tell you anything. I'm sorry that I made you feel like that was a one–way street just now. The truth is, I've never had anyone feel like fighting side by side with me before. I'm not so sure that I *am* worthy of that. And I've never had anyone save my life before, either. So, I'll make you a promise. You can say anything you want to me at any time, and I'll always be open to discussions, just not to demands. I'll do the same for you. Deal?"

She wrapped her arms around me too. Her head was on my shoulder, and I felt her nod before I heard, "Deal."

This was the most vulnerable I had ever seen Kari in the just over two months that I had known her, and it made me want to protect her that much more. So, I knew exactly how she felt; I got where she was coming from, and it's a very uncertain place, even for someone as strong as her.

She leaned her head back, looking into my eyes again. "You're wrong, Marlin. You are so very much worthy of how I feel right now. You can't imagine what it was like when I got here after the explosion and found you were missing, then after we pulled you out of the water, you weren't breathing. I thought you were gone. I've never felt that huge a loss in my life, that big of a hole in my heart. To have just found you, only to lose you. Promise me that you'll be careful. I know Jack is your cousin, but there are so many unanswered questions around him and so many answers that aren't that certain."

I pulled her head back against me. "I'll be fine. Because I'll have the hottest-looking bodyguard on the East Coast with me. If you still want to go, that is. Seeing your face after you started to walk out of here, I guess I got a taste of what that night was like for you. I just got a wake-up call as to what this is, you and me, and what you mean to me. I don't want to screw this up, Kari. Nothing is worth that." Now she pulled my lips down to hers, and we kissed in the middle of that smoky stateroom for more than a minute, until we heard footsteps overhead.

"Marlin? Kari? Are you guys here?" Murph called from the hatchway.

"Down here. Just be careful where you step in the salon, most of the decking that's left is sketchy." I said.

The splintering, crashing sound let me know that my warning was too little, too late. Kari and I stuck our heads out into the salon to see that Murph had found the weakest part of what was left of that deck. The salon and galley deck is elevated about three and a half feet higher than the fore and aft staterooms, creating room for the engines. Murph was now standing down in the engine room bilge, having fallen through the salon deck, which was now at chest level around him. Fortunately, he was unhurt.

"I'm good, I'm good. Man, are you guys ever going to have your work cut out for you while we're gone. You're gonna have to take this whole section down to the frames. All the paint and hoses are gone off these engines too, they'll have to come out to get checked over." It was just dawning on Murph the enormity of the task ahead of us.

"I wanted to rebuild them pretty soon anyway. I'd have taken a trip or two with her if they had fewer hours. Now, we'll be able to use the old girl to run around the bay some next year." I could tell by the look Kari gave me that the idea appealed to her. I knew she liked vintage boats but guessed that she probably hadn't done much cruising in one. I hoped to remedy that.

We climbed up from the lower stateroom and helped Murph back up and onto the aft deck just as Lindsay arrived. We formulated our plan where she and Kari would ride on *Why Knot*, while Murph and I would tow them slowly down the start of the Virginia Inside Passage, a channel that began right in front of *Mallard Cove* and led northeast, dumping out behind Skidmore Island, at the bottom of Magothy Bay. A couple of miles up that bay in the small settlement of Magotha is Albury Boat Works, Kari's cousin's business.

Fifteen minutes later we had cleared the breakwater with both boats and had made our northeast turn. Murph and I were sitting on *Marlinspike*'s lean seat.

"You and Kari still seem to be getting along good."

I nodded. "She's the whole package, Murph. Smart, pretty, tough, and she loves boats and the water as much as I do."

"Glad you see all that, and that you appreciate her for it."

I nodded. "Seems that you and I are both are pretty lucky, finding great women that love the water and who'll put up with us." I looked over at him and grinned.

"Very true. But, you guys have been getting pretty serious in just a short amount of time," Murph said.

"Now you are starting to sound like Lindsay. But I guess we are. Then again, after last Friday, I almost ran out of time. All that's happened this last week has changed me, so it can't help but affect how I feel. I'm not taking as much for granted, certainly not Kari. I know what I've got in her, and that's something I don't want to lose."

"Smart man."

I replied, "Lucky man. Sometimes that's a better thing to be."

WE GOT *Why Knot* tied up next to the huge ways at Albury's, which they would use to haul her out of the water when they opened in the morning. A ways is a device with a steel track that extends into the water on what looks like a steep boat ramp. A cradle on a wheeled platform rolls down into the water, then chocks are moved in from the sides, supporting the sides as the boat is hauled out. The ways at Albury's was the last big one on ESVA, capable of hauling anything up to and including shrimpers and ocean-going tugboats. There had been one at *Mallard Cove* up until a few months ago, but Murph, Lindsay, and Kari had decided to remove it as part of their renovation plan, making Kari's cousin, Carlton Albury, one very happy man with no local competition.

In addition to owning the boatyard, Carlton was also the head of the county board of supervisors. He realized that their plan for the new *Mallard Cove* meant more business, jobs, and tax revenue for the county, so he pushed their approvals through quickly. About as fast as they removed the *Mallard Cove* ways, giving him a small monopoly.

The trip back to *Mallard Cove* took less than ten minutes since we were no longer towing anything and could run at a fast cruise. But we still got back too late for the Beer-Thirty-Bunch, so we ended up on the party deck at the houseboat. It started to get a bit chilly as the sun went down, but I finished cooking on Murph's big grill just as that happened. I wanted to thank everyone for their help today, so I had picked up steaks and jumbo shrimp earlier, on the way back from the storage unit. We went down into the living area beneath the party deck to eat. I had something that I wanted to spring on the three of them afterward.

I started in. "You guys know how Baloney plans to get an additional boat this winter and set B2 up in it next spring? He got me thinking. As fast as the hotel and second restaurant are getting finished, you're going to be close to opening in the spring."

Kari interjected, "We will be open. I'm way ahead of schedule."

I said, "Even better. So, there will be a lot more people around, but not every one of them is going to be into fishing. I've been doing some digging into what some similar places have to offer, and I've come up with two very popular things; parasail rides and eco-tours. Look at the parasail boats in VB and Ocean City, they are packed all season long. So, I want to buy a parasail rig and a big, shallow draft outboard. It's easier to find qualified local crews for both of those than it is to find good fishing captains for those big sportfish rigs. These will be great amenities for your hotel guests, and we'll also probably pull in day trippers off the road who will end up eating and drinking in the restaurants. What do you guys think?"

Lindsay spoke first. "I think it would be a win/win for the four of us." Murph and Kari agreed.

"Good. So, then would you guys give me an exclusive on each? It's one thing to have a friendly competition between charter boat crews, but I've read about some of these groups that have come in undercutting other eco and parasail boats and have wrecked things for both of them. If I see there's room for more equipment and crews, I'll add them."

Murph said, "That sounds like something that we could agree to, but how can you buy two more boats when you are just keeping your head above water now?"

I explained about my insurance "windfall" from the boat bombing. "Murph, where I am now is like you would have been if you had just kept the marina and not taken in your partners and expanded your operation. I've already paid off my loans on both of my work boats, way ahead of schedule. I'm going to use some of the insurance payment as a downstroke, and I won't have any problem getting a loan for two more boats."

Lindsay said, "I think that works for all of us, what do you say, Kari? It sounds like you are rubbing off on him."

"I'm a bit prejudiced, but it sounds to me like a great deal."

"Done! You have a monopoly, Marlin. Or, should I say, Commodore? Now you'll need a really big hat." Murph chuckled at his reference to the famous pirate movie quote.

The rest of us were pirate movie fans, so we all joined in, laughing. I was happy they all agreed with my plan. I expected some hesitation, but I guess it was an even better idea than I thought. "She may be rubbing off on me more than you think. I've been tossing the idea around in my head about finding someone for some part-time guiding next summer, too. Having my second boat sitting at the dock all the time makes no sense, and with the new scheduling system, it will be easier to book things farther in advance. More income from assets that I already have."

"There may be more of your uncle in you than you thought." Kari smiled.

I smiled back, happy because I might have risen a notch or two in what she thought of me. While I had found out long ago that I wasn't interested in living in Uncle Jack's corporate world, I recently discovered that I wasn't averse to expanding my little sphere of capitalist influence. I owed that partly to Kari, who inspired me as I watched her handle this property and project. It was her plan that was starting to take Murph and Lindsay way beyond what they had originally envisioned, creating a much larger income stream for them with a smaller investment. That's what got me thinking about expanding my footprint. I didn't want to just keep getting by.

. . .

We weren't asleep yet when I saw her raise up on an elbow and look over at me in the semi-darkness. There was just enough light coming through the window from the moon as well as the post lights on the dock to see the outline of her head.

"Marlin?"

"I'm up for it again if you are."

"That wasn't where I was going."

"Oh." Male ego deflation. Only the ego.

"I wanted to say that I'm proud of you. Expanding like that takes a lot of guts, it's a big leap."

She probably couldn't see it, but I was smiling. "Thanks. I have this corporate hotshot girlfriend, and I have to keep pace with her."

"Don't do it for me, do it because it makes you happy."

"It'll make me happy, especially when it helps by providing us with a larger income. But I don't think I would be doing it if I hadn't met you. You're inspiring, and as I said, you make me happy."

She was quiet for a moment. "Thanks. Nobody has ever called me inspiring before."

"You are."

"Wow, you give compliments and you're a great cook. You just might be a keeper."

I could still only see the outline of her head, but I knew the smile was there. "Stranger things have happened." I felt a finger on my face, searching for the smile that was on mine as well. It lingered on my lips.

"Marlin?"

"Hmm?"

"About that other thing, I'm up for it again if you are." She chuckled, already knowing that I was.

17

THE VISITOR

I walked Kari to her car after an early breakfast at the *Cove,* she had an office day scheduled up at *Bayside*. My charter was in a half hour, and I had just enough time to get the tackle all set and ready.

The big fish weren't cooperating today, we only caught some small schoolies and not even a full limit's worth. I tried different areas, and different lures, but the result was just the same. Some days are like that. My charter client was relatively new to fishing with me, but an old hand at the sport. He knew that I was working hard to find him some big fish to catch, and fortunately his tip reflected the effort, not the result. He did mention that the box lunch from the *Cove* that I now included in full-day charters was the best he'd ever had. I made a mental note to tell Kari about that.

I got everything cleaned up and put away just in time for the Beer-Thirty-Bunch. I grabbed a six-pack from the marina office's new Ship's Store on the way.

"Tough, that's what it was today. Nobody home but peanuts at the tunnels." Baloney had about the same luck as me today. "Hey, Shaker, good to see you back. Get the Chris up on the hard?"

"They were going to do that this morning. I haven't been up there yet; Kari's been handling it with her cousin. We're going to get started on her this weekend."

"Yeah, you've been makin' yourself scarce since you got back from the hospital. You back up to snuff?" Baloney looked concerned.

"Yep. Right as rain."

"I heard they caught the guy who did it." Baloney added.

"Something like that. He won't be around here again."

Baloney nodded and swiped one of my beers. Concern comes with a price around here. Then Lindsay and Murph showed up, and he lit up like a marlin on a bait when he spotted the brand of beer they brought with them. He looked down at the one he swiped from me and scowled slightly, but he didn't pour it out.

I got a text from Kari saying that Eric Clarke was due in at *Bayside* in a while, and he wanted to have a dinner meeting with Casey, Dawn, Cindy, and her. He was a northern Virginia billionaire who was a partner in *Bayside*, the *Bluffs*, and *Mallard Cove* and was also building the first house in *Bayside Estates*. She was going to stay overnight at her garage apartment up there rather than drive back down late tonight. I was disappointed but glad that she was playing it safe. I texted back that I'd see her tomorrow.

I hung out with the gang for a while longer, then headed back to *OCT*. I was halfway down the dock when Lindsay caught up to me.

"Flying solo, stud?" She grinned.

I looked sideways at her. "If I'd had had a sister, she probably would have been as annoying as you."

"Doubtful. She'd have had to work at it. I come by it naturally."

I sighed. "Kari has a dinner meeting and is going to stay up there tonight."

She nodded. "I know, she called me and asked that I keep an eye out for you."

"Why'd you ask then if you already knew the answer? And I need to have a babysitter now?"

She grinned. "Icebreaker. Conversation starter. Great pickup line, though I take it you've never heard it before. And no, you idiot, you don't really. But your girlfriend has a case of 'new relationship nerves.' She wants to be down here and is worried that you might be ticked off because work took her away overnight. I'm supposed to keep you busy, so you won't be lonely. I told her I'd be glad to since soon I won't be able to annoy you for four whole months. At least, not in person anyway." She cocked her head. "You do know she has it that bad, right?"

"If I'm so terrible, then why did you push her at me at first?"

"Geez, Marlin, you can be so dense at times. You're not terrible, at least she seems to think you aren't. I meant that's why she's falling for you. From the look on your face, I'm guessing she hasn't told you that part yet, at least not in so many words. And I didn't 'push her at you,' I merely pointed out what should have already been obvious but wasn't. You know, like I'm doing now."

Lindsay suddenly looked serious, "Then I was worried you guys were going too fast right before you got yourself blown up. I think that's what sealed the deal with her you know. She's had the whole 'need to protect you' thing going since then. Which is why I'm supposed to be babysitting. You know, it might not be a bad thing for you two to take a night off; take a short breather. Or not. I take it from that look you have it as bad as she does. Remind me to buy some flameproof sheets for the big bed before I leave, so that I still have a home to come back to." She gave me a smug look.

For a guy who over-analyzes everything, I hadn't done that with my newfound relationship. Because, well, new ones can be scary. It's the unknowns, and the things you think you know, but aren't quite a hundred percent certain about. Nobody wants to take the big relationship leap by themselves. The one where you start using the big, scary, "L" word. No one wants to say "I love you" only to get an "Aw, how sweet" or, "That's nice" in return. Frankenstein can't even conjure up bigger nightmares than that does.

Frankly, I hadn't gotten into a serious relationship this fast before in my whole adult life. Not that it has never happened, but at least not since Susie McGuire in my senior year of high school, and the memory of that breakup still stings. It came right at the quasi-adulthood point of life. I know, I'm a full-fledged adult now, and that relationship has nothing to do with where I find myself at present. Except all our past experiences do, even the ones at the end of high school that can warp you as you pass through that door on the way to adulthood. Then again, my worst breakup came a few years ago in a relationship I had gotten into probably the slowest and most cautious of any I've had. So, I guess it isn't how fast you get involved, it just depends on the partner...

"HELLO? Marlin? Are you in there?"

Lindsay looked amused and had been trying to get my attention for quite a while. "Sorry, I was thinking about something. What were you saying?"

"Gee, I wonder who you could have been thinking about. Love can be so distracting at times."

"Funny, it...what? Who said anything about love?"

"Neither of you, so you're right, it is funny. She's too young, you're too old, she's a partner in the project, it could get messy, she's too perfect..."

"I never said she's too perfect!" I said hotly.

"Which proves my point; you're an idiot. She is perfect for you, and I can't believe I'm saying this; you are for her as well. Like I told you before, if only you two nitwits could see what the rest of us have a front row seat for."

Do you remember that I said there are times when keeping silent can be a really bad thing? This was not one of those times. Though Lindsay found my silence even more amusing.

"So, tonight I'm going to buy my two favorite men dinner at the *Cove*. We'll have cocktails on *OCT* and go over in a little while."

"Exactly when did I become one of your two favorite men, Linds?"

"A few seconds ago, when I realized that you really are perfect for Kari and that you wouldn't intentionally ever break my friend's heart. C'mon, I'll go mix us some drinks and you can text her that there's some blonde at a bar trying to get you drunk." Lindsay cracked up seeing the look on my face. "I was serious about that drink, but kidding about the text. You are so gullible!"

~

AT DINNER, Kari was on point with her report on the *Mallard Cove* construction progress. And everyone at the table was blown away at how the *Cove* had already way exceeded its initial profit goals. They all realized that they had the beginnings of a very hot property on their hands.

Dinner came with a couple of bottles of wine, so Kari was glad that she wasn't driving back to *Mallard Cove* after eleven p.m. Her apartment was only two minutes away, down a road that shouldn't have any traffic, otherwise, she would grab one of the resort's empty rooms. But she hadn't been to her apartment in a week and felt that she should at least check on it.

She shut her car lights off as she went down the drive at the side of her landlord's house. They were both retired and turned in early every night. Kari parked beside the stairs that led up to her apartment over their garage. She flipped the light switch at the bottom of the stairs that turns on the single jelly glass light at the top of the stairs, but nothing happened. Thinking the bulb had burned out, she started up the stairs in the dark. When she reached her door, she found that it was ajar, and she knew she hadn't left it that way. Even with her pistol in her purse, suddenly she was scared. She silently and slowly retreated down the stairs and went back up the driveway to her landlord's door. Taking out her cell phone, she called her cousin Billy Albury, the sheriff of Accomack County. He said to wake up her landlords and get in their house with them until he got there.

BILLY LED two of his deputies up the stairs where he found that the door had been forced open. They proceeded to do a room-by-room search. They didn't find anyone hiding, but what they did find was disturbing. He went to the stairs and called for Kari to come up. He took her to her bedroom where propped on a pillow was a picture taken with a zoom lens from quite a distance. It was of her and Marlin together on the aft deck of the *Why Knot* that night he had cooked for her, the second night they had stayed together. The day before Marlin almost died.

Kari called Rikki, then gathered some clothes and drove back to *Bayside* and that vacant room.

I WOKE up a little after five a.m. The *Cove* will be open in a half-hour, then I can get a quick breakfast, and pick up the box lunches for my charter. I looked out the side window at the water, the reflection from the dock light showed that it was smooth as glass. It doesn't mean that the mouth of the Chesapeake will be, but if there are ripples here in the basin, that usually meant there were rollers in the bay.

I glanced out through the glass in the door leading onto the party deck. I had left the blinds on it open because Kari wasn't here with me. But I saw that someone was; a dark figure was silhouetted against the low dock lights and was now creeping silently toward the door. I reached over to the built-in nightstand and grabbed my nine-millimeter Glock, the one that was identical to Kari's. The figure grabbed the knob and silently tried to open the door, being careful not to rattle it. Through the glass I drew a bead on the person's center mass, holding my breath with my finger on the trigger. If the intruder breached my door, he was going to die. The figure stopped, turned away, then silently and slowly headed for a deck corner. My heart was beating out of my chest as I padded barefoot across the room, and turned the knob as quietly as I could. I flung the door open, catching the intruder in the middle of the deck.

I yelled, "Freeze, you son of a bitch! Let me see your hands! Slowly, or I'll shoot!" I advanced across the deck as the door rebounded loudly off its stop and latched shut, but my total attention was on the intruder. So was the light from my laser sight that I had just turned on.

"Marlin, please don't shoot. It's me, Dave, from ESVA Security. If you have your finger on the trigger, please remove it. Can I turn around now?"

Before I could answer Dave, Murph came bounding up the stairs in his boxers with a flashlight and a pistol, and Lindsay was a few seconds behind him, similarly equipped and attired. She had hit the deck light switch at the top of the stairs.

Murph demanded, "What the hell is going on? Dave, why are you here, and Marlin, why are you out here, naked?"

Lindsay smirked, "Wow, Marlin, now I see what Kari sees in you, or rather, in her. But I usually wait until after at least the second date to get this casual."

Lindsay may have been topless, but she was getting the Full Monty from me. I turned and ran over to the door, only to find it locked. It was one of those that can be opened from the inside and remains locked outside unless you turn the little knob in the middle or use your key. Which was on the nightstand. Dammit! There was now only one way back into my room. It led right past Lindsay, down the stairway, and then up the ladder in the galley. Screw it. I needed to find out why Dave was here when he had been pulled off this job two days ago. And I had no secrets left to keep from Lindsay at this point anyway. I went back over to the group but turned off the light switch next to the door first.

"Party pooper." Lindsay apparently wakes up in rare form, even before coffee.

Dave began, "I guess nobody called you. When Kari got home last night, she found that her place had been burglarized. Nothing was stolen, but a picture of you two that looked like it had been taken from that deadrise you told us about was left on her pillow. We don't know when it was left because she hadn't been there in a week, so it could have been done by Shifflett, but we don't know for sure. Rikki pulled me off a job in Richmond at two a.m. and sent me here to watch over you. I gave this place a visual from the dock, then checked the property perimeter for anybody who might be watching. I had just finished that and then came up here, checking to make sure your door was secure. I was going to sit in the chair and wait for you to get up."

"I almost shot you, Dave." My voice was shaking almost as much as my hands.

"You have no idea how much I appreciate the fact that you didn't, Marlin." He chuckled. He was one very cool customer.

"Where is Kari, and why didn't she call me? Why didn't anyone call me about this? My God, I came within a hair's breadth of shooting you! Is Kari all right?"

"Again, thank you for using some restraint. As to Kari, I don't know where she is, Marlin. I'm assuming that she isn't at her apartment, but that Rikki has her covered, and she's fine. And I have no idea why you weren't called. I'll promise you this; I'm damned sure going to call you from now on before I ever come over again."

We all suddenly realized someone was climbing the stairs. Instantly, two flashlights and four pistols were trained on...Kari, who hit the light switch at the same time. I almost shot a friend for the second time in five minutes. If I wasn't shaking enough before, I was really shaking now.

"Marlin, why are you naked? And, Linds, the same question?"

"Because I almost shot Dave! Because nobody thought it was a good idea to call me and tell me what the hell had happened to you, or where you were! And the four of us almost shot you as well!"

I'm not usually prone to swearing, but if there was ever a time to, this was it. I was scared, furious, and in love, all at once. Wars have been started over far less.

"Dave, Murph, why don't I go make us some coffee, and we can give these two some privacy? Not that there's a lot of that left around here this morning." Lindsay led the two of them downstairs.

"Why are you naked?"

"Because you didn't call me! Now I'm locked out."

Kari took out her key and opened the door, and I followed her in. "What does me not calling you have to do with you and Lindsay being out here naked together?"

"Is that your biggest issue right now? And she wasn't naked, she had on boxers."

Kari shook her head as if trying to clear it, "Okay, then why was she topless?"

"I guess because she sleeps that way!"

"And you were naked because you sleep that way, too?"

"Yes! You know that I do!"

"And you know how she sleeps..."

"Okay, you caught us. She and I were outside screwing on the party deck, and we invited Murph and Dave to watch. What do you think?"

"I don't know what to think right now."

"Well, Kari, I know that I think you should have called me to tell me what was going on so that I didn't shoot Dave when he showed up unannounced. But you didn't, and that's what almost ended up happening."

"I didn't want to wake you. I know that even texts wake you up. That's why I drove down so early, to tell you about it when you got up. I was trying to be considerate, Marlin. Why are you so angry at me when you were the one that was outside with my friend, naked?"

"Because two people who love each other need to communicate better than this!" Oh, crap. I didn't mean to say that right now.

"I told you, I was letting you sleep, and I didn't want you to worry! I can take care of myself; I don't need you for that. And who said that I love you? I sure as hell didn't!"

I wanted to go crawl under a steamroller. "You're right, you didn't. My mistake. My big mistake. One I sure as hell won't ever make again." I picked up my clothes and my pistol and went out the door, slamming it behind me. I got dressed on the bottom entrance deck and walked over to the *Cove*.

18

COMMUNICATIONS BREAKDOWN

Ten minutes later a fully clothed Lindsay found me at a corner table in the empty bar, my back to the door. She took a seat across from me.

"I'll come get my stuff off your houseboat as soon as my charter's over, Linds. Sorry about this morning." I really was.

"Don't worry about it. I'd have given you a peek at the girls if you'd only asked," She smiled and winked. "Besides, I got a lot more of a show than you did."

"That wasn't what I was talking about."

She sighed. "I know it wasn't, Marlin, I was trying to be funny and I'm not good at it. I was making coffee in the galley and overheard you two. I wasn't eavesdropping on purpose; the ladder hatch was open, and you guys were pretty loud."

"Doesn't matter, Linds, I don't care."

"You do too care, and you know she didn't mean that stuff."

"Honestly, I don't know what she meant."

"Marlin, you gotta admit, it did look, well, different. That was quite a scene she walked in on. And she'd already been through a lot last night. If she and I had swapped places, and Murph had been in yours, he'd be icing his gonads right now, trying to get them to drop back down from where my kick repositioned them."

I chuckled a little and nodded.

"By the way, I don't sleep topless, I sleep like you do, au natural. I grabbed a set of Murph's briefs on the way out. Otherwise, the explanations would have gotten a whole lot more complicated."

She grinned, looking at me until I did the same, if only for a second.

"Mar, I wasn't wrong."

"Mar?" That caught me off guard.

"If you can shorten both mine and my home's names, I can shorten yours."

I knew she was trying like hell to cheer me up, and I appreciated it. Mar it is. I nodded.

"Mar, I don't need to tell you that she is one very strong woman. She was feeling vulnerable and confused, and I guarantee that is not a place where she's used to finding herself. So, she lashed out, in a way that she never, ever should have. I know how much that must have hurt you, but believe me, she didn't mean it. You have got to believe that."

"Linds, it's not that I don't believe you, but I only have what she said to go on. She made things really clear; that I'm the biggest idiot on the Shore right now, a real fool."

"Because you listened to me. Which I'm trying hard to convince you to do again, right now. Because I was right then, and I'm right now."

"No, because I listened to my heart instead of my head, and believed what I wanted to be true, instead of what really was."

"Don't do this to yourself, Mar. Don't beat yourself up."

Kari said, "Marlin, Lindsay's right. And you know we're not supposed to go anywhere without Dave, and you should never sit with your back to the door." She had come up behind me.

Lindsay got up and let Kari have her chair. She patted my back as she left. She nodded to Dave as she went by him on her way out; he was now sitting at the far end of the bar, watching over us, just out of earshot.

"Yeah, well, you're not the only one who can take care of themself. I'm through with babysitters, and with a lot of other things."

"After you left, Lindsay and Dave talked to me. It hadn't sunk in about how you came so close to shooting him. I should have called you, I'm sorry. I'm sorry about a lot of...those other things."

"Don't worry, I'm getting used to having people jump to wrong conclusions about me. First I was supposed to be a drug kingpin, now I'm some player who screws around with his friend's girlfriend, on the girl he thought he loved. I guess for some reason people find it easy to believe anything bad about me. Then again, I understand how easy it is to jump to conclusions. I just did it too, convincing myself that you loved me. I'm so damned stupid. So now I know how foolish it feels, 'cause I've seen it from both sides."

She winced when I said, "thought you loved," past tense, and started to reach for my free hand. But I pulled it away and wrapped it around my coffee mug. I didn't want her to see how bad it was shaking right now.

"You didn't jump to a wrong conclusion, Marlin. I was just scared to admit it or say it, even to myself."

"Well, do us both a favor and don't."

"You were right, Marlin, I do love you."

"Trying to convince yourself of that now? Don't bother."

"For the record, you aren't the biggest idiot on the Shore, I am, for hurting you like I just did. I'm so used to being independent, and not having to check in with anyone. I realize now what that almost caused this morning. I should have called or texted you, you're right. I was freaked out about the break-in. And I freaked out hearing you say what I hadn't had the courage to, but what I knew was true."

"This was not a case of 'checking in' with me; it wasn't a summer camp bed check. This was about letting me know that your life was possibly in danger again, dammit! Who sent Dave over here?"

"I asked Rikki to. I wanted to make sure you were safe." Kari looked concerned.

"Kari, if I had found that picture on my pillow at midnight, I'd have called you before I even called the cops, because you'd need to be looped in. I would feel the need to tell you as soon as I could. Only after that would I call Rikki and get you some protection. Also, for the record, I never feel like I need to 'check in' with you; I feel the need to talk, to communicate, and that's something completely different. I was right about one thing this morning; communicating is what people who truly love each other do. That's why you didn't. And why I should have known right then that I was wrong."

I threw a twenty on the table, picked up my two box lunches, and walked out.

MY CLIENT TODAY was Paul again. I was glad because we had a really good understanding of each other. He could read me, and vice versa. I always had a good time fishing with him. Fortunately, the rockfish were cooperating with us again today. When it came time to head back in, I asked him if he had anywhere to be. He had already figured out that I didn't. We ended up staying out an extra hour and a half. I didn't even clean our fish until long after the Beer-Thirty-Bunch had left, just as I had hoped. I really didn't want to run into anyone.

After I cleaned the fish and the boat, I went over to get my gear off *OCT*. I planned to get a hotel room until I could find an apartment. I knew that Kari wouldn't want to go back to hers, and Murph and Lindsay still needed a winter boat sitter, so she could have that gig. This was the second part of this whole nightmare that I had told Lindsay I was so worried about; having to see Kari around here all the time, while feeling like an idiot. Right now, about the only thing that would make me feel somewhat better is finding the son of a bitch behind Shifflett, so I could shoot the bastard myself.

Lindsay and Dawn had picked out a little ice cream shop table set for *OCT's* entrance deck, on the far side away from the finger pier. Kari was waiting there. Not good. I really hadn't wanted to see her and had hoped she wouldn't be aboard. She looked up as I stepped onto the deck.

"I won't be here long, just need to get my clothes, then I'll be gone."

She said, "Can we talk, Marlin?"

Damn. I wanted to be anywhere but here right now. But I walked over and sat in one of the stupid-looking, cold, tiny metal chairs that were about the right size for a doll's butt. Yeah, anywhere but here.

"I tried calling you, but it kept going to voicemail."

"I shut it off."

"I wanted to talk with you."

"I had a client on the boat, I couldn't have talked anyway."

"Dave was ticked that you left."

"Dave is getting paid to be ticked. I don't get paid when I'm sitting at the dock. Where is Dave anyway?"

She said, "That was part of why I needed to talk with you. They found Shifflett's fingerprints on the photo, meaning it wasn't a recent break-in. Dave got pulled off of us."

"I'm glad. Then you can still use the apartment."

She nodded. "I could."

I squirmed; this damned seat was just for looks as far as I was concerned.

"That was a long charter."

"Yeah. I'm wet and I'm cold, and I smell like fish. And these metal seats aren't cutting it. I'm going to go get my stuff and find a hotel." I said.

"The other reason I wanted to call you was because my best friend once told me that two people who love each other are supposed to communicate better. And I don't want to lose my best friend. Because I love him."

I looked over at her. It was too damned easy to get lost in those eyes, and they can make you believe anything. I looked away.

She said, "If you want, you can shower here. I'll bring you some clothes. Then please can we talk? I mean, really talk? If you still want to leave after that, I'll even help you pack. But please hear me out, first."

"Where are Murph and Lindsay?"

Kari replied, "They're over on the Rybo. They wanted to give us some space tonight, so we can work things out if you still want to. I really hope you do. Because I do."

I WAS in *OCT*'s great rainfall shower when Kari came into the bathroom. She handed me a vodka around the shower curtain edge, though I hadn't even asked her to make me one. But I could sure use it right now.

"Thanks. So, what did you want to say?" No sense prolonging this any longer than necessary.

"I thought I had it all planned out, Marlin. I'd say something witty and clever that would make you want to stay. I've been thinking all day about what that was. The truth is, no words can make you stay if you don't want to. We both know there's one reason for you not to go, and only one. It just depends on if you still feel that way."

I stayed under the water stream, thinking and rerunning in my head what had happened. I tried to see it from her side like Linds had been doing. Kari was right, there was one big reason for me to stay, and another reason for me to leave: pride. It was also the reason why I took my time answering. I stuck the empty vodka glass out of the curtain, and Kari took it from me.

"Do you want another?"

I mumbled my answer.

"What?"

I mumbled the same thing, only softer.

"Marlin, I can't hear you. What did you say?"

She set the glass on the counter and opened the curtain slightly. I grabbed her and pulled her into the shower, fully clothed. She shrieked, but in a good way.

"What I said was, 'Kari, you need to get out of these wet clothes.'"

She laughed, "You're crazy!"

"Yep. But not crazy enough to want to lose my best friend."

. . .

I SLEPT like the dead from two a.m. until five-fifteen a.m. I could tell that Kari was already awake, lying on her side with her head against my shoulder and an arm across my chest. I said, "Good morning."

"Good morning. Don't shoot, I'm communicating here."

"Funny gal. Hey, did you know that you and Lindsay sleep the same way?"

"I thought she wore Murph's boxers."

"No, she sleeps nude, but I was talking about how she likes to put her arm across my chest like that, too...OUCH! Dammit, that was my sore shoulder!" She had punched me. Hard. Then she snuggled in closer.

"Marlin, can we be serious for a minute?"

"I was hoping for a bit longer than that, but okay. Ouch!" Same shoulder. "I'm all ears, dear."

"I was thinking about yesterday and..."

I sighed. "You were replaying it in your mind, over and over again. Don't. Let it go. I do the same thing, and it only gets me in trouble. I keep recalling the same things."

"Everything I said." She sounded sad.

"Huh? No. Lindsay's boobs." It was too dark for her to see my smile and the grimace that came when she hit my shoulder again.

"Dammit Marlin, I'm trying to be serious here."

"And I'm trying to avoid revisiting a minefield, Kari. You want serious? This is it. We draw a line from the point I got back from my charter and do a reset. I think a good place to start would be the shower." I braced for the hit that never came.

"That was a great reset."

"I liked it."

"For the record, Marlin, I knew I loved you when I got to the *Why Knot* after the explosion, and I thought you were gone. I was lucky enough to get a second chance, but I still didn't say anything.

"I guess it's not really in my makeup to talk about feelings. I guarantee that I'm the youngest project coordinator that many if not all of my contractors have ever worked with. It's my job to be tough, if I don't get and keep the respect of all of them, I might as well go home, because then I'd be done. I'm learning to switch off that disconnect when I'm with you. But talking about feelings is tough for me. I'm used to hiding my vulnerabilities.

"Most people never get a third chance, but I'm glad you gave us one last night. I'm sorry that I almost denied how I felt."

I laughed. "Almost? Kari, you didn't dip a toe in the river of denial, you were hip-deep wading in it. But let's not go back and rerun that video."

"I know I made you feel awful."

"You have no idea, and I never want you to. Let's leave it that way. I understand and appreciate that you are a very complex woman, Kari Albury and it's part of what I love about you. When you want something, you aren't afraid to go after it. You aren't afraid of much, but you sure were with this. I felt like the car the dog was chasing. I stopped at the corner and you caught me, but then didn't know what to do with me."

"Marlin?"

"Yeah?"

"I know what to do with you now."

SHE ALMOST MADE me late for my charter. When I left *OCT*, she had gone back to sleep, not needing to be at work until an hour after me. I love working on the water, and I don't mind getting up early for it, but today I'd have loved to have stayed there an extra hour. Or longer.

"THANKS FOR HAVING me to lunch, Kari." Lindsay was meeting her at the *Cove*.

"It's the least I could do after what you did for me, for us. He didn't want to talk to me before you talked to him."

Lindsay shook her head. "Yes, he did. He just didn't realize it, and you didn't either. It's fun understanding you two better than you understand yourselves. I'm going to miss you guys while we're gone. You're so much fun to watch."

"Yeah, we were a regular riot last night. Again, I'm so sorry that I thought that you and Marlin—"

"It's not every day you come home and find your boyfriend naked with a topless woman, and it turns out there's a perfectly logical and innocent explanation." Lindsay laughed. "Besides, when you think about it, if I wasn't with Murph, and Marlin wasn't with you, is it that far-fetched to think that he and I might—"

Kari said quickly, "Yes, it is! I hadn't thought about it before that happened last night, so yes, that makes it completely far-fetched."

Lindsay roared. "I am so just playing with you right now! That would be like kissing my brother. I'm just glad that you knuckleheads finally see what you have. I don't know that many couples who could have come through last night unscathed."

"I wouldn't say unscathed. I hit him in that sore shoulder after he compared my boobs to yours when we were in the shower."

Lindsay started laughing again. "He did? Seriously?"

"Yes. But it was just his idea of payback humor." Kari looked perturbed.

Lindsay grinned, "I won't ask you what he said."

"Good. Don't."

"Hah! His stock just keeps going up and up. Both of yours do."

Kari smiled slightly, "I owe you, we owe you, big time. I don't know what would have happened if you hadn't talked some sense into both of us."

Lindsay laughed again, "I know you guys would have found your way. But I'm leaving in a week and a half, so I knew if I wanted to see it happen, I had to help. You were the tough one to convince, my friend. Which, when you think about it, is funny. Since you were the one who wanted him in the first place."

"There's just something about Marlin. I don't know how to explain it."

Lindsay nodded. "And that, my friend, is how you know it's for real."

19

A FINAL GOODBYE

Kari and I were lying in bed at about eleven p.m., having turned in after a fun evening of cocktails, and fantastic burgers that Murph cooked on his grill. Great company and equally great conversation, with just the four of us. I'm going to miss them while they are gone down south. But I was also really looking forward to getting my boat back in shape and moving back to my own place. It wasn't that *OCT* wasn't comfortable and spacious, it was. I just didn't like having to depend on the generosity of others for a place to sleep.

"I'm glad I'm coming with you tomorrow. There are just too many unanswered questions around your cousin," Kari said.

She was snuggled against me on her side as usual. Or, what was becoming our usual. I loved these talks in the dark. She's so smart and observant, and I've obviously had the wrong glasses on when it comes to reading my family members.

"I'll give you that. But it's probably all coincidence. In any case, we do this last thing for my uncle, and we don't have to see Jack again unless we want to."

"I like the way you say 'we,' both for tomorrow and into the future."

"So do I."

"We don't leave the dock until nine, right?"

"Correct."

"So, we can sleep in."

I chuckled. "Like that'll happen."

"Let me rephrase my question. So, we don't have to get up early."

I chuckled again. She swatted me.

"You can be such a child." Using her exasperated tone now.

"A regular kid at heart. You bring out my inner child."

She said, "Let me try this again. We don't have to get out of bed early, right?"

"I wasn't planning on it."

"Perfect."

HAVING the *Cove* next to the boat is really convenient. We were just walking out after having a late breakfast and "sleeping in." Jack and Carter were walking up the dock, and they both seemed as surprised to see Kari with me as we were to see Carter with him.

"Good morning. I didn't realize we were going to have such a large crew, Marlin."

"I could say the same thing, Jack."

"I figured it would be just family."

"Kari is my family, Jack. You need to get used to her being around." I had been taken aback by his jumping on offense, and I wasn't going to let him get by with it. You want to ride on my boat, you play by my rules.

"She certainly is easier on the eyes than you, cuz, so having her along is a plus. How are you this morning, Kari?" He smiled at her as he used his special smooth voice again. I'd seen this with him and women so many times before.

"Fine, Jack, how are you? Hello, Carter, good to see you again."

Kari wasn't going to play Jack's game. Polite, but dismissive. Like I said, observant and smart.

"Hey, Kari. I'm glad you're coming along. Grandpa would have liked you."

"Marlin mentioned me to him, but unfortunately I never got to meet him."

Jack looked at me, now ignoring Kari "Where exactly are we going?"

"Norfolk Canyon, it's about seventy miles out. It's the place where we used to fish a lot, where he and I spread Dad's ashes, and where I caught my first white marlin that day with Uncle Jack. And we had better get going since we have a lot of water to cover."

I handled the wheel as Kari handled the lines. Jack did not attempt to hide the fact that he was checking out her butt as she undid the bowlines. I knew he was doing this deliberately trying to provoke me, but I didn't know why. I wasn't going to play his game. Not today, Jack.

Kari hopped up on the leaning post with me, and Jack sat on the front console seat with Carter. I had my clear isinglass "telephone booth" already installed for the winter. This was a large, mostly clear plastic, and canvas-edged wrap that hooked onto the four deck legs of my half tower, wrapping around three sides. It keeps the cold wind and spray off anyone behind it. Also, unless Kari or I yelled, they couldn't hear us in that front seat.

"Someone forgot to take his anti-asshole pill this morning. He's acting like you just stole his prom date."

I nodded. "He was checking you out as you were untying us."

"Well, all that proves is you're related." Kari gave me a sly look as she hooked her arm around mine.

The ocean had little two-foot rollers, and we had a light breeze off our stern. I was more worried about the trip back. The wind was forecast to pick up all afternoon as the front had picked up speed and would now pass through early tomorrow morning. Depending on how much the wind increased, we could be in for an uncomfortable and wet run back in. Gold Lines are known for their ability to carry a large payload, their width, and their reverse chines, which help with stability and planing at lower speeds. But at higher speeds in rough head seas, they tend to pound and throw bow spray. Not fun.

I scooted over a bit to let Kari run the boat. Again she gave me a sly look, knowing exactly what I was up to. I wanted Jack to see her in charge. I figured that crap he pulled back at the dock was to show dominance. He didn't know that she was used to dealing all day with macho male idiots who thought she was just some young pushover. They learned, and fast. So, Jack, meet Captain Kari.

By the time that we got out to Norfolk Canyon, the wind had increased to about twelve knots, and the seas were a steady three feet. We needed to get this done and get turned back around. I had a waypoint on my GPS marked "Dad," and Kari was steering to it. We watched the sonar as the bottom suddenly went from six hundred feet to almost two thousand. We had reached the canyon. She started throttling back as we neared the mark, then spun back bow first into the wind.

"I'll turn us beam-to when you're ready," she said.

I nodded. I had heard firsthand accounts of nightmarish incidents involving the scattering of ashes at sea. You really want the wind at your back.

I hopped off the lean seat and joined Jack and Carter. "We're here."

Carter had been holding a box on the way out. He opened it and removed a plain beige urn. He stood up with it and started to pass it to his father, who shook his head. Then he passed it to me. I didn't think anything of it as I took it from him.

"Jack, you want to say a few words?" I asked.

He shook his head.

"Carter?"

"Rest easy with Grandma, Grandpa. I love you, and I'm going to miss you. Now you need to say something, Marlin."

I knew the twenty-third Psalm by heart, so I repeated it, then followed with, "Glad that I was able to give you a ride, Uncle. But I wish that we were fishing today instead. I love you too, and I'll also miss you, so much."

I nodded to Kari, who swung us beam to, as I took the lid off the tightly sealed urn. I scattered the oatmeal-looking contents in the lee of the hull, watching as some sank and some drifted across the surface of the water. I didn't bother looking at Jack, I just went back and sat next to Kari. She had pointed us toward home, and I amended the GPS waypoint to read "Dad & Jack." She got into the throttles, getting us up on a plane.

We weren't able to make the same speed as we did coming out, since we had an almost dead on head sea. An hour later we were looking at a steady sixteen knots of wind, and four-foot rollers that were starting to get closer together and form whitecaps. Kari and I were now standing, leaning back against the seat. She looked over at me and indicated the wheel, silently asking if I wanted to take over. I shook my head. I could see how happy she was with my having so much confidence in her.

Jack and Carter finally had enough of the bouncing and spray they were getting on the front seat, and they retreated to where we were standing. Only, there wasn't enough room for more than three against the lean seat. Instead, we made a little room on the sides so they could at least get part of their bodies behind the protection of the telephone booth. The temperature was still in the low sixties, and it wouldn't start dropping until after the front came through tonight.

Jack looked at Kari running the boat and said angrily to me, "She's beating us to death!"

"Wrong, cuz. She's handling the absolute worst sea conditions for this hull perfectly, and I didn't need to tell her how. She's as good as me or better. But you had better hang on, because we've got another hour or more of this, and it's only going to get worse."

I was right, on both counts. The Gold Line hull with twin engines on a transom bracket has a big balance flaw. It doesn't like to hold back; it wants to get on a plane and run like a thoroughbred. It takes an experienced hand to trim and run it correctly in these conditions. Kari had instinctively found the delicate balance that allowed her to get the most speed and comfort possible right now. She knew her boats. By the time we were back in sight of ESVA, the wind was a sustained twenty knots, with gusts to twenty-five. The front had fooled the forecasters again, accelerating as it neared the East Coast. We hit a couple of eight-footers on the way in, and Kari was into the throttles the last half hour, working us through the waves.

Conditions like that take their toll on you, but when I looked at Jack, he was exhausted. A lot more so than a man in good health in his early fifties should be. He had been hanging on to an overhead support that I had wrapped with nylon cord to make it non-slip so that it could be used for that very purpose. The long sleeve of his shirt was soaked, and the water's weight had pulled it down, revealing a series of purple patches and ugly bruises up by his wrist.

"Jack, are you all right? Your arm looks terrible." As pissy as he'd been, I was still concerned about him. I had to cut him some slack since we had just buried his dad at sea.

"I'm fine. I'm seeing a doctor tomorrow. I just had to finish this first. Carter, you need to drive us home, I'm too tired."

Carter nodded and didn't look surprised. I got the feeling this wasn't the first time he'd been put in this position lately.

After I tied us up in the slip, Jack turned to Kari and said, "Kari, I'm sorry about what I said back there. You did a hell of a job getting us back in."

It was uncharacteristic of him, a glimpse behind the mask. The apology was real.

"Thanks, Jack. Sorry, I couldn't make it a smoother ride; it is what it is when it's that rough."

He nodded. He looked at me for a long time, then turned back to her. "Take care of Marlin. You'd have to go a long way to find a better man."

She smiled. "I will. He's the best man I've ever loved."

Carter had to help Jack over the Gold Line's wide covering boards. Jack looked like he had aged ten years since the beginning of the trip. Murph and Lindsay passed by him and walked out on the finger pier.

Murph asked, "Was that your cousin?"

I nodded.

"Must have been rough coming back with the wind springing up early like that. Looks like a rum front to me. I've got the first round at the *Cove*."

"Let me get her washed down, and I'll join you three."

Kari looked at me, "We'll do it together."

I shook my head. "The mate always washes the boat, Cap. I'll see you inside."

She started to argue, until she saw me raise the hose nozzle with a smile on my face, then she saw the wisdom of my words. Twenty minutes later, I took my place beside her with Murph and Lindsay at a table in the bar. It was almost two-thirty; the sea condition had slowed our return trip considerably. An appetizer plate of calamari was waiting for me, and a server brought a vodka on the rocks with lemon, not a minute after I sat down.

"Somebody ought to tell the owners of this place that they are doing a great job with it." I looked around the crowded room, "On second thought, I guess they already know."

I saw three grins on my friend's faces that were looking back at me.

Kari held her glass high and said, "To great uncles, and even better nephews."

I raised my glass with Murph and Linds, "I don't know about the second part, but I'll drink to the first. To Uncle Jack."

They all chorused, "To Uncle Jack."

I couldn't help thinking of the old adage about one door closing, and another one opening. Uncle Jack was now at rest. That world of his that I had always felt so safe in, where it felt like anything was possible, no longer existed. But looking at my three great friends who up until a few months ago had been strangers to me, I realized that I now had my own world. All four of us were in it, and anything was still possible. Looking at Kari, I realized that she was the biggest proof of that. She was laughing at something Linds had said, that I had missed. She looked over at me and tilted her head, asking a silent question. I took her hand and squeezed it as her answer.

Our "rum front" lasted another hour and a half in the bar, then continued until almost ten on *OCT*. At some point, we had pizza delivered, because, by that time, none of us were in any condition to drive anything or anywhere.

This impromptu party was our celebration of Kari and me putting all the tough stuff behind us. My uncle was gone, the guy who tried to kill us was dead, and we were going to get *Why Knot* in perfect condition again, then back home where she belonged.

Kari and I went up, peeled out of our clothes, and got under the covers together. We listened to the wind howl outside as the real front made its presence known along the coast. We were safe on *OCT*, and in each other's arms, enjoying the storm and each other. This storm would pass through by morning, welcoming the first real cool air of this fall season. But the thing about storms is, that there's always another one coming, and not all of them have to do with the weather.

20

COUNTING ON CARBS

This was the first time since we'd been staying here that the sun was up before we were awake. I saw a mop of black hair on my chest and whispered loudly, "Linds, you gotta get out of here before Kari gets back."

She lifted her head, and two bloodshot eyes glared at me through several strands of hair. "Very funny, butthead. Speaking of heads, ouch! I hurt myself last night." Kari replied.

"Yeah, you were the only one that was drinking. Made a real spectacle of yourself, too." I chuckled.

"You know, a month ago I had a nice quiet life, in a nice quiet apartment. An uncomplicated life. Hadn't had a hangover in forever. Then you came along. Remind me again why I love you?"

"Because I'm cute." I gave her my best fake-looking smile.

"Maybe ruggedly handsome, but cute is definitely not the right word."

"How about ruggedly handsome and sexy." I gave her what I thought was my "leading man" pose.

"Don't do that, it's creepy. You know what's sexy?"

I pretended to be hurt. "I was hoping it was me."

"Not unless you are made of carbohydrates. Save the sexy for later."

"How much later?"

"When my head quits pounding, later. I need carbs for that to happen."

"One ton of carbs, comin' up. Belgian waffles. The *Cove's* tropical ones with bananas, pecans, and toasted coconut. With a mountain of bacon. Yes, I know it doesn't have carbs, but it's *bacon.* Plus, a quart of fresh orange juice and a gallon of coffee. What the heck did we ever do before you guys opened that restaurant?"

"Lead on, you sexy talker. And in answer to your question, you starved, of course. Except at dinner. You're almost as good at grilling as me."

She kissed me and I started to caress her back. She broke off the embrace and forcefully said, "Later! Food now. And aspirin."

IF WE THOUGHT that we were bad off, Murph and Lindsay walked in looking worse than even we felt. They spotted us and bypassed the half-hour-long line of people waiting for tables, taking our two empty seats after shedding their coats. The temperature had plummeted to the low forties overnight.

"Hey, guys. Glad you already had a table; I'd have died before we got through that line. You two get hit by the same truck as we did?" Lindsay asked.

Kari replied, "Yeah, it was a semi. I didn't get the plate number, but it had a bumper sticker that read 'Got Carbs?'" She grinned a little. The aspirin she took on the boat and the orange juice that had arrived a minute earlier had started to take the edge off.

Murph didn't say anything until he ordered, clearly the worse for wear of the four of us. He unfolded a paper he picked up out of the rack out in front and scanned the headlines. He wasn't being unfriendly, he was just wounded, the worst casualty of last night. I figured we wouldn't hear much out of him until after he ate. That's why I was so surprised by his outburst.

"Holy crap! Marlin, did you read the paper?"

"No. Why?"

"Listen to this story; 'Did Richmond Billionaire Have Hidden Heirs? The Last Will and Testament of Richmond's wealthiest man, Jack Denton, Sr., was entered into probate late last week in Naples, Florida. According to sources who have seen both the Will and an accompanying video, it directs that twenty-five percent of the family trust which owns all of the late Denton's assets is to be divided equally among his grandchildren, and the remaining seventy-five percent, worth an estimated seven billion dollars, is to be divided equally between his 'children.' According to those same sources, identical wording was also used in the video, which features a well-known Henrico County judge attesting to both the contents of the Will as well as Denton Sr.'s 'sound mind.'

"To date, Jack Denton Jr. is the only publicly known or recognized offspring of Denton Sr. Depending upon if any additional children are identified, and the number of those children, control of Denton Enterprises might not go to Denton Jr., as most had assumed.

"Calls requesting comment from both Jack Denton Jr. and the Henrico County judge that reportedly appeared in the video were not returned by press time."

All three sets of my friends' eyes were now on me, as the color drained from my face.

Murph asked, "Did you know he had more kids?"

"No! And I still don't. You can't believe everything you read in the damned papers!"

I wanted to keep denying that it could be true, but things started coming back to me. My uncle's strange behavior, and most of all the note that he left for me on the plane. Maybe that's what he wanted to apologize for; hiding the fact that I had another cousin. Or, was it cousins? No, it couldn't be. This was all crap. My head was spinning now, only partially because of last night's alcohol.

Did I think he might have had affairs? Let's just say that I knew he wasn't a candidate for sainthood, and that he appreciated the female form as much or more than most other men. But to my knowledge, he had at least been discreet while my aunt was alive. I don't know if she knew, or just chose not to. I know this, she loved him fiercely, flaws and all. And this was all that mattered to me.

If, and in my mind, it was a huge if, I did indeed have another cousin or cousins out there, then he, she, or they could only be the product of an accident or accidents, purely unintended consequences of something undoubtedly casual. I felt sorry for the poor bastards; not growing up in a loving family with both a dad and mom like I had.

I suddenly realized that things at the table had quieted down, and that's when I noticed our food had arrived. I also noticed that what little conversation was being carried on, it was all small talk. Murph and Lindsay weren't looking at me, and the looks that Kari was giving me were those of concern.

I said, "Relax, guys. It's all a load of garbage, designed to sell papers and advertising. Sensationalism sells, whether it's true or not. And this isn't true. Now you understand part of why I hid my family connections; they are targets for the tabloids and con artists." I looked at Kari, who had ordered the same thing as me. "How's your food?"

"Just what the doctor ordered. You should try yours; you haven't touched it." She looked even more concerned.

The others were over halfway finished when I finally started in on my breakfast. After they finished, Kari talked to Lindsay about having a sendoff dinner next Saturday for the two of them. She and I would host it in the private room here at the *Cove*. She planned to invite Dawn, Casey, Rikki, and Cindy as well. We hadn't all gotten together again since the night *Why Knot* exploded. We wanted everyone to have a good night together before Lindsay and Murph left. I suspected it might be her way of distracting me from this latest nonsense as well. I was good with that.

After breakfast, Kari and I walked back to *OCT* and went up to the guest room. Kari closed the hatch over the galley ladder, then sat down with me on the bed, and grabbed my hand.

"If you need to talk about it, you can."

I shook my head slightly. "It's just tabloid crap."

"I know that you admired him..."

"I *loved* him, Kari. Don't get those two things mixed up. Admiration is earned, love you can't help. Case in point, you love me. You just can't help yourself, because I'm cute." I grinned the biggest, most fake grin of my life. Of course, she saw right through the deflection. Only an idiot wouldn't have. I don't know why I tried.

"You know that I've already told you once today about being cute. But I get it, you don't want to talk about it. Whenever you're ready, I'll be here." The look she gave me right then was pure compassion, and I truly loved her for it.

"What's to talk about? Did I know that he screwed around? Yes. That was his business, not mine. And he was a widower for ten years, so he was a free agent. But it's still crap about there being more children out there."

"You loved but didn't admire him. Is that why?"

"Probably. Okay, I guess we are going to talk about this now, huh?"

She lightly shook her head. "Not if you don't want to. But I am curious about one thing. Before we spent that second night together, you told me that you weren't a short-term kind of guy; that you weren't into one-night stands."

"I'm sure there are a lot of guys that aren't."

"Marlin, how many serious relationships have you had?"

I couldn't breathe for a minute. I really didn't want to go down this road. I stayed silent.

"I'm not asking you to be mean; I'm asking for a reason. If it helps, then you should know that I've only been in two before us. In my twenty-four years. I guess I'm both a late bloomer as well as being very picky. And I think that may be why I felt drawn to you; I felt that we might be a lot alike in that respect. There wasn't that bravado about you. Not that you lacked confidence, but you were, and are, a gentle and non-pushy guy. And by the way, you're the only guy that I've ever moved in with. I mean, I guess I've moved in with you since you haven't asked me to leave yet; it just kind of happened and wasn't planned. I figured you kind of needed me at the time."

She had just bared her soul, probably farther and deeper than she had with any other person. If this conversation continued, no doubt I'd end up doing the same. I looked into her eyes again, I was right, they were so easy to get lost in. But they were windows into her soul, and I knew what I was reading there. I drew a deep breath, then I started unloading things that had never been shared and had never seen the light of day before.

"Five, in my thirty-two years. Only one lady that I've lived with, for actually less than a month, and that ended a year and a half ago. You are the only person who has ever stayed on the boat with me. And yes, I'm asking you to keep staying here and to move back aboard with me when we get her finished. If you want to. We can even make any changes to the boat that might make it easier for two of us to live on her since we have to rebuild her anyway." I paused for a minute, just long enough to see one very happy smile of agreement.

"I wasn't a late bloomer, but there were just long gaps in between relationships. Why? Who knows, other than me being a bit of an emotional cripple. I always said that being desperate only finds you desperation. Or, maybe I was scared, who knows? But I do know where you were headed; you want to know if it was because I watched someone I love be less than faithful? I'm no Sigmund Freud, but I'd guess that it might have had something to do with it. Was that why I couldn't admire him? I never really thought about it before, but I guess it is. Ironically, he gave me a copy of his memoirs, inscribed 'to a much-admired nephew.'"

"Did he ever fish before you two did?"

"As a kid and a young man he was a huge white marlin fisherman. After he started building his business, he used to love going with me, but he hardly ever picked up a rod unless we had more than one fish on. He was always working, reading reports and stuff."

She said, "Like he was still at the office, but watching you fish at the same time."

"I never really thought about it that way, but yeah, I guess you're right."

"Did your dad ever fish with you?"

"Once, with Uncle Jack and me. At Norfolk Canyon. It wasn't his thing."

She looked curious. "Yet he named you Marlin."

I shook my head. "It was my mom who named me. Told me that she had always liked it."

"Did she fish?"

"No, she didn't even like to eat fish."

Now it was her turn to take a deep breath as she took my second hand. She looked into my eyes and asked the question that was about to change our life together forever.

"How long have you suspected that you were his son, Marlin?"

"What?" All of the air went out of the room in an instant; I felt like I was in a vacuum. I could no more breathe than I could that night underwater. She had that compassionate look on her face again. Suddenly it wasn't as sweet as it had been. "That's insane!" I wanted to get up and go outside, but I couldn't stand. I started shaking.

She said softly, "I'm so sorry, Marlin."

"I can't be that guy. I'm not that guy, Kari. My dad was my father. He had to have been."

She pulled me to her, and I was still shaking. She said, "It all fits, Marlin. He was trying to tell you, but he ran out of time."

I was shaking my head violently. "No! He can't. I can't. They couldn't have."

"The Will and the video with the Henrico County judge, he did that because he knew it couldn't be successfully contested."

I said, "If it really was me, then why not just name me in it? Why keep me hidden?"

She said, "If I had to guess, I'd say he was giving you the choice and leaving it up to you, whether or not you wanted to claim him after he was gone. He knew that you kept your being related to him quiet, right?"

"Yes, of course. We talked about it, and he understood."

"Marlin, he knew that once he made it public, there was no putting the genie back in the bottle."

"So, he left it up to me whether or not I wanted to be branded a bastard, and have my mom be thought of as an adulteress."

She looked at me sadly, "Bastard is a word that fortunately has lost favor in recent years. It's so unfair to hoist that title on someone who had no choice in the matter and make them pay for something their whole life when they hadn't even had a say in it."

I don't know why Kari had come into my life at the time that she did, but I was so grateful that she had, and that she was still here. It was time to share some things and empty the skeleton closet. I'd never wanted to tell anyone these before, but now they were weighing heavily on me.

I told her about the special connection that I'd always felt with... Uncle Jack. I still couldn't call him "my father" or "my dad." My dad was the man who raised me, and who restored *Why Knot* with me, no matter who my biological father was. But there were other clues, things that backed up what I still wanted to think of as Kari's theory. I still wasn't convinced that it was a fact. Or, at least I wasn't willing to concede that; not yet. Had I had fleeting suspicions over the years? Yes.

I knew that when Jack Jr. had been born, there were complications with the birth that left my aunt unable to have any more children. She and Uncle Jack had wanted a large family, but it just wasn't to be. I also knew that my parents had hit a rough patch and separated for a short time around when I would have been conceived. Mom had hinted at that when I went through my first breakup as a teenager. So, she might have been vulnerable, and Uncle Jack was a very smooth man when he wanted to be, just like Jack Jr.

When I was in second grade, I remember my teacher asking each of us in the class, if we could pick a new name for ourselves, what would it be? I of course answered, "Jack Denton." I'd never repeated this since that day.

I had been surprised and happy about Uncle Jack telling me that he was proud that I had become what he called a great fisherman and that I was building up such a solid client base. I had been worried after I completed my internship and then quit college, that he'd see me as a failure. That was when he gave me that signed book. But like I said, the measure of Jack Jr. was done all by profit dollars.

While I was telling her all this, Kari was silently hanging on every word, still holding my hands. I repeated the part about my first conversation with my uncle on this last trip. She did giggle a bit when I got to the part where he called my last girlfriend Tiffany's name a stripper's stage name. But I thought I detected a hint of jealousy in the giggle. Then I repeated the story of my interaction with Jack Jr. just after that, and she got a very serious look on her face.

Finally, I had unloaded everything from Uncle Jack's and my past. I was emotionally drained and felt about as vulnerable as I had ever been. But it felt good to have leveled with Kari. I could see her wheels turning as she digested everything. Finally, she looked at me, still holding my hands.

"Marlin, I don't think there's any doubt that you are Jack Sr.'s biological son, at least not in my mind. I'm guessing here, but I doubt that your dad knew, especially with the close relationship he had with Jack. But your mom had to have named you Marlin because Jack was such an avid marlin fisherman. No doubt it was a reminder to him of your real relationship. It'll be easy to prove, Marlin, with a DNA swab. You're the other heir and entitled to half of that seven billion dollars. Which would come with huge consequences, and as you've pointed out, not all of them are good. Your unc...er...Jack Sr. must have had all that in mind when he left it up to you to decide. When he said, 'Then keep doing it like you're doing it, and don't let anything change your life.' He wanted you to keep being happy. As he said, he didn't want to wreck your life any more than he already had. He knew your world and your happiness was about working on the water, and his was building a huge conglomerate; two completely separate orbits. So, you've got a big decision to make. And you and I have a big decision to make, together."

I smiled. "If this is a proposal, the answer is yes." I was trying to deflect again.

She smiled back. "Maybe one day, Marlin, but not today." Her face turned serious. "This is what I think; Jack Jr. knew about your real relationship to his dad and him. All that sedation and the bums' rush in Naples was to keep Jack Sr. from being able to tell you about it. Then trying to keep you from the funeral was all to start distancing you from the family.

"He tried to kill us both, Marlin. He knew we were together, he even had trackers put on both of our cars, and had that picture left in my apartment to make sure I wouldn't want to stay there. He wanted to be certain I'd be with you when the boat exploded. If the fire and the explosion had both been as intense as Shifflett had anticipated, there wouldn't have been a trace of the tampering, and it would have been just another old gasoline boat exploding and burning. You would be dead, long before it would become public knowledge that there had been another heir. Somehow, someone in Naples got access to that Will and the video and sold it to the news. That shouldn't have become public record until after it cleared probate, and by then it would have been too late. Jack has to be crapping bricks right now."

Kari's toughness had started to resurface as she realized the implications of what had happened. I was glad because we both needed her business mind and her toughness right now. I was feeling as vulnerable as a softshell crab in a school of slob-sized rockfish.

Kari continued. "I didn't tell you yet what I saw yesterday, but now it fits. Marlin, you were never supposed to come back from that boat ride. When those two got soaked on the front seat, I saw the print of a pistol in a holster on Carter's ankle. Maybe he knew I was also carrying, or maybe he realized he couldn't have easily explained away two people going overboard in an accident, even in those rough seas. Remember how Jack declined to spread the ashes and to even say anything? You were bent over the gunwale, the perfect position for a bullet to the back of the head, and the blood spray would have been away from the boat. But remember how pissy Jack got when he realized I was coming, too? We spoiled his plan, and it was almost foolproof. His 'get out of jail free' card was the note from his dad detailing how the two of you were supposed to do this together."

It was chilling, to realize that my own cousin, or brother, had planned to murder me not once, but twice. I wish there was any way I could say that I found it a total fantasy, and completely unbelievable. But I can't. Then it hit me that Kari had saved my life yet again by being in the right place at the right time. When I looked at her, I recognized that face. Contractors dreaded it.

"I'm guessing that you have a plan."

"This is business to Jack, Marlin. We have to treat it the same way. And in business, I always have a plan, as well as a backup plan. Remember those decisions I was talking about? You have another to make. You're going to have to decide if you are willing to let a couple more people in on your secret."

I said, "Who?"

"Casey and Dawn."

21

PAYBACKS

So, that was how we found ourselves invited up to lunch with Casey and Dawn aboard the *Lady Dawn.* Kari had told them that we needed privacy for a confidential meeting. We had lunch at their dining table, then walked across the salon that was large enough to put both of my outboard boats inside with room left over. Kari and I settled on a comfortable couch while Casey and Dawn took flanking, overstuffed chairs. You could see all through lunch they were intrigued; they knew that Kari wouldn't waste their time asking for advice in private unless it was for something big.

Kari then asked for their total confidence, and both readily agreed, anxious to find out what the mystery was all about. We had decided on the drive up that she would present our case because she was the best, most succinct speaker between the two of us, and more emotionally disconnected. Except about the part about her almost getting blown up, too. It didn't take long before both Casey and Dawn moved up to the front edge of their chairs. When Kari finished, they both sat back, absorbing the details. Finally, Casey spoke.

"The most obvious thing is, Marlin, that you are going to have to make a decision about claiming your part of your father's estate."

It was the first time that someone else had used the term "your father" with me referring to Uncle Jack. It felt really weird.

Dawn spoke up. "From what you two have found out, I don't think there's any doubt that you are Jack Denton's son."

"And you can almost, but not quite, make a case for attempted murder. And even though the news has broken about there being another heir, you're still in danger. Both of you are until you get things locked down. We'll have to talk to a lawyer, even though I don't think you are there yet with the evidence about the attack. But we all know someone who can help us with that, now that we know what and who we're looking for," Casey said.

Kari asked, "I take it by 'we' and 'us' it means you'll help us?"

Dawn laughed. "Of course, we will. Yes, we work together Kari, but you're my friend. That's the only way we'd have wanted you in as a partner in *Mallard Cove*. We don't have any partners that aren't also our friends. And Marlin has become a friend now, too."

"So, how do you want to play this; what are your thoughts, Marlin?" Casey asked.

I replied, "It's complicated, that's why we came to you two for your advice. I want the money, but I don't want the money."

The look on Dawn's face was priceless; like she was sitting here with a total moron.

I said, "Let me explain."

"Please do. This I want to hear." Casey had a similar look.

"First, after we prove that he was behind trying to kill us, Jack has to pay for what he did. Not in years, his lawyers would probably get him off anyway with all of his and their connections. But to avoid any negative publicity and the possibility of jail, it should be worth say, ten million apiece for Kari and me. If he doesn't take that deal, he'd be an idiot."

Dawn asked, "What about justice for that Shifflett murder, and catching his killer?"

Kari railed, "Screw him. He wanted to kill us, and he got what he deserved. Whoever shot him will probably end up shooting another scumbag, and he'll either get shot or arrested in the process. Right now, we're still breathing, and we want to keep it that way. Jack isn't using outsiders anymore that we know of since he and Carter were going to kill Marlin themselves."

I jumped in. "Here's the deal. Uncle Jack was so glad that I was happy and told me that I should 'keep doing it like you're doing it, and don't let anything change your life.' I watched that business divide Jack and him, and how it became all-consuming with each of them. It's no longer even about the income with Jack as much as it's about the power. He's even willing to commit murder in order to keep it. Three of his ex-wives, who all hate his guts, will for the next few years control fourteen percent of Denton Industries until their kids come of age and inherit the stock. His other three adult children will control only eleven percent. So, Jack could either court me to side with him or kill me. He made his choice, and it's going to cost him.

"But I don't want to control that company. In fact, I want nothing to do with it. I had my look inside corporate life when I did my internship, and it's so not even close to being me. That was probably the best lesson Uncle Jack ever taught me. So, I want to take his advice, and make sure I don't change my life."

I looked over at Kari, and then back at both Casey and Dawn.

"Well, maybe just a little. And I have to think about the future if I ever get married and have kids. Not that ten million wouldn't take care of me and any future family. But here's what I have in mind." I laid out my plan, and they both had some good suggestions. After that, Dawn had a plan of her own.

"Here's what I think you two should do. Instead of running back down to *Mallard Cove*, stay here with us tonight, we have three empty staterooms. That gives Casey and me time to digest this plan before dinner," Dawn suggested.

Kari replied, "We had planned to stay at my apartment if the landlord has fixed the door latch."

"So, you have a change of clothes with you anyway?" Dawn asked.

We nodded.

"Perfect, but I insist that you stay here. We have plenty of security, and Jack can't get at you here. Marlin, you look wrung out, and I have the perfect solution for that. We've got our private heated pool and hot tub over in the woods across the parking lot. I've erased a lot of tan lines over there, so take that hint if you're so inclined, it's very private. I think I remember you saying you are a waterfowl watcher, Kari, and after last night's front, we should see the first flights arriving this evening. Watching them is something that Casey and I love doing as well. Why don't we meet on the upper deck for cocktails and see how many come in."

"Thanks, Dawn."

"Good, then that's settled. Come on, I'll take you over to the pool."

She wasn't kidding about private. First off, we were already on the gated side of the marina. Second, it took a magnetic keycard to get through a security fence. Then there was a winding path through the trees, and an oasis on the other side with a big paver block deck, heated infinity edge pool, and hot tub, each with a breathtaking view of the Chesapeake. There was an outdoor kitchen next to the pool that was to die for; you know how I love my little grill on the boat. But the most incredible feature of this place that was nicknamed "*C3*" was a building that contained a huge dining table, pool table, bar, big screen TV, steam room, and changing rooms. To top it off, the whole side of the building that faced the pool and bay was glass. That view was stunning, like something out of a magazine. Dawn went into the changing rooms and came out with two fluffy terry robes.

"There's beer and wine in the bar, and if you decide you need them, an assortment of bathing suits. But I love a skinny dip in the hot tub when it's in the low fifties like right now. From what Linds has told me, I figured you two might be fine with that." She winked and smiled at us. "Okay, see you two around five thirty, if not before."

I watched as Dawn left. I looked at Kari, "Want to get suits?"

"I was thinking more along the lines of wine. Don't you think suits would just get in the way?" Her eyes twinkled and went well with her sly smile.

Going back and forth between the hot tub and the pool was a real rush, the temperature difference was like hitting the "runner's wall."

This place was incredible, as was the view. The one of the Chesapeake was as well.

Dawn was right, I was wrung out. I needed this place, almost as much as I needed Kari right now, and to have both together was indescribable. I got lost in her eyes several times, and then we gave each other back rubs in the hot tub that turned us both into human jellyfish. Then chasing each other in the pool, and back to the hot tub, playing like a pair of river otters. Everything else ceased to exist, as did everyone else. I'd never been so relaxed, nor more in love. I knew the two of us were going to have a tough week ahead, but right now there was only the here, and the now. You have no idea how much I needed this. Well, I guess you do, at that.

"HEY, KIDS, HOW WAS THE WATER?" Dawn had a big smile.

Kari beamed, "Amazing. We needed that disconnect, thank you both so much."

We were up on the entertainment deck of *Lady Dawn,* which had its own hot tub, bar with built-in stools, U–shaped booth and table, and a flying bridge with full controls. A retractable roof went from the helm back to the hot tub, and on the far end of the deck, a hydraulic davit and Casey's eighteen-foot Maverick flats boat named *Predator II*. Between the hot tub and the boat were numerous cushioned teak deck chaise lounges, four with folded blankets. It was on one of these chaises where I had found myself that awful morning, though I didn't remember all these details from that day. But to be honest, the first half of that day was still really fuzzy.

We walked up to the bar with Casey and Dawn. Their steward, another beautiful redhead named Andrea O'Neil, was bartending. We both asked her for vodkas on the rocks.

Dawn was still smiling. "I know this has all been a shock, and a real emotional day for you, Marlin."

I nodded. "It was, it is, but I'm so grateful to have had Kari with me to help sort things out."

"Lindsay was right, you two do make such a cute couple."

I turned to Kari, "See? I told you I was cute."

"She said we were a cute couple, as in the two of us together, not you, knucklehead!" She swatted me as Dawn laughed and Casey laughed.

Dawn continued, "I've been getting updates. Linds is proud of herself for successfully playing matchmaker."

I said, "We're kind of happy about the whole situation, too."

Up until now, Casey had been pretty quiet, and I felt like he had something on his mind. I was right.

"So, in talking this over, Dawn and I think you have more than just a good shot at pulling this thing off, assuming that Rikki can come up with that piece of information for you. And like you said, Marlin, your brother would be crazy to turn down your settlement offer as well as your other offer if he's half the businessman that I've heard he is." Hearing Jack referred to as my brother felt weird and uncomfortable.

Casey continued, "So, I guess you'll be pretty set, Kari. The big question for Dawn and me is, will you be leaving McAlister and Shaw now? We'll still be friends even if you do, but we'll have to change some plans if that's going to happen."

I could tell this caught Kari off guard. "Not unless you are planning to fire me. I was kind of hoping that I could talk you into letting me invest in more projects with you if this settlement happens. You both know I'm not the kind of person who would be satisfied sitting at home watching the stock market. Half a year ago I started by answering the phone here. Then I got to help sell the *Estates*, and now I'm doing project design and management. It's exciting. I love what you have me doing and the challenges that come with it. Wait, you said future plans? As in something already concrete?"

Casey and Dawn were both smiling now, very relieved. They knew what Kari was capable of and had planned their future expansions with the thought of her still being part of their team. Especially the next project.

Dawn said, "We know that you have your hands full with *Mallard Cove* for the next year. But we've had our eyes on a huge vacant piece of waterfront property over in Lynnhaven. We finally got the owner to sell us a three-year option on the parcel. He was tough to deal with, very gun shy after being hounded by the new owner of the marina next to it on Long Creek. Here's the part you'll both love, the guy driving him nuts was Glenn Cetta, and this property is next door to the marina you used to call home, Marlin. And he's now missed out on another deal that we're part of." Dawn chuckled as she saw the expressions on both Kari and my faces.

"Anyway, that's where we're going next after you get finished with *Mallard Cove*. And we'd hate to break up the partnership; you can have a larger piece of this one, and we're going to offer shares to Murph, Lindsay, Eric, and Cindy. But I'm already getting ahead of myself. We have an idea for a slight change in *Mallard Cove*, but we'll talk about that at some point down the road."

Meanwhile, the four of us kicked back on the chaises, watching the first really big and loud groups of Canada geese arrive, as well as two flights of huge Tundra Swans. The blankets were a smart idea, as the temperature started to drop as the sun got closer to setting. There's something so unmistakable about a fall Chesapeake sunset. This one was spectacular, lighting up the few wispy clouds over toward the Western Shore with a myriad of hues, from pink to bright orange. The final rays disappeared about the same time as the liquid in all our glasses. I love it when a plan comes together.

22

LODGE MEETING

The thing about having powerful friends is that they usually have other powerful friends. Casey and Dawn were no exception. After breakfast, Casey, Kari, and I were airborne in Casey's plane, headed for DC, and the office of a friend of Eric Clarke's. Billionaires always have great attorneys, or they won't stay billionaires for long. This guy was one of the best, having even been an advisor to two presidents. I'd heard of him of course and seen him on television numerous times. Judging by his ego wall, this was going to be one very expensive bill. But if everything worked out, that wasn't going to be an issue.

We laid out what we wanted to do and avoided talking about things that might compel an officer of the court to have to report to the authorities. Things like Jack's conspiracy to commit murder. If things are inferred but not stated, a sharp attorney can still get the picture, while avoiding the subpoena. He was one of the sharpest.

I could tell he liked our ideas, as well as our brand of justice. He would have all the documents put together by late this afternoon. He would make room in his schedule to go to the meet once it was set up. We would be providing the plane, of course. Yeah, this was going to get expensive, really fast.

An hour later back at *Bayside*, Casey, Kari, Dawn, and I met with Rikki in McAlister and Shaw's conference room. She brought a picture along with her of a broken cell phone in what looked like an evidence bag.

"You were right, Marlin, we were able to backtrack the calls from Shifflett's burner phone and found a sequential number that he called right after your boat exploded. That phone had called another sequentially numbered phone a minute later. We triangulated the location of that call, and it was in the vicinity of Brantley Plantation. As in, somewhere within its eighteen hundred acres. Whoever received that call was on Jack Denton Jr's estate at the time."

I nodded. I had expected it but still had hoped that somehow we had been wrong. "Rikki, do the police have this information?"

"No, we were able to get this on our own. Don't ask how." She had her own version of a sly smile on. "They haven't discovered the third phone, nor its location."

"Good. Well, does anyone else have any thoughts before I do this? Once I make this call, there's no going back."

Kari said, "Marlin, it was another call made days ago by others that was the 'no turning back' point. Let's do this."

There were nods all around the room. I punched the number into my phone and put it on speaker. Jack picked up the second ring.

"I'm kind of busy right now, Marlin."

"I kind of thought you would make time for your own brother, Jack."

There was silence, then he told someone to give him the room and close the door on the way out. "What do you want, Marlin?"

"You already know what I want. But it's not so much what I want as what you do."

"What do you mean by that?"

"I mean I'm just assuming that you and Carter want to stay out of jail."

More silence. "I have no idea what you're talking about."

"One call, Jack, and you two are done. If you don't get convicted in court, you'll already have been convicted in the court of public opinion. One call, Jack."

"I don't want to talk about this on the phone."

"I didn't think you would. That's why we'll be at the lodge at Brantley tomorrow at ten a.m."

"We?"

"You didn't think I'd come there alone, did you? I'm bringing my lawyer and some friends. I'd advise you to have your lawyer there with you, to look over the documents I'm bringing. But you probably should have a good criminal defense lawyer on speed dial, just in case you do something dumb, like deciding not to sign. Oh, and tell Carter to leave his leg iron at home. You know, the one he was going to use on me on the boat. See you tomorrow, Jack." I hung up.

There was silence in the room for a second, then a lot of smiles and more than one "Well played." We had an outline, but I was winging it. Nothing was signed yet, but Jack was scared. To tell the truth, I was too. This whole thing tomorrow hinged on a big bluff. Everything we had was circumstantial.

Kari and I walked out with Rikki. "I like the way you handled yourself in this, Marlin. And I understand that you are quite a fly fishing guide, too. I'm a bit of a fishing fanatic myself. I'd love to get together and fish sometime."

"Sounds good, Rikki. Let's make some concrete plans, maybe when you're down at the dinner this Saturday night."

"You're on. See you tomorrow for the trip."

She split off, heading back to her office, as we went over to *Bayside*'s *Rooftops Grill* for lunch.

"You won't be jealous if I fish her, right?" Rikki was very stunning, with white-blond hair and ice-blue eyes.

"First, I'll only start getting jealous if you quit looking at me like you always look at me. Second, no. Cindy is her partner."

"I thought Cindy worked with you guys?"

"Not that kind of partner, doofus. I mean she's taken. Just like you are."

"Oh. Ohh. See, I haven't even paid attention to other women since I met you."

"Riiight, and it had nothing to do with you being clueless. As in not picking up on the vibe that I was into you before Lindsay had to beat you over the head about it."

"Nothing whatsoever."

"Un, huh. No, Rikki is quite an accomplished angler; she and Casey took first in the Virginia Beach tournament early this year. I think you two would fish well together. Maybe you two should team up in the tournament we want to run out of *Mallard Cove*."

If she was that good, that might just be a plan. Another thing to talk about on Saturday, or maybe tomorrow, if things go well.

We got an early start the next day, with almost a full plane load. Casey, me, Dave, Dawn, Kari, and Rikki. We picked up the lawyer over in DC, then headed to Richmond. The three women were dressed less conservatively than their normal work attire on purpose. Everybody except the attorney knew I had to really sell this, and I needed every bit of leverage I could get. If there's one thing Jack loves, it's beautiful women. And I was hoping they would help distract him enough to maybe keep him off his "A" game.

We were met on the ramp at Richmond by two big, black SUVs with limo-tinted windows, looking like they were straight out of the president's motorcade. Two female security agents and two male ones met us with the cars. All four were dressed like Dave, with black suits and black sunglasses and obvious bulges under their arms. If you are thinking this was all theatrical, you're right. We weren't about to miss a trick. But I was half expecting Jack to have some security there if he was as unnerved as I suspected. By the way, our lawyer wasn't surprised a bit, he never even blinked. This wasn't his first rodeo, and why he gets the big bucks. I still didn't know how big, and right now, I didn't want to think about that. I'd only be on the hook for the tab if things went horribly wrong.

. . .

Brantley Plantation goes back hundreds of years and is comprised of eighteen hundred acres of farmland on a peninsula in the James River. It's forty-five minutes east of Richmond, and just upriver from Jamestown, where one of our ancestors had been an investor in the Virginia Company. I think that one reason Jack wanted Brantley was that it had originally been granted by the King of England to another investor of the Virginia Company. Since then it has belonged to Shakespeare's son-in-law, an early president's son, two governors, and a conglomerate. Technically, it is now owned by another conglomerate, since Denton Industries holds the title. Like it holds the titles to dozens of my cousins' homes here and abroad, the four airplanes, and a fleet of vehicles.

This is partly why Jack is scared to death to lose control of the company. If that happens, he could be out of everything from his home to his car, as well as his job. His whole lifestyle goes up in smoke. You see, he may be worth three and a half billion dollars on paper, but that's just a numbers game. In reality, he isn't worth that. Those numbers are just an estimate, based partly on the value of Uncle Jack's (I still can't call him my father) private stock portfolio, but the biggest part of the estate is the company. Everything is in a massive web of trusts, to escape most of the death taxes. The company's current valuation is based on sales of similar companies that sold at their most advantageous point. Meaning, that there was a good market, and over half the shareholders wanted to sell. If you don't own over half of a privately held company, you've got nothing to sell. Meaning that three and a half billion may be toilet paper on a good day, depending on how pissed his exes still are. And the truth is, even if you own more than half and want to sell it, it's only worth what someone is willing to pay for it then. And fire sales have a nasty habit of turning ugly and cheap.

So, Brantley Plantation is listed as a farm holding of Denton Industries. There are various small houses on the property used by some of the higher-ranking farm employees. They get "free" rent as part of their compensation, but they pay tax on that rent's value. Not a lot of tax, just like Jack. The Plantation residence is a drafty old early eighteen-hundreds brick manse. The oil bill to heat it runs over five grand a month in winter. Jack gets taxed on only about that much as his rent valuation, to live in a mansion. The pool, the shooting range, trap and skeet ranges, the ten thousand flowers that are planted every spring, the docks, the helipad — all of it are farm expenses. If the eighteen-hundred acres worth of corn or soybeans can't pay for it all, Denton Industries does, out of pre-tax earnings. They hold company parties at the lodge every year, so that helps make it look legit, too.

The lodge part was built in the nineteen eighties by that first conglomerate, as a getaway place for their corporate execs. You can imagine how plush it is, though somewhat dated now. That's our destination today. I chose it on purpose, rather than at Jack's house or office in Richmond. More theater. The corporation that built it went into bankruptcy, partly because the execs were more interested in holding wild hunting parties out here than running the public company they worked for. This is how Jack picked it up for pennies on a dollar. He never pays full price for anything. That was going to change today.

We pulled through the gates. A farmhand in a utility vehicle spoke into a walkie-talkie, no doubt alerting those in the lodge. It's showtime. We drove down a half-mile tree-lined asphalt driveway, then took a left at a fork, and headed to the lodge. We pulled up on the circular drive in front of the huge, two-story, wood board and batten-sided structure. There was a wide covered porch in front, with stairs in the middle. Two security guys stood at the top of the stairs, one on each side. Our five agents stepped out as one of the two said, "That's far enough. You five will have to remain outside."

Dave smiled wide, "Annnd that won't be happening."

Jack's security guys closed ranks at the top of the stairs, barring passage, as the rest of us piled out of the vehicles.

Dave continued, "You two need to stand aside. One way or another, we're going inside. The one way is nice and easy. The other way is stepping on your bruised and bleeding bodies."

As if on cue, all five of our agents unbuttoned the fronts of their coats, to give themselves more mobility. Like I said, theater. The two at the top of the steps moved aside. Hospitalization must not be part of their compensation package.

We walked through the double doors that I had been through on a couple of occasions before, always with Uncle Jack. Twin stairways led up either side of the front hall to the ten guest rooms. Half a dozen Tundra swans and two dozen duck mounts adorned the plaster wall at the back side of the stairs and over the wide open doorway. Through that entrance was the main sitting room, over a hundred feet deep, with a vaulted ceiling over thirty feet high. It was fitted with numerous couches and chairs. The room itself was trimmed with a small forest's worth of dark wood paneling. A huge fireplace was piled with burning oak logs to our right. There was an open doorway that led to the formal and informal dining rooms just past the fireplace, also to the right. On the left side was another doorway that opened into the card room. At the far end of the room was a massive glass bay window with a stunning view of the James river, seventy feet away, and twenty feet below. I'd watched freighters make their way past, to, and from the Port of Richmond, on more than one occasion. Jack was seated in an overstuffed chair down by the window, right where I knew he would be. We weren't the only ones employing theatrics. He was flanked by Carter and Dennis Peel. Behind them was another guy, who I judged to be more security. On the left sitting on a couch was a "suit;" no doubt Jack's lawyer. More crapped bricks were added to the growing pile when they saw who our lawyer was. Any doubts about if I was playing or not just evaporated.

Dave motioned to two of the agents to clear the rooms on the other side of the doorways. Both came back in and nodded. Dave then focused on the other security guy. "You need to leave."

"Like hell. I stay."

Dave motioned to the two female agents, who started advancing on the guy.

Jack looked at him and said coolly, "John, why don't you take a smoke break out on the porch."

John wasn't happy but did as he was told. I was glad we brought Dave and four other agents, instead of just one.

I addressed our lawyer and Jack's. "Gentlemen, why don't you give us a few minutes?"

Jack nodded to his attorney, who followed ours into the card room, out of earshot.

"Who the hell do you think you are, coming in here giving orders?" Peel came around Jack's chair and started advancing on me.

I have to tell you, I'm no fighter. But this asshole has had it coming for a long time, and I must have been saving it up. He never saw my fist before it connected with his nose, knocking him backward into a couch, blood spurting out of both nostrils.

"You broke my nose, you son-of-a-bitch!"

I said loudly, "You tripped and fell against me, you clumsy ass, and now you want to blame that on me?" I lunged forward as if to do it again, and he flinched sideways, spreading more blood across a very expensive-looking couch.

"Dennis, go bleed outside before you ruin my rug, too." Jack frowned.

Dennis glared at me and went the long way around the couch, the farthest end from me as he left. Our four Richmond agents fanned out around the room, one behind Jack and Carter. I have to hand it to Jack, as he feigned some semblance of calm. But Carter looked nervously behind him.

"Well, Marlin, at least you left me with something good to look at." The smarmy voice again, as he looked Dawn, Kari, and Rikki up and down. It was working.

"You know, Jack, keep it up and they'll be the last women you see for the rest of your life. And Carter there, I have to say, I'm really disappointed in you, cousin. I always liked you. You just had some very bad influences."

Casey and Dawn went over and sat on a couch, looking amused. Kari stood next to me, and Rikki walked to the edge of Jack's peripheral vision. Once the women had his attention, the idea was to split them up so that he couldn't concentrate as well. It seemed to be working.

"The thing is, Carter, jail is no place for a young fellow like you. If you come out at all, you'll be looking very, very old."

"Did you come over here to waste my morning, Marlin, or was there a purpose to this visit?" Jack was trying to take back control of the situation.

"Really, Jack? You know what the purpose is. But what you don't know is that we have proof that you tried to have both me and Kari murdered because of it. Nice touch, by the way, taking out both of us; fewer things pointing to just me being the target."

"I don't have the slightest clue as to what you are talking about."

I turned to Rikki, who reached into her briefcase bringing out an evidence bag with the burner phone pieces and a sheet with a list of calls. I saw Carter go pale. I now knew who made the call, but I figured that I knew who was in on it, too. Jack stared angrily at Carter.

"It was cold and raining on the dock, Dad! They were picking up the garbage the next day anyway."

"Carter's fingerprints are on the phone along with the hitman's. We got his prints off the hand grab on my boat. We also have a copy of the receipt for the three sequentially numbered burner phones bought by the dead hit guy, and a video of him making that purchase. Plus, this is a list of all the phone calls and locations of the phones, including the one where Shifflett's boss called here to say that I was dead. All gift wrapped with a bow for the State's Attorney. Just think, Jack, Carter's ass is gonna get traded for some guy's mashed potatoes in jail. More than once. Each day." I smiled at Carter, who looked ready to ralph. We really hadn't found the phone, nor did we have his fingerprints. Not knowing I was bluffing, Jack was now pale. Gotcha!

"What do you want, Marlin?"

"I want it all, Jack, so I can break your company into little bitty pieces so small that it can never be put back together. I want to bust up what you've spent your life creating, what you almost succeeded in killing Kari and me over. I want to ruin you and your family."

"You little bastard! If my father hadn't laid that whore mother of yours, there wouldn't be any question about it all being mine! But that doddering old man had such a sweet spot for you, his little fishing buddy, his carnal accident. You'll never take this company away from me!" The veins were standing out on Jack's neck now.

"I already have, Jack. I want you to feel what it is like to lose it all because you almost did that to me. It's funny because that just made Kari and I appreciate each other so much more. Thanks for that, brother.

"So, Jack, now you know that I *can* ruin your precious company, that I *can* ruin your life, and that I *can* have Carter gang raped in prison before breakfast. But you know what else? I think you've now learned exactly what I'm capable of, and that I'm not playing. So, now you need to know what I really want. In doing that, I'm going to throw you a lifeline; after all, we're brothers.

"When we came in here, Kari and I were willing to settle for ten million each, to keep you and sweet meat out of the pokey." I looked up at Kari. "See what I did there? Pokey? Sweet meat? Think he understands the full consequences? We're about to find out." I looked at a confused and nervous Jack, "Because you brought my mother into this, the price is now fifteen million each. That's just to keep you two out of jail, and to keep this, including our real relationship, confidential."

I could see the wheels turning.

"How do I know you'll keep your end of the deal?"

"Because of the second deal, which we'll get to in a minute. But if you don't ante up the thirty to the two of us, there's no sense in talking about the second deal, because you both are going to jail, and I'm coming after the whole thing. With the help of your exes, I can already break it up anyway. Your only shot at keeping this intact and you keeping control is by agreeing to the first one. What's it going to be, Jack?"

"Agreed."

I smiled. "Hey, Carter, you can start breathing and unpucker your butt again. Okay, now we come to what's mine. I see you don't like that phrase. Good, I said it just to irritate you.

"Jack, you are a very generous guy. An extremely generous guy. Since no other legitimate heir has, nor ever will come forward, in keeping with your father's love of fishing and the water, you have decided to donate half of that seven billion to a foundation dedicated to preserving the fisheries and habitat that he so loved. And in return, the foundation agrees to sell back all Denton Industries stock it receives from that donation over a period of thirty years, at the current valuation. Just think of the tax write-off you'll get. You won't pay another cent of tax in your whole life! And over the years you'll be paying for that stock what should amount to mere pennies on the dollar by the time that last payment is complete. Oh, and before you think of playing stupid shell games with the stock, you and sweet meat are going to personally guarantee the full amount."

"I don't personally guarantee anything, Marlin."

I knew I had him right then. "Wrong. You didn't personally guarantee anything. Past tense. Until today. But you're such a generous guy, you're going to do that in this case, or Kari and I withdraw our offers on the first deal. So, do we call in the lawyers? I would if I were you. Mine costs a fortune per hour, and as part of the deal, you agree to pay his fees and our expenses for this. Including our Shaw Air charter fees."

Jack nodded tersely.

"Honestly, Jack, I don't understand why you're so upset. You're getting tax credits, all the stock back at what will eventually amount to a discount over thirty years when I could just keep it. And this way you never have to see my smiling face again. Unless you do something stupid."

"What are you getting out of all this? Do you want me to give this away just to buy it back? Is that it?"

"I get what I wanted in the first place; nothing. Well, I guess fifteen million isn't really nothing. But here's what's so funny Jack, I saw what it did to you and Uncle Jack. And yet I ended up as the one son that he truly admired. That must eat at you. Oh, wait, there is one other thing I forgot to mention, I'm the executive director for life of that foundation which you'll never have anything to do with. It is a part-time but very well-paid position. And then there are the paid board positions, too. Did I introduce my board? Kari, Casey, Dawn, and Rikki, meet our biggest benefactor. He's about to make headlines as a really great guy. Now get the damned lawyers in here before I change my mind and feed Carter to the boys in cell block A."

23

THE BIG ASK

Back in the SUV heading toward the airport Casey said, "That was the damnedest negotiation I've ever seen. You know, for a little while you were the richest friend I've ever had. Even richer than Eric."

I noted the "friend" part, and I was happy about it. "Only equitable title, Casey." I used a real estate term I learned from Murph, who probably learned it from Casey in the first place. It meant having the right to something without having closed on it yet. "Haven't you ever flipped an option before?"

"I have, that's how I got started in real estate. But it darned sure wasn't for nothing in return." He was looking at me differently. Like maybe I could use a good head shrinker.

"It wasn't for nothing. It was to keep my life on my terms, basing it on being happy. That was truly the biggest lesson I learned from my uncle. And now I get a chance to help protect the fishery where I and so many others make our living, and that would make him happy as well. Oh hey, Rikki, I kind of sprung that director thing on you back there, sorry about that. Let me back up and extend a more formal invitation. You up for it?"

"Why me, Marlin?"

"Let's just say you were highly recommended as an angler, and I figured then I might have a better shot at stealing you for next year's *First Annual Mallard Cove White Marlin Tournament*. Bribery is good for the soul, as they say. Kari, Casey, and Dawn aren't eligible to fish it, with all of them being partners in *Mallard Cove*. And about the foundation, if you are as serious an angler as I've heard, here's a chance to do something even more than just catch and release. We'll be highly funded, but extremely low-key ourselves. Kind of our little secret society. This way we decide our best course of action, not public pressure from one direction or another."

She smiled. "Then I'm in, on both."

Kari looked over at me. "I can't believe we just got fifteen million dollars, each."

I shook my head. "We haven't, at least not yet. He has forty-eight hours to transfer the money. Hold your breath until then. But it'll be there, and I guarantee it'll be coming out of Denton Industries some way, not from his pocket. That's why I know it'll be there. The thing is, Carter is his Achilles heel. When I saw Jack go pale at the idea of Carter going to jail, I knew he was ours. You can see that Carter is being groomed to be the next head of the company, and frankly, Jack looks ill. But I was not going to have that son-of-a-bitch say that about my mom and get away with it. I'm just glad that he never realized that I didn't want the world knowing that I was a bastard, because of what it meant about how I ended up being..." I couldn't continue.

Dawn spoke up, "Marlin, there were three bastards in that room; one sprang a sudden nosebleed, and you weren't either of the remaining two."

I nodded my thanks. Kari squeezed my hand and said, "You know, for a guy who claims to not be a good businessman, you certainly did great back there. Everything centered on you selling them the idea that we had Carter's phone when all we had was one that looked like it."

"But we knew what happened. And now because of the recordings Rikki just made, and thanks to Virginia's 'One Party Consent Law,' they would be admissible in both criminal as well as civil courts. If you remember, I said that corporate life isn't my thing. I hate that stuff, but I never said that I wasn't good at it." I grinned about as wide as I could.

BACK AT *BAYSIDE*, Dave and Rikki started to head back to the ESVA office. Dave turned to me first and said, "By the way, nice right cross, Marlin." He grinned.

I smiled back. "Best one of my life, Dave, and it felt damned good, too."

Casey said, "Marlin, why don't you ride down to *Mallard Cove* with me and let Dawn and Kari ride together."

He obviously had something on his mind, so I agreed. I found out what it was on the drive down, and I loved it. I couldn't wait to see the look on Kari's face. We pulled into the property and drove back between the boat barn and the hotel with Kari right behind us. We all got out and Casey pointed out over the basin and the breakwater, to the view of Smith and Fisherman islands, and out into the Atlantic in between.

"So, how soon do you think we can have some sketches, Kari?" Casey asked.

Kari looked blank. "Of...what?"

"Our new office building. Dawn and I are thinking of two stories over an open parking area underneath. Something cool, and nautical, but also nondescript; we don't want to draw too much attention to it. But we do want covered deep porches on the end facing the basin and the Atlantic. What a view." Casey and Dawn were trying not to grin.

Kari looked really confused now. "So, this is going to be a rental?"

Dawn nodded. "Yes. M & S Partners will be taking the top floor, and we already have a tenant lined up for the first floor."

"Who are M & S Partners?" Kari asked.

Casey replied, "That's our new management company that's going to handle all the marina property partnerships, and do future acquisitions, development as well as design. We figured this was kind of centrally located between the entire Eastern Shore and the mainland; the areas we want to concentrate on."

"Okay. So who is the renter?" Kari was still wondering about the new structure.

"That would be the Mid-Atlantic Fisheries Foundation. You know, that thing you're on the board of?" I was grinning because I already knew what was coming.

Casey looked at Kari, "So, you'll do it?"

"Well, yes, I can get you some preliminary sketches by tomorrow."

"No. I mean, so you'll run M & S Partners for us?"

It took a minute for it to sink in. "You're serious?"

Dawn said, "We are. Of course, it means that you'll still be working out of here instead of *Bayside* when you are through building *Mallard Cove*, but you'd be coming up there probably a few days a month for meetings. And we also need to get started planning on Lynnhaven right away, we'll have a long road for approvals over there. You'll be one busy lady. So, does that work for you?"

"Yes. Yes, it does. Thank you both, I won't let you down."

"We know that. I told you we had plans for you. Now I guess we need to go have a talk with the other two main partners of *Mallard Cove* and get their approval on the new rental property, but I don't anticipate any problems there." Dawn grinned.

I added, "I have a little bit to tell them too."

WE FOUND Murph and Lindsay on the dock between *OCT* and *Irish Luck*.

"Well, the prodigal kids return home. What kind of text is 'Be gone for a few days, talk later.'" Lindsay was irritated with Kari.

I got between them. "My fault. Things were going on that you couldn't know about yet. That I wasn't sure about."

"You knuckleheads didn't run off and get married, did you?"

Kari chuckled. "I'd never get married without you being there, Linds, you know that."

"I'm not so sure, especially with the way you two's hormones have been raging."

All six of us went in and sat down in *OCT*, then I made them promise to keep everything in confidence. Then I related what happened since Murph read us that article in the paper. They both sat silently until the end.

Murph looked at me. "You're insane. And you know this means you can forget about any future discounts, pal." He was joking. Kind of.

I laughed, "How did I know that was coming? Hey, you two want a couple of jobs?" I explained about the foundation, which they loved. They were both in.

Casey then explained about M & S Partners and hit them with the new building idea, which they enthusiastically endorsed. He told them about the Lynnhaven parcel, and they were excited about throwing in on it as well.

I went upstairs and dug out one of the bottles of Uncle Jack's vodka. He'll always be Uncle Jack to me. I took it downstairs and made six glasses, explaining that I felt it only proper to toast the new foundation's board and Kari's future at M & S with it. Uncle Jack would certainly have agreed.

After Casey and Dawn headed back up to *Bayside*, I told Kari we needed to go over and meet with her cousin. It looked like I was going to need more of the boatyard's help repairing the Chris because I had a lot of work ahead of me around here over the next few months.

Carlton's boatyard did some boat building as well as repairs, and I was starting to formulate an idea in my head. But I was going to let that percolate a bit.

"I know it won't be historically correct, but I'm thinking of ditching the gas engines and installing diesels. A lot safer, and now we'll work to make her more ours than my dad's and mine and put her back the way we want her. What do you think?"

"Whatever you are comfortable with, Marlin. But I do like the diesel idea."

Carlton turned out to be a great guy, who was willing to work with us, doing as much as we wanted him to, but leaving the varnish and finishes to us. After seeing some of the boats they were working on, I was comfortable letting his crew do a lot of the structural work.

LATER, sometime around midnight, we were in bed but still awake. We had done a bit of our own private "celebrating."

"Marlin, you know how you said that when you were around your uncle, you felt like you were living in his world like it was almost a bubble where anything was possible?"

I sighed. "Yes, I miss that."

"I understand because I feel that way around you. Anything is possible. Look at how much has happened in my life since I met you, and especially how much has happened since we've started seeing each other."

"Well, I am supposed to be in my sexual prime right now, you know." I braced for the hit that never came.

"Deflect all you want, but I'm serious, Marlin."

"I'm glad you feel that way, Kari, but it's not about me. We just happen to make a really good team together, and we have some great people around us. You have found what you are great at, and Casey and Dawn recognized it. You've got a great future ahead of you, and it'll be fun to watch."

THAT SATURDAY NIGHT she and I hosted a grand sendoff dinner at the *Cove* for Murph and Lindsay. It was all the Beer-Thirty-Bunch, Casey, Dawn, Rikki, and Cindy. I sat in between Kari and Rikki and had great conversations coming from both sides.

As Cindy and Rikki were leaving, Rikki said, "I'm looking forward to fishing together, Marlin. So often the best part of fishing with someone can be the stories and conversations. So far, except for tonight, every time I've been around you some stories came out of it that I can't talk about with too many other people. I have a feeling there'll be more of that."

I smiled. "Sure seems to be that way lately. We'll see what happens, but I have a funny feeling that may very well be right." Rikki was probably the most badass person I knew, so that was almost a "given."

Before Dawn and Casey left, they came over to Kari and me and handed us keycards to their gate at "*C3*," that private pool complex. They said that there were fewer than a dozen friends that had them, and all of them and as well as the two of us are encouraged to use it like it's our own. I knew this was a lot more about a symbol of friendship with those two than anything else, and I appreciated it for what it meant. We were now officially part of their inner circle.

MONDAY WAS A SAD DAY. We untied *Irish Luck*'s lines from the finger pier for Murph and Linds, then watched our two good friends head off for four months of adventure and warmth. It did mean that we moved downstairs to the larger quarters which gave us more access to the living room/salon, but it wasn't worth the tradeoff. I already missed those two before they were out of sight, and I knew Kari did, too. Thankfully, we each had a busy week ahead. And I had a few surprises in store for her, she had a big one for me, but the biggest surprise would come in a phone call mid-morning.

"HELLO. MARLIN."

The caller ID had forewarned me by a couple of seconds, but I still was surprised.

"Jack." I mean, what do you say to the guy who had, well, you know what he had done? Now, it was a question of what he wanted. The thirty million had been transferred, but I thought this might be about the foundation "donation," and there was a shoe about to drop. There was one, but not what I thought, and it was a few sizes larger. It would also make me take a quick, hard look inside myself.

"I saw that doctor as I told you I would after our boat ride."

I thought, yeah, the one I was never supposed to come back from. But I stayed silent.

"I have leukemia."

I figured that day and at Brantley that something was wrong with him, but I hadn't suspected anything this bad. Again, I stayed silent and let him talk.

"He is treating me with some new chemotherapy regimens, but he isn't that confident that they'll work long term. My only hope will likely be finding a stem cell donor."

I said, "You mean a bone marrow donor?" I had heard about the procedure, and it didn't sound like a picnic for either the donor or the recipient.

"No, that's different. They discovered that there were stem cells within the marrow which was the real reason those transplants worked. Now they use a blood separating machine in a process similar to when people donate blood platelets. Almost painless, and much less invasive. But first, we have to find a donor match. A match within the family is best, but so far there is none among mine. The chances of success are the best when the donor and recipient have the same parents or one common parent. It's likely that we wouldn't be a match, but it's still possible that we might. You could be my only chance for survival, Marlin. I'm asking you if you would be willing to be tested."

You would need a chainsaw to cut the irony of this situation. I'd like to say that I didn't hesitate and immediately answered him, but I'd be lying if I did. At least I didn't pause for much more than a second or two.

"I'll do it."

I could almost hear the sigh of relief. I knew he was really out of options to have made this call.

"Thank you, Marlin. They'll send you a kit, and you just take it to any doctor and get blood drawn, they'll take it from there."

I gave him the address to send the kit, and he said they would overnight it. He hung up after saying "thank you" another time. I wondered for a split second if it had been me making the call to him if he would have said "yes." I thought I knew that answer; I had gotten it the night *Why Knot* exploded. In reality, I was doing this for my cousins/nieces and nephews, the ones other than Carter, who still loved Jack as "Dad," and were oblivious to what he was capable of. I wasn't going to be the reason they lost him if I really could help.

I MET Kari for lunch at the *Cove*. It turned out that we both had news to share. She was stunned about Jack, but not at all surprised by my answer, which made me happy. Then she hit me with her news.

"My mom's throwing a birthday party for me this Saturday."

"Pardon me?"

"No, you have to go."

"That wasn't what I meant but, okay. I didn't know your birthday was coming up."

She sighed. "That's because you're clueless. Did you not see the gift that Linds and Murph gave me before they left?"

"I thought they were being awfully nice, now I know why."

She shook her head. "You can be so dense."

"What, like you know when my birthday is?"

"Of course I do, it's April first. I thought it was so appropriate." She smirked.

"Funny lady. I thought you weren't so tight with your family."

"I am, and I'm not, it's...complicated. But it is my twenty-fifth birthday, and that's kind of a big thing you know."

"I had better block out Saturday so that I don't get booked."

"Already done. Sunday, too. You're giving me a whole weekend of you for my birthday."

"Great! Then I don't need to get you anything else."

She frowned. "Guess again. Did you forget that I mentioned it's kind of a milestone?"

"I was kidding. I already knew what I was going to get you."

"You just didn't know when to give it to me."

"Right."

"Um, there are a few things you should know about my family. I'm the oldest of three sisters, but I'm my Daddy's little girl. As I said, I am close to my family, and not. I've been out on my own since I got my two-year degree. My one sister married a waterman that's several years older than her, and Dad's not happy about it. My other sister is in her last year of high school, and her boyfriend is a couple of years younger than me and they're pretty serious. He's a mate on a charter boat at the *Bluffs*. Again, Dad's disappointed. I think he wanted doctors or lawyers as boyfriends and sons-in-law."

I could see a pattern forming here. Remind me to keep my back against the wall when I'm around her dad. "So, he's going to be just tickled pink to meet me."

"Give him some time to know you, Marlin, and he will be. He just wants what he thinks is best for me, and he's worried about my sisters. So, let's just focus him on your articles, and what you want to do here with the new boats."

"Right. I mean, it's not like I'm a waterman or anything. Though I make my living, well, on the water."

"As far as anyone can tell, you do."

I looked thoughtful, "Maybe we can convince him that I'm just doing research before I go into maritime law!"

"Funny guy."

I could tell that she was nervous about her father meeting me. She probably thought I couldn't be more nervous than her. She would be wrong.

After lunch, I made a mad dash to one of my favorite shops over in Virginia Beach. I had a rush order for them that a true Shore woman could appreciate. I hoped. Then my next stop was to see Carlton Albury about an idea I had. I needed to see how flexible his boatyard was.

24

PUT A LID ON IT

That evening I looked up from the couch when she walked in, I was surrounded by papers on each side of me and on the coffee table in front. She came over and kissed me, then picked up a stack to make room enough to sit next to me. She looked puzzled.

"What is all this stuff?"

"Half of it is foundation startup related from our new, much less expensive, and local attorney. We're killing trees so that we can save fisheries; go figure. Almost the entire other half are boats that I'm interested in for my new gig. You know, the parasail, eco-tour, and sailing tours."

"I didn't know about the sailing tours."

"Another head boat idea. Tours, weddings, et cetera."

"Knowing this will come in handy on Saturday, being able to tell my folks what you do."

"You didn't tell them about..."

"You know better than that. I haven't even told them about the money we got from Jack because that was part of the agreement. I did, however, tell Mom about my promotion. And she knows about you, and that we have the same address."

She grinned, after seeing me squirm. Meeting her family for the first time, with them already knowing we're living together. And her father hates watermen, which is what I'll be in his eyes. Lovely.

"And what's this?" She picked up a line drawing of a flying pelican with its wings partially extending beyond a square turned at a forty-five-degree angle.

"The logo for the new boats and my old ones, kind of ties the operation together. Also, a bit of a nod to Uncle Jack since he'll be posthumously financing it. You like it?"

"Marlin, it's perfect, I love it. Right out there where people can see it, but they won't have a clue about what it really means."

"Exactly." Reason number two thousand twelve of why I love this woman.

She picked up a folder and was about to open it when I reached over and stopped her.

"That's not ready for you to see yet." I took it out of her hand.

"Aw, c'mon, Marlin!"

"Your birthday is coming, young lady. You don't get to open your presents before then."

"So, it's a present! Cool."

I rocked my head back and forth in a non-committal way. "Well, maybe. I haven't decided yet."

"You teaser."

"There will be other presents, for certain."

"Ooh, presents with an 's' as in plural. I like that!"

I nodded. "I hope you'll like them; I think you will."

"Since they're from you, I know I will."

The next day the box arrived from the cancer center in Richmond. I called my doctor's office in Virginia Beach, and they agreed to get me right in. I gave the phlebotomist the box, which turned out to have a few empty vials. It wasn't the first set she'd seen for donor screening, and I thanked her for making room in her schedule.

"We're always glad to do this and know that getting this done right away is so important. We'll take care of shipping it all back, and there's no charge to you at all."

I hate needles and have always had a phobia about them. But today I didn't even feel anything, and was surprised when she announced, "Okay, all through."

Now, we just have to wait and see what happens.

I HAD charters the next two days, so I stayed busy but not nearly as busy as Kari. In addition to project management, she had now jumped headfirst into the office building sketches that would eventually be turned over to the architect. She also was digging into research on allowable structure types and sizes as well as any variances that had been granted on similar properties around Lynnhaven. This was a huge property and finding the highest and best use to maximize its long-term profit potential was now totally on Kari's shoulders. She was under a ton of pressure and taking it all very seriously. But I was about to meet her biggest source of pressure, and it was about to get much, much worse.

But she wasn't the only one who was getting stuff piled on their shoulders. Friday afternoon I got another call from Jack.

"Marlin, you are the match, in fact, a perfect match, despite the statistics. Are you still willing to do this?"

This time I didn't hesitate, "Yes." While I hadn't expected it, I was prepared for it.

"Thank you, Marlin."

"Just to be clear, Jack, I'm not doing this for you, I'm doing this for your six kids."

"I have seven kids, Marlin."

"Not to me, you don't. Carter's dead to me, just like I was supposed to be to you two."

"I understand. Well, if this current chemo doesn't work, we'll be doing the transplant in about two months."

"Fine."

"Marlin, please be careful, you're my only hope."

"Right." I hung up. Be careful, says the guy who wanted me dead.

I called Kari. "I'm pregnant; I'm now living for two."

"HAPPY BIRTHDAY!" I had snuck into the galley and made her breakfast, which I was now serving her in bed.

"What time is it?"

"A little after seven. How do you like how I blacked out the windows with blankets so you could sleep in?"

"Sleeping in on my birthday means like nine o'clock, Marlin."

"Normally, you would be right. But not on this birthday, being such a special one. It's not every day you turn a quarter century old, you know. And you have special presents that must be put to good use." I brought back in two huge, flat triangular gift-wrapped packages, and two small square ones. I set them against the wall.

"Let me have them!"

I shook my head. "Eat, first."

"You are a mean man, Marlin Denton." She tasted my special birthday pancakes. "Okay, a mean man who can cook."

I took the tray away and handed her the first triangular package. She was confused when she ripped open the paper to reveal a large piece of cardboard that I used to conceal the shape of the present. When she got to the real part of the gift, she was floored. A custom-made black flounder rod, wrapped with green and gold threads, which were her favorite rod colors. Under the finish, down near the grip in gold letters was: "Kari Albury, Badass Shore Woman."

Before she could say anything, I handed her one of the square presents which turned out to be a top-of-the-line reel for the rod. The next triangle was a matching rockfish rod with a similar inscription, and the second box was its reel.

"Marlin, I love these."

"Good. Breakfast is over. Now begins phase two of 'Operation Birthday.' Up and at 'em, we're going to go break that rod in at the tunnel island."

"We have to be at my parent's at noon."

"Then we better get cracking." I yanked back the covers. "Nice suit for your birthday, but you're going to need some clothes, it's cold out there."

WE DID BREAK her rod in on several school-sized rockfish. Unfortunately, the "slobs" weren't cooperating. But it was fun, and she had a ball. We raced back in on *Marlinspike*, got cleaned up, and made it to her folks' place up in Melfa, VA with five minutes to spare. Along the way she pointed out the community college where she had gotten her degree and the now-shuttered CPA's office where she had worked before coming to work with Casey and Dawn. She was the epitome of a "small-town girl," who was expanding her horizons and doing well.

I pulled up in front of her parent's house and we got out. A big man who looked to be in his fifties opened the door and broke out in a huge grin when he saw her.

"Birthday girl!" The smile shrank a bit when he swung over to me, and then my truck.

"Daddy!" Kari raced ahead and hugged her father as I walked up. "Daddy, this is my boyfriend, Marlin Denton."

He saw her looking expectantly at him as I said, "Nice to meet you, Mr. Albury." I stuck out my hand, which he took after hesitating.

"Same here, Denton." It was said in a tone that screamed "not really." Kari didn't seem to notice.

We went inside, and she introduced me to her mom, who was very pleasant, and to her sisters and their significant others, and several cousins including Billy Albury, the sheriff of Accomack county.

"Heard you were in the boarding party on that kidnapping ring a few months ago. That took guts, Marlin."

At least I had one friend in the crowd. "I was just covering my friends. I wouldn't have been much of a friend if I hadn't."

"Still, not a lot of people would have."

It turned out that Billy was a big fisherman, and he had read a few of my articles. We had a great conversation about what we were seeing as trends in the bay fisheries and fishing in general.

Then I spotted his brother, Carlton, in the crowd, and he waved me over.

"What did she think of the sketches?"

Putting my finger to my lips in a "shush" sign I said, "I haven't shown her yet. I figured I'd wait until tonight, then spring the idea on her as the last present of the day."

He beamed. "Nice. Well played, Marlin. What else did you get her for her birthday?"

"Fred Heide flounder and rockfish combinations in her colors."

Carlton whistled. "Remind me to charge you top rate for everything from now on."

"I'll call you about that first thing in the morning." We both laughed.

"We made quite a bit of progress this week, Marlin. Got the salon roof off, and the engines out. Chasing down the burned wiring now. I sourced out a pair of diesels that should fit nicely, too."

I smiled. "That's great, Carlton. I'll stop by early next week and check it all out. Hey, have you seen Kari?"

"She's out back with her father. Be careful around my uncle, he's as protective of her as a mama bear with a cub. And don't tell him I compared him to a mama anything, either." He grinned.

"So, Mom tells me this guy is a waterman."

Kari shook her head. "He's been a guide, captain, and writer, but now he's looking into adding some tourist boats at *Mallard Cove*."

Her dad snorted. "Looking into it huh? Sounds like a waterman. Mom says you're living with the guy, too. What's he, ten years older than you?"

"Seven, and I love him."

"You just met him!"

"I've known him a few months, Daddy."

He shook his head. "What did this waterman get you for your birthday?"

"The most beautiful set of flounder and rockfish rods. He took me out fishing first thing this morning, and it was wonderful."

He sighed. "Mom told me about your big promotion. I'm so proud of you, kid, you're going places. I worry constantly about your sisters, and where they'll end up. But I've never worried about you, at least until now. Don't let this fella drag you down and take up time that you should be spending on your job. Now's the time to concentrate and advance, and not get bogged down by some waterfront loser."

"He's not a loser, Daddy. And he doesn't bog me down. I've been thinking that I might even marry him at some point if he asks me."

His heart was breaking, and she could see it. Hers was now, too.

"I wish that you knew him as I do."

"He even have a house?"

"He has a boat. Carlton is fixing it up, it had a gas leak and exploded."

"Good God! It's a death trap. So, where are you two staying?"

"On a friend's houseboat. But just until the boat is fixed." Kari realized how bad this all sounded, and she wanted to tell her dad everything, but she had promised Marlin that she wouldn't. It made her angry because while she understood his reasoning, he didn't understand the position it was putting her in and the damage that was now happening to her relationship with her father because of it. All because of him.

He reached into his pocket and brought out a ring, sliding it on the third finger of her right hand. "This ring was your great-grandmother's. She had it on when she came over from Ireland when she was twenty-five. Never took it off until the day she died, and you shouldn't either. She was the oldest of three girls, too, and I've been waiting until your twenty-fifth birthday to give it to you.

"Sweetie, your grandmother would have never made it here to America if she had gotten tied up with some fella instead of reaching for her dreams and making them come true. There'll be plenty of time for other fellas after you have made your mark, and you'll have your pick of the ones your own age."

KARI WAS MOSTLY silent on the way back to *Mallard Cove*. I don't know what I did wrong. I laughed at everybody's jokes, her mom seemed to like me, and her dad, well, to be honest, I think he barely tolerated me. Then I noticed the new ring on the third finger of her right hand. A Claddagh ring and the heart was pointing outward.

"Where did the new ring come from?"

"My dad. It had been my great-grandmother's. She had it on when she came to America, and he said she never took it off."

"Most people don't, they just switch it around, depending. So, did he put it on your finger himself?"

"Yes, why?"

"And he asked you not to take it off."

She looked confused. "That's right."

My turn to be quiet. Message received, and understood, Mr. Albury. But my being quiet now just made things worse.

When we got back to the marina, Kari said that she was going to go and catch up on a few things in the office trailer and would be home later.

"Why? It's your birthday! And a Saturday."

"Yeah, so? I took the morning off to play with you, and now I need to pay for it. It's not like Casey and Dawn don't work on some Saturdays. You know they put a lot of faith in me to give me this promotion, and I can't just go running off whenever you feel like playing. I have responsibilities, Marlin, and I take them seriously. In fact, I may end up working some tomorrow, too."

She headed toward the trailer, leaving me sitting in my truck, speechless. That must have been a doozie of a pep talk her dad gave her about work. Then again, I can only imagine what he must have said about me.

I went back to the houseboat and started digging through the pile of boat listings, and then I made a call.

Kari came home a few hours later, still in a mood.

"Kari, I don't know what I did to make you angry, but I'm sorry it was on your birthday, of all days."

"It wasn't anything you did intentionally. It's just that I now have so much piled on me at work..."

"This suddenly piled up after you talked to your dad."

"He just reminded me of a few things is all. Responsibilities."

"And told you how much he hates me."

"He doesn't hate you."

"That ring he put on your finger is an Irish Claddagh ring. You know they are a sign to others of the relationship status of the wearer, right? On the left hand, the heart pointing out means engaged, and pointing in means married. On the third finger of the right hand, pointing in means in a relationship, and unavailable. Pointing out means available and looking. That's the way he placed it on your hand."

"He probably didn't know, or just put it on wrong."

I smiled sadly. "You don't believe that any more than I do." I noted that she didn't change it.

"I still have to work extra hard to impress Casey and Dawn. I don't want to lose my job or..."

"Or, your dad will be upset. Probably at me. I know." I finished her thought for her. "You know that opening an office here was only partly about location. Casey and Dawn figured the long commute every day would get old, and in the long run, it might end up costing either them or me, you. They didn't want either to happen. That was part of my chat with Casey on the way back down here the other day; he told me about their reasoning. They were willing and happy to make that change to keep you. Does that sound like they are unimpressed with you, and your work or that you're on the brink with them? They know that you work eight days a week when it's needed, and five when it's not. They don't want you getting burned out.

"I've been thinking, too. *Why Knot* has been almost perfect, if not a little tight, for my needs by myself. But if we are truly going to be long-term together, living on her full time would end up being a challenge. I figured my, or our, options are either buying a house, a larger boat, or this."

I opened the folder I had taken from her earlier in the week and took out a series of sketches of a house barge. It was a bit larger than *OCT* and had more amenities. "I've been talking with Carlton this week, and he said that his yard could easily handle building it. We can move onto the Chris until it gets built when Murph and Lindsay get back. What do you think about the idea?"

She shuffled through the sheets. "The houseboat? Or being together 'long term' as you put it? I don't know, Marlin. What if we started building it, and we didn't end up staying together? You'd be stuck with something that reminded you of me all the time until you could sell it."

"Yeah. It was just a dumb thought. Forget I said anything." There was no putting that genie back in the bottle now; this wasn't good. I took the folder from her, closed and tossed it on the coffee table. Then I picked up another stack of papers and concentrated on digging through it. Kari got up and returned a few minutes later with two vodkas. She took the papers out of my hand and replaced them with a glass.

"I didn't say no, and I'm not packing. I just said not now." She looked concerned.

"As I said, it was just a dumb idea."

She replied, "Maybe thought-provoking?" She obviously wanted to mend bridges and wasn't going to touch my addition of the word "dumb." She changed the subject quickly. "What do you want to do for dinner?"

"I picked up some stuffed pork chops yesterday and I'm going to grill them after I have another one of these. You get sides duty in the galley." Now it was my turn to not want to talk.

"I can do that."

FORTY-FIVE MINUTES later I headed out into the gathering dusk with my third vodka in one hand and a plate of raw meat in the other.

Fifteen minutes after that, Kari came running out with her pistol in hand, after hearing several gunshots.

"Marlin! Are you okay?"

"Yeah, I'm fine. But Dennis Peel isn't." I pointed to a body lying on the dock. "You need to get back inside; I don't know if he has anyone else with him."

"You're bleeding!"

My sleeve had started turning red.

"Flesh wound. Or, this is better vodka than I thought, and it doesn't hurt that bad because of it. I'm glad that Murph went for the upgraded model with thicker metal." I pointed to the bullet holes in the grill top that I had just raised when Peel opened fire from the dock. That was what had given me the time to pull out my pistol and return fire as I had ducked behind the grill. It had become my habit to carry concealed after everything that had happened, and heeding Rikki's advice. But I was just lucky that asshole couldn't shoot as good sober as I can, even after two and a half vodkas. I was also lucky that he didn't hit the propane tank.

Kari said, "We need to get you inside too; let's look at that arm and call the police."

I had another call to make while she was doing that.

"Why would you send Dennis to shoot me if you need my stem cells?"

"What! I didn't send Dennis to shoot you, I fired the son-of-a-bitch this morning after we figured out he had been embezzling from the company. Are you all right?"

I believed him. "Just a scratch. But let's just say that Dennis won't be filing for unemployment."

"Holy... He knew that you were my match, and he knew why. This wasn't about you as much as it was about me; he wanted to take away any chance I might have. Well, and maybe payback for that broken nose."

"Yeah, well, none of that can come out. I'll say I knew he worked for you, that he and I had words on occasion through the years, but he was unstable and had been angrily fixated on me for quite a while for no apparent reason. And by the way, you are a distant cousin, and we never talked tonight, got it?"

"Agreed. Sorry, Marlin."

"Yeah, you mean this time." I hung up on him.

THE STATE POLICE took my gun for ballistics and impounded the small outboard that Peel had used to gain access to the dock inside the security gate. They also took the video from the dock security cameras that clearly showed him firing first, with no warning, totally unprovoked. I called Rikki to let her know what went on and asked her to tell Casey and Dawn. Then I called Murph, who was in Jacksonville, Florida. He freaked, partly about me, and partly about the negative publicity. I assured him that we were "trying to put a lid on things" as much as possible. He missed the irony of the whole "grill lid saving my life" thing. I told him there was no reason to return home.

Kari took me to the hospital where they checked out my wound. It had indeed been caused by copper jacketing from the bullet that peeled off when it passed through the stainless grill lid. The fancy name is shrapnel. It got swabbed, bandaged, and I got a tetanus shot.

I was going to call my new attorney on Monday morning, and sic a forensic accountant on Peel's estate. We were going to find that stolen money, and nobody in his family was ever going to benefit from it. Whatever award I got from the lawsuit I was going to file was going straight into the foundation.

We grabbed burgers at a drive-thru on the way back to the marina. The chops were burned, and likely had some shrapnel embedded in them as well.

After we got back to *OCT*, I built another vodka. I could lie and say it was for the pain, but screw it, I just wanted another vodka. I was still pretty shaken up. I downed the booze, showered, and hit the rack, followed shortly by Kari.

"I've been thinking about the houseboat idea, and maybe we should go ahead with it."

I looked at her. “Me getting shot at is not a reason to go ahead with anything; the houseboat is a dumb idea.”

“You almost died tonight. Again.”

“Right, and that is not a reason to start making commitments when I’m apparently a bullet and bomb magnet. The only real reason to, Kari, is something that I’m figuring out that we don’t have, at least not yet, and we may never end up with.

“Look, your dad is right, you have a great career that has just gotten started, and I should be focusing on expanding my business as well as building the foundation. Let’s just see where things lead us because you were also right, we might not be headed in the same direction.

“They say when you take tests, you shouldn’t change your initial answer, because it’s usually correct. And I always lean on you because I can depend on your having honest and well–thought–out answers. You were right about this before.” I hated to say that, but I believed it now. And she didn’t argue like I halfway hoped that she would. “You only have to look at your right hand to know that’s true.” She looked at the ring and realized that she hadn’t changed it, as I rolled over and went to sleep.

I WAS PACKING an overnight bag when she woke up around four a.m.

“What are you doing?”

“I’m going up to New Jersey overnight to look at a fifty-four-foot Irwin ketch for the fleet.”

“At four o’clock in the morning?”

“Couldn’t sleep. I kept thinking about what we were talking about. I really think this trip can help me better clear my head. It’ll give you some time to do the same, too.”

“I thought you wanted to build the houseboat.”

“The houseboat is just a thing, Kari. As you pointed out, it’s not something that I’d build just for myself. You build houses and houseboats to hold a life that you’ve already built together with someone. I’ve got the Chris for just me to live on. I got ahead of myself, and apparently way ahead of us. Frankly, right now we need to figure out if there's something that we'll ever want together. Being by myself will do me some good, it'll let me think, and hopefully, it'll do the same for you. I love you, and I hope I'll see you when I get back tomorrow night."

I KEPT my phone on silent the whole trip and was actually beyond the service area going through a lot of the farmland in Maryland and Delaware. On the ferry across the river, I sat and read my texts, most of which were from Lindsay, and almost all contained the words "idiot" and "moron." I had one from Kari, which simply said that she loved me and was thinking about me. That was the only one I answered, saying: "Me, too." Then a minute later I got a picture of her right hand with the ring's heart pointed inward. It was something, I guess.

I looked at the Irwin, which needed some work. The price reflected that, but not enough in my opinion. I passed, found a nice little family-run motel, and crashed for the night. I woke up early but took my time leaving, not knowing what I'd find when I got back. Lindsay had gone silent; you can only curse someone out for so long in texts without getting blisters. Her fingers were probably bleeding.

On the way back through those same fields, I found that overnight they had become filled with snow geese which had arrived for the winter by the thousands. The only thing I could think of was how much Kari would love seeing this.

I got back to the houseboat about five-thirty, and Kari was on the sofa holding a vodka, I went to the bar and made myself one as well, then went and sat beside her.

"Did you buy a sailboat?"

"I did not. The price just wasn't there, and the guy was hard-core Jersey, and didn't want to negotiate."

"Well, when things aren't right and you know they never will be, only a fool doesn't quickly walk away."

I figured we weren't talking about the sailboat anymore. She looked at me silently. Finally, she said, "I guess you've noticed that I'm still here. Meaning I hope that at some time we'll reach a point where we'll want to have a permanent life together, and we'll both want to build something to hold it. When is not up to me, or you, but up to us."

I opened a picture on my phone of a field full of snow geese, with flocks landing in the distance. "The only thing I could think of while I watched this was how much you would have loved seeing this in person."

"Only if I was beside you, Marlin, not there all by myself."

"Yeah, it all kind of lost something for me without you being there too."

She took my right hand and turned it palm up, then placed her great-grandmother's Claddagh ring in it. Then she held both her hands straight out, palms down, and looked at me with those incredible eyes that were silently asking me what I wanted. I slipped it on her third finger, with the heart pointed out.

Oh, by the way, that was the third finger of her *left* hand...

EPILOGUE

You're probably wondering if we told her family about the money, the foundation, and everything else. That would make life waaay too easy. So no, we didn't, mostly because we legally couldn't talk about the settlement. Now two months later, her father still hates me and is certain his rising star of a daughter is going to end up losing everything because of her lowly waterman fiancé. They say you marry the entire family, and guess what, they are marrying me as well. God help them.

KARI and I both went over to Richmond, where I underwent the stem cell harvesting procedure. We were there for six days, staying in a suite at a hotel that was paid for by, you guessed it, Denton Industries. You really didn't think it would come out of Jack's pocket, right? Anyway, I received daily injections of Filgrastim, a solution that promotes stem cell production in my bone marrow. The needles are tiny, and even for a person with needle phobia like me, they really don't hurt. By that fourth day though, my joints were aching like I had a case of the flu. It was all those extra stem cells wanting out. And out they came, over four hours. One line came out of my right arm, up into the separator, and then the reduced stem cell blood got put back in through the left.

Sometimes it can take two separate days of collection to hit the amount needed, but I was a really good donor and was done a little after noon on the first day. I had even produced extra, which was frozen for later use or research. Now I know what a milk cow feels like. Within an hour I had started feeling much better, and all of the flu-like symptoms were gone by the next day. Enough to feel frisky, order room service, and stay an extra day on Denton Industries' dime.

JACK'S DOING GREAT, ahead of the curve in what is a long process that includes varying amounts of isolation and physical therapy. This procedure brings you literally to the edge of death and back again. But it's worth getting that return ticket. Though it'll be a year or more before his life resembles anything like normalcy. In the meantime, he gets injections to rein in my stem cells a bit, to avoid his body rejecting them. The dosage keeps getting lowered, allowing more of those little buggars to roam free in Jack, who is now cancer free.

BY THE WAY, did I mention the part about Jack and I now being twins? It's true. The way this thing works is that the day before the transplant they inject him with a medicine that destroys his bone marrow. For the next few hours until the transplant, his body cannot produce red or white blood cells or DNA. It's about as vulnerable as you can get and still be alive. Your DNA is produced by your bone marrow. My stem cells were actively at work, rebuilding his bone marrow, which in turn now produces my DNA. In Jack. It won't do anything for his attitude and outlook, but now he's going to hate some of the old foods he loved, and crave some of the ones he wouldn't have touched before. I'd be lying if I said I wasn't smiling about that right now.

. . .

Oh, I know what you might be thinking, I just lost the only evidence that Jack and I shared the same father, now that his original DNA is destroyed. I'm not that dumb. He had to get a mouth swab as part of the settlement agreement, and we have his old DNA profile attached to that agreement. And sadly, yes, it was conclusive; I didn't defraud him.

So who leaked the Will and Jack's phone number to the press? My guess is that it was Clara. I say 'guess' because we still haven't talked, and I can't even find her. She apparently went into hiding. But I found out that Jack had Peel fire her after that last time I saw her in Naples. They never saw eye-to-eye, and once my uncle was gone, so was she. While that leak was no doubt retaliation against Jack, it also might have been her looking out for me as well, I don't know.

Linds is back to speaking to me again, and so is Murph, who took the brunt of Hurricane Lindsay when I went radio silent. I so owe him "big time" when he gets back.

Why Knot is coming together nicely, and her semi-sistership, *Tied Knot,* is being built right alongside her. She'll be two feet wider and four feet longer than *OCT*, when she's done. On the top deck she'll have an outdoor kitchen to die for, and a private hot tub with a sundeck area. That deck is enclosed with solid wood sides that are three and a half feet high and has a covered bar area. While it's not quite as private as Casey and Dawn's place in the woods, it should be good enough to erase a tan line or two. Carlton's crew is making great time, and she should be finished and in her slip by this summer.

Have we set a wedding date yet? Not really. Kind of letting Kari's dad get over the shock first. It's a slow process. I can guarantee one thing though; we aren't getting married without Lindsay being in town. I want to be able to go on our honeymoon with all my appendages still intact.

THAT'S ALL FOR NOW, but not for long. It seems like there's always something going on around *Mallard Cove*. So, like that guy who sells clothes on television says: "I can guarantee it!"

The adventures of the gang from *Mallard Cove* continue in Coastal Adventure Book #3, Coastal Paybacks.

GLOSSARY OF NAUTICAL TERMS

I grew up on the water in South Florida, and I have an extensive boating background. I've worked on boats, built them, re-built them, and spent a good amount of time in boatyards. I've always loved boats, and ever since I was a pre-teenager, I haven't gone longer than six months without owning at least one. Most of my friends are boaters, too. So it's easy for me to forget that not everyone is as familiar with the jargon as my friends and me, which is something that I've now been reminded of on more than one occasion. (My apologies to those readers that I ended up sending to the dictionary!) To make amends, here's a (growing) list of uniquely nautical terms and words that have been included in several of my books. Bear in mind that these definitions are based on my own usage and experience. Things can be different from one region to another. For instance, you can fish for stripers in Montauk, New York, but here in Virginia, we fish for rockfish. But the true name for the target species is "striped bass."

So, here are the definitions of some of the more confusing words, at least as I know them. We'll start with a half dozen simple ones, then move on to those that are more complex:

- **Bow:** the front of the boat.
- **Stern:** back of the boat.
- **Port:** the left side of the boat.
- **Starboard:** the right side of the boat.
- **Aft:** the rear of the boat.
- **Forward:** (fore) the front of the boat.
- **Bow Thruster:** a propeller in a tube that is mounted from side to side through the bow below the waterline, allowing the captain more maneuverability and control when docking especially in adverse winds and currents. Powered by an electric or hydraulic motor.
- **Bulkhead:** boat wall.
- **Center Console:** a type of boat with a raised helm console in the middle of the boat with space on each side to walk around. Most also incorporate a built-in bench seat or cooler seat in the front.
- **Chine:** The longitudinal area running fore and aft where the bottom meets the side. It can be rounded or "sharp." They hurt when the boat rocks and it meets your head when you are swimming next to it. Trust me on that.
- **Circle Hook:** a fishhook designed to get caught in the corner of a fish's mouth. Greatly reduces the mortality of fish that are released or that break the line.
- **Citation:** at an airport, it's a type of jet made by Cessna. But here in Virginia, it's a slip of paper suitable for framing, issued by the state confirming that you caught a fish that's considered large for its particular species. Or it can be a speeding ticket, either on water or land. I like the fish kind better.
- **Covering Board:** a flat surface at the top of a gunwale usually made out of teak or fiberglass, that's used as a step for boarding and for mounting recessed rod holders.
- **Deck:** what floors on boats are called.

- **Fighting Chair:** a specialized chair that can be turned to face a fish. Mounted on a sturdy stanchion with a built-in gimbal, the chair allows the angler to use the attached footrest to use their legs and body to gain more leverage on a large fish. Most of today's fighting chairs are based on the design by my late friend John Rybovich.
- **Fish Box:** a built-in storage box for the day's catch. They can be either elevated in the stern, or in the deck with a flush-mounted lid. Some of the higher-end sportfish boats have cooling systems or automatic ice makers that continually add ice throughout the trip.
- **Fishing Cockpit:** the lower aft deck on a sport fisherman that usually contains a fighting chair, fish box, baitwell, and tackle center. Surrounded on three sides by the gunwales and the stern. The cockpit deck is usually just above the waterline, with scuppers that drain overboard. Can get flooded when backing down hard on a big fish.
- **Flying Bridge (Flybridge):** a permanently mounted helm area on top of the wheelhouse. Can be open or enclosed.
- **Following Sea:** when the waves are moving toward the boat from behind the stern.
- **Gaff:** a large, usually barbless hook at the end of a pole, used for landing fish. They come in different sizes and lengths.
- **Gangway (Gangplank):** a removable ramp or set of stairs attached to the side of larger boats to allow easier access for boarding from a dock. Usually hinged to allow for tide variation.
- **Gear:** marine transmission which has forward, neutral, and reverse.
- **Gimbal:** there are a few types, but the ones in my books are rod holders with swivels built into fighting chairs.
- **Gin Pole:** a vertical pole next to the gunwale usually rigged with a block and tackle and used for hauling large

fish aboard. These used to be quite common until John Rybovich invented the transom door fifty years ago.

- **Gunwale (pronounced gun-nul):** aft side area of a boat above the waterline, also the area on either side of a fishing cockpit.
- **Hatch:** a hole in a deck or bulkhead with a cover that may be hinged or completely removable. On a sport fisherman, the door into the wheelhouse may be called either a hatch or a door.
- **Head:** a bathroom, or a marine toilet.
- **Helm:** the area that includes the steering and engine controls. In many sportfishing boats, the controls are mounted on a helm pod, a wood box with radiused edges that juts out of a cabinet or bulkhead.
- **Keys Conch:** a person born in the Florida Keys. You can be born in Miami and move to the Keys an hour later, then live down there the rest of your life, and you will still NEVER be a Conch. They are usually very tough and independent characters.
- **Lean Seat:** a high bench seat usually found behind the helm of a center console. Designed to be leaned against or sat upon. May have storage built-in under the seat section.
- **Mezzanine Deck:** a shallow, raised deck on a sportfish just forward of the fishing cockpit, and aft of the wheelhouse bulkhead. Usually contains aft-facing bench seating for anglers to comfortably watch the baits that are being trolled behind the boat.
- **Outriggers:** long aluminum poles on sportfishing boats that are raked up and aft from up alongside the wheelhouse. They are extended outward when fishing, having clips on lines that carry the fishing lines out away from the boat, creating a wider spread.
- **Pilot Boat:** a smaller boat designed to handle all kinds of seas, whose sole purpose is delivering and retrieving a

captain with extensive local knowledge to larger boats approaching or leaving a port.

- **Rod Holder:** As the name suggests, a device that a fishing rod butt is inserted into to hold it steady. There are recessed types that are mounted in covering boards, and exposed ones attached to railings or tower legs.
- **Salon:** a living room area of a boat's cabin.
- **Scuppers:** deck or cockpit drains.
- **SeaKeeper Gyro:** a stabilizing gyro that almost eliminates roll in boats.
- **Shaft:** attaches a propeller to the gear.
- **Sheer Line:** the rail edge where the foredeck meets the side of the hull.
- **Sonar/Fish Finder:** electronic underwater 'radar' that displays the sea floor, and anything between it and the boat.
- **Sportfisherman (Sportfish):** a unique style of boat designed specifically for fishing.
- **Spread:** the arrangement of the baits being towed while trolling.
- **Stem:** the forwardmost edge of the bow.
- **Stern:** the farthest aft part of the boat, also called the transom.
- **Tackle Center:** a cabinet in the fishing cockpit or the center console which holds hooks, swivels, leads, and other fishing supplies.
- **(Tuna) Tower:** an aluminum pipe structure located above the house or the flybridge designed to hold spotters or riders, and may or may not have an additional helm.
- **Transom:** stern.
- **Transom (Tuna) Door:** a door in the stern just above the waterline, designed for boating large fish, but also useful for retrieving swimmers and divers.
- **Trough:** the lowest point between waves.

- **Wheel (Propeller):** slang for a prop.
- **Wheel (Steering):** controls the boat's direction.
- **Wheelhouse (House):** the cabin section of a boat which sometimes contains an enclosed helm.

A FEW AUTHOR NOTES

If you enjoyed Coastal Cousins, I'd be grateful if you would leave a review on its page at Amazon.com. And please feel free to email me at contact@DonRichBooks.com if you would like to let me know what you liked about this book or the series. I'd love to hear from you! Thanks so much for reading this story, and I hope you'll continue to follow these characters in their future episodes.

You can sign up for my Reader's Group at www.DonRichBooks.com and find information about upcoming releases!

ABOUT THE AUTHOR

Don Rich is the author of the bestselling Coastal Adventure Series. Don's books are set mainly in the mid-Atlantic because of his love for this stretch of coastline.

As a fifth-generation Florida native who grew up on the water, he has spent a good portion of his life on, in, under, or beside it. He now makes his home in central Virginia. When he's not writing or watching another fantastic mid-Atlantic sunset, he can often be found on the Chesapeake or the Atlantic with a fishing rod in his hand.

ALSO BY DON RICH

Check my website www.DonRichBooks.com for the current list of all my book titles.

The Coastal Beginnings Series:

(The prelude to the Coastal Adventure Series)

- COASTAL CHANGES
- COASTAL TREASURE
- COASTAL RULES
- COASTAL BLUFFS

The Coastal Adventure Series:

- COASTAL CONSPIRACY
- COASTAL COUSINS
- COASTAL PAYBACKS
- COASTAL TUNA
- COASTAL CATS
- COASTAL CAPER
- COASTAL CULPRIT
- COASTAL CURSE
- COASTAL JURY
- COASTAL CURRENCY
- COASTAL CRUISE

Other Books by Don Rich:

- GhostWRITER

Here's A Tropical Authors Novella by Deborah Brown, Nicholas Harvey, and Don Rich:

- **Priceless**

Go to my website at www.DonRichBooks.com for more information about joining my **Reader's Group**! And you can follow me on Facebook at: https://www.facebook.com/DonRichBooks

I'm also a member of TropicalAuthors.com, where you can find my latest books and those by dozens of my coastal writer friends!

www.ingramcontent.com/pod-product-compliance
Lightning Source LLC
Chambersburg PA
CBHW071433200726
48294CB00002B/619

* 9 7 8 1 9 5 9 1 2 6 2 8 7 *